D1570094

The Trojan Generals Talk

ILLINOIS SHORT FICTION

A list of books in the series appears at the end of this volume.

Phillip Parotti

The Trojan Generals Talk

Memoirs of the Greek War

UNIVERSITY OF ILLINOIS PRESS

Urbana and Chicago

Publication of this work was supported in part
by grants from the Illinois Arts Council, a state agency,
and the National Endowment for the Arts.

This book is printed on acid-free paper.

"A Trojan General Talks," now entitled "Merops in Mysia,"
was first published in the *Sewanee Review* 95 (spring 1987).

Library of Congress Cataloging-in-Publication Data

Parotti, Phillip, 1941–
    The Trojan generals talk : memoirs of the Greek War / Phillip
Parotti.
      p. cm. — (Illinois short fiction)
    ISBN 0-252-01510-X (alk. paper)
    1. Trojan War—Fiction. 2. Troy (Ancient city)—Fiction.
3. Greece—History—To 146 B.C.—Fiction. I. Title. II. Series.
PS3566.A7525T76 1988
813' .54—dc19   87-34282
                                                CIP

for my mother

The Trojan Generals Talk

A Note on the Trojans

In the beginning, long before the sacred citadel of Ilium rose high above the Plain, Dardanos founded Dardania. In those days the numbers of the Troad were not one but many, sheltering their clans across the well-watered slopes of Ida, where the West Wind empties his rain. There Dardanos gathered the clans and made them into a people and in time gave them his own son, peerless Erichthonius, to be their king, and a rich king he became, grazing across the Plain more than three thousand mares which were made love to by Boreas himself. In the mists of myth, wealthy Erichthonius had a son named Tros called Lord of the Trojans, and Tros himself sired three noble sons: Ilus, bronze-armed Assaracus, and the godlike Ganymede, who was made cup-bearer to Zeus in honor of his youthful beauty. Ilus was father to the blameless Laomedon, who enlarged the boundaries laid out by his parent and erected the high, white towers of Troy overlooking the Plain. To Laomedon in the years of his glory were born five noble sons: Tithonus, Priam, Lampus, Clytius, and Hicetaon, scion of the War-god, and of these Priam eventually ascended the throne to become King of holy Ilium and Lord of the Troad.

A leader to his people, royal Priam sired fifty sons of his own who lived in comfort in the Trojan citadel, in chambers of polished stone. Directly across the courtyard Priam erected twelve broad apartments, and there his bright-eyed daughters slept with their well-appointed husbands. Nineteen of Priam's sons were the offspring of his marriage to Hecuba, daughter of Dymas and the nymph Eunoë; the remainder were born to Priam's concubines. Of Hecuba's sons, Hector, Bulwark of

Troy, was the eldest and strong in his glory, while the others—warriors like Polites, Helenus, Deiphobus, and, finally, Paris—were known to be men of lesser light who walked forever in Hector's shadow. In the end it was one of Hecuba's sons, Paris, who brought Troy down in flames.

According to the Muse, on the night before Paris was born Hecuba dreamed that she would deliver a flaming brand. From this nightmare, she awoke shrieking, screaming that the whole of the Troad was on fire. At once Priam consulted seers; the seers, interpreting the queen's dream, advised that her infant would threaten Troy's very existence and that the dictates of wisdom urged the child's destruction as soon as it was born. Subsequently, before nightfall on the following day Hecuba was delivered of a strong and healthy prince, the boy known eventually as Alexandros of Troy, repeller of men.

Torn between love and duty and loathe to shed his own son's blood, Priam shunted, gave way to the promptings of his heart, and ignored the signs from the gods. Instead of killing the child himself, he reluctantly gave the baby prince over to chance, handing him into the keeping of a shepherd of the people. This man, all too familiar with the seers' warnings, made haste toward Ida, and there, on a high, forbidding crag, he exposed the child to the elements and made his solitary way back to Troy, certain that he had fulfilled the will of the gods. In fact, Hecuba had outwitted him, contravened Priam's intentions, and conspired to save her son. This she accomplished by means of an agent known only to herself—Agelaus, Priam's chief herdsman. He it was who followed the shepherd of the people onto Ida's heights without being seen. There, in the same hour that the infant Alexandros was exposed, he was rescued by Agelaus, secreted in the folds of his wallet—from whence the boy later took the name *Paris*—and delivered into the hands of a trusted subordinate, a Mysian, who raised the boy quietly on Ida as his own. And as the years passed, Priam waxed secure in the illusion of Troy's safety.

Meanwhile, across Ida's heights Paris grew strong in the stalk of his youth. Knowing no restraints like the ways of the people, he ran free like the wind, and the high crags echoed with the music of his song. There, in pursuit of the stag, he mastered the power of the bow, and there too he learned to soar with the freedom of an eagle, and there, finally, he saw the water nymph Oenone, pure in her beauty, and gave her chase and seduced her and deserted her in the hour of her hot salt tears, and in that hour, as a punishment for his crime, Zeus the Thunderer commanded him to render a judgement.

The judgement of Paris came about in this way: to the wedding of Peleus and Thetis—the destined parents of Achilles—Eris the Strifebringer was not invited. For revenge the spiteful goddess unleashed her wrath by rolling a golden apple against the feet of the wedding guests, and the apple's inscription—*For the Fairest*—set Hera, Athene, and Aphrodite immediately to bickering over the rights to possession. Reluctant to decide the matter himself, Zeus instructed Hermes the Guide to lead the three goddesses to Mount Ida, and there, by the Cloud Gatherer's order, luckless Paris was made final arbiter of the dispute. In her own way, each goddess attempted to lure Paris into awarding her the prize: Hera offered him power; Athene offered him prescient wisdom and hard military might; but golden Aphrodite offered him the most beautiful woman in the world, and instantly overcome by his sensuality, Paris gave Aphrodite the apple, earning her immortal protection but earning as well everlasting enmity from both Hera and Athene. Thus, the judgement of Paris precipitated the fall of Troy.

Weeks passed and then months, and in time, at Aphrodite's prompting, Paris made his way down to the Plain, and there, before the high citadel at Ilium, he met and bested his brothers in a series of boxing contests and raised their ire, and in the ensuing crisis, when it was thought that he might be killed to satisfy his brothers' passions for revenge, Agelaus stepped forward and identified the youth as long-lost Alexandros, son of Priam and prince of wind-swept Ilium. At first no one believed the herdsman, who was hard pressed to save his own life by substantiating the claim, but then Hecuba came forward, confirming Alexandros's identity by means of a birthmark, and in that moment Priam swelled with joy as he received his son back into the bosom of his family. Even so, not all Trojans rejoiced at Alexandros's return: the seers warned again that if the youth continued to live, Troy would surely perish, and this time Priam's own daughter, sapient Cassandra, echoed their warnings. In his fury Priam silenced the seers, citing his son's survival as a sign from the gods, and then, after first declaring that Cassandra was mad and therefore not to be believed, he confined her to the temple of Apollo as a punishment for her plain, blunt speech. And within a matter of months, at the head of a Trojan embassy, Paris sailed for Sparta on a mission of peace.

At Aphrodite's urging, the winds conspired to give Paris a swift journey, so in a short time he beached his broad-beamed ships at the head of the Laconian Gulf and made his way upcountry to Sparta. There, for the first time, he met Helen, daughter of Zeus and Leda and wife of red-haired Menelaus, who was himself the son of Atreus and brother of Agamemnon. Having been hatched from the delicate shell of a swan's egg, Helen's perfect beauty was so fair, so fine, so pure that it dazzled men's eyes and minds, and Paris was no exception: in the same instant that he first saw her, his passion to possess her overcame his judgement, and urged on by Aphrodite, he resolved to make her his own. Thereafter, Paris's pursuit of Helen was shameless, but even so, the Spartan queen resisted his advances until, during her husband's absence, Paris abducted her, disregarding the fact that nearly all of the Argive kings, who had once been Helen's suitors, were sworn by treaty to come to her defense in the event of just such an outrage. On the island of Cranaë, with Aphrodite's blessing, Paris finally seduced Helen, and thereafter she was his to hold at his will. At last, then, before a fair wind and full, Paris returned to Troy, carrying Helen and a large portion of the Spartan treasure with him, and there, indeed, the whole of the Troad became so enchanted with Helen's beauty that they resolved never to let her go.

Knowing that the Greeks would seek Helen's return, Priam prepared Ilium for war, fortifying the land and calling up his bronze-armed allies from the length and breadth of the earth. In time, after launching more than a thousand high-beaked ships from their Argive beaches, the Greeks arrived, invading the Plain in their fury, and the dusty Troad burned red with war. Even then, the Greeks sent envoys to remonstrate with Priam, to urge Helen's return, but Priam remained firm in his resolve, and as the war commenced, so it continued for nine bitter years while the wide, dusty Plain ran wet with warriors' blood.

Reluctant to fight for a quarrel and cause in which he did not believe, loath to risk both life and honor for no higher purpose than to protect a brother's adultery, Hector had the war thrust upon him against his will, but then, for the duration, in defense of wife, child, hearth, and home, he fought hard and well in command of the armies of the Troad. Even at the beginning, even as the Greeks stormed ashore across the long, white beach at the foot of the Plain, lordly Hector was first in battle, first to kill his man—impulsive Protesilaus, who leapt from the first high-prowed ship to attack Ilium until Hector took the situation in hand and brought the man low with a spear-cast. And then the war raged full for three long days until both contending armies sank to their knees from exhaustion. Thereafter the war passed into a deadly stalemate of bloody thrust and parry that dragged on and on, ravaging the land and sapping the strength of both Greeks and Trojans alike until finally men began to believe that it might never end, that the killing might become eternal.

In the war's ninth year—worn to the point of exhaustion, frustrated by the endless nature of the conflict, disgusted by the ceaseless flow of blood, bitter—Hector resolved to break the stalemate and concentrated his armies on the Plain. Then, without hesitating, he went swiftly over to the attack, striking the Greeks hard on their front with the clear intention of burning their ships and driving the whole Argive army into the sea, and against all odds he nearly succeeded. But Hector's initial success in the battle was predicated upon Achilles' absence, for Achilles, having quarrelled with Agamemnon, was sulking in his hut, refusing to fight. Thus, while Achilles remained out of the fight, Hector remained a dangerous threat to the whole Greek enterprise, and many Argive warriors fell before his spear-cast until, at the close of the second day, he killed Patroclus, Achilles' friend and squire. Then, Achilles could no longer remain inert: having sent his friend in place of himself to face Hector and die, Achilles had no alternative but to revenge the death. On the third day, just as Polydamas had warned, Achilles broke from the Greek camp at the head of his Myrmidons, and immediately he succeeded in splitting the Trojan ranks, trapping half their number for hard slaughter against the banks of Scamander. Responsible for the disaster but powerless to turn back the tide of battle, knowing full well that his desperate gamble to save Troy had failed, Hector remained strong in his integrity, and in that hour he stood by his decision and faced Achilles and died fighting beneath the high, white walls of Troy. All Ilium mourned his passing, for Hector was Priam's last great hope.

During the weeks and months which followed Hector's death, the war dragged endlessly on, and slowly the Greek grip tightened around Troy. Twice more, with the help of fresh allied armies—the Amazons led by bright-eyed Penthesilea and the hard-fighting Ethiopians commanded by Prince Memnon—the Trojans made strong attempts to break the Greek hold on the Troad, but in both instances merciless Achilles shattered the Trojan assaults, reducing their strength to resist by annihilating more and more of their numbers. In the end the Trojans were forced to withdraw into their citadel. And then, on a clear morning and calm, from the top of the wall, Paris took careful aim and shot a sharp-barbed arrow deep into Achilles' heel, killing him instantly, and in that hour the Trojans took hope, and their hope proved the beginning of their end.

Not long afterward the Trojans awoke one morning to find Aurora blushing a brilliant pink to the east while to the north, at the foot of the long, dusty Plain, they found the whole of the Argive camp deserted and the broad Hellespont smoothly empty of their ships. All that remained to give mute testimony of the former Greek occupation was an enormous wooden horse that seemed, at the distance, as high and wide as Ilium's great tower. Warned repeatedly by Cassandra and warned again by noble Laocoön to beware of an Argive ruse, the hopeful Trojans threw caution to the winds, embracing too readily the appearance of their final deliverance, and in the same hour royal Priam stood before the people, calling for them to rejoice in their long-awaited victory. Drugged by hope, the Trojans gave themselves over to celebration, dragged the great horse up from the beach, and pulled it even into the heart of Ilium, dedicating it as an offering to Athene.

The Trojan dance of victory lasted late into the night, but then, after the weary celebrants retired to their beds and the long-awaited sleep of peace, the high-beaked hulls of the Greeks slid silently ashore at the foot of the Plain, returning en masse from their day-long hiding place in the lee of Tenedos. As the Argive army poured quickly and quietly ashore and up across the Plain toward Troy, the Greeks in the horse emerged, throwing wide open the impregnable Trojan gates. And in the same hour, amidst fire and darkness, the great slaughter commenced. At the height of the chaotic battle, Paris was struck down from the walls of the palace by Philoctetes' arrow, and against the high flames of

Troy all Ilium saw him fall. The royal family, including Priam, Hecuba, and even Hector's little son, Astyanax, were put to the sword in the throne room by bloody Neoptolemus, Achilles' savage offspring. Cassandra, Andromache, other Trojan women, and the remains of Priam's treasure were carried off by the Greeks when they recovered Helen and finally set sail for home. Lord Aeneas, his father, son, and a small band of followers escaped into Mysia and from there to the West, where Aeneas's seed was destined to found Rome, but all the other warriors and princes of Troy, even unto the boys and old men, died fighting, going down hard beneath the high, bright flames of Ilium, and in the morning, across the whole of the ash-white Troad, there were no survivors save the circling kites which floated lower and lower in the sky.

Apart from myth, the fall of Troy may be supposed to have taken place between 1250 and 1185 B.C. Lately, some suggestion has been made of a vague link between Priam's Troy and the vast Hittite empire to the east, in central Anatolia, which based its strength and prestige on the immense citadel at Hattusas. Curiously, at about the same time that the Dorian invasions overran Argive Greece, destroying forever the victors at Troy, similar barbarian invasions struck Hattusas, bringing the whole of the Hittite empire under an endless, dark shadow. With the fall of the Hatti the milieu of the Trojan War passed finally into oblivion, and on the following morning a new age dawned. Forever after, Aurora has blushed the color of iron.

Map I Achaia

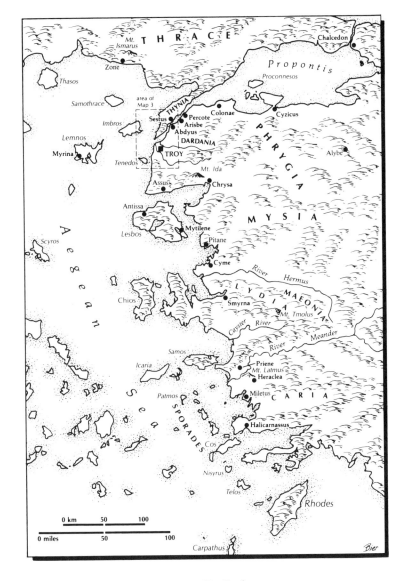

THRACE

Mt. Ismarus

Zone

Thasos

Samothrace

area of Map 3

THYNIA

Sestus
Percote
Arisbe
Abdyus
DARDANIA

Colonae

Cyzicus

Propontis

Proconnesos

Chalcedon

PHRYGIA

Alybe

Imbros

Lemnos

Myrina

Tenedos

TROY

Mt. Ida

Assus

Chrysa

MYSIA

Antissa

Mytilene

Lesbos

Pitane

Scyros

Aegean

Cyme

River Hermus

Chios

Smyrna

LYDIA

MAEONIA

Mt. Tmolus

Cayster River

Meander River

Samos

Icaria

Sea

Patmos

SPORADES

Priene
Mt. Latmus
Heraclea

Miletus

CARIA

Cos

Halicarnassus

Nisyrus

Telos

Rhodes

Carpathus

Bier

0 km   50   100

0 miles   50   100

Map II Troia

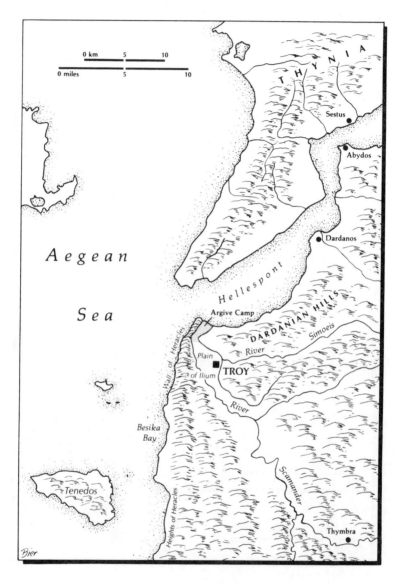

Map III Ilium

Map IV Asia Minor

As is the generation of leaves, so is that of humanity.
The wind scatters the leaves on the ground, but the live timber
burgeons with leaves again in the season of spring returning.
So one generation of men will grow while another dies.

Glaucus to Diomedes
Homer *Iliad* 6.146–50
Richmond Lattimore translation

Keas on Ida

The Plain? —I have never gone back. I saw it last in flames, over my left shoulder, on the black night some fifty years ago when Abas, my strong-armed squire, half-dragged, half-carried me up through Ida's passes to escape destruction.

—We had gone into position that afternoon across the slopes of Gargaron, Ida's peak of the many springs that are sacred to the Father of both gods and men. My Lord Aeneas had selected me to command, promoting me from his staff, where I had served nine years, and charging me to defend to the last man our lines of supply that led from the mountain fastness of Mysia down past our dark citadel at Thymbra and on across the Troad toward the high, white walls of Ilium. He promoted me, as I say, appointing me to command a mixed formation of some four hundred veteran spearmen drawn by lot from contingents already blooded in the field—Dardanians, Lycians, Cicones, Carians, Maeonians, even an odd Thracian or two. Individually each bronze-armed warrior had already proved himself, but collectively the men were weak with hunger, battle-weary, worn to the point of exhaustion after weeks of bitter, endless struggle on the Plain. I had no time to come to know those men—no time to learn their names, their homes, the numbers of their children, no time to bind their spirits to me, no time to train or mold them into an effective, reliable unit. Instead, from the moment we were formed, from the moment we received our eagle-tipped standard, we were considered ready for service in the line. Then, without so much as an hour's delay, the high command thrust us immediately into action. When the Greeks struck us on that first dark night, they annihilated my entire command.

—Pardon? —No, my Lord, *no*. I can allow myself no such luxury: the numbers of the enemy were irrelevant. That was long ago, as you say, and the passing years have given me much time for thought, but the result remains always the same. Now, as then, when midnight winds blow cold over Trojan bones, the responsibility is mine, mine alone, for on Gargaron *I* commanded and I failed utterly to defeat the Greeks.

—Draw yourself closer to the fire, my Lord of the Hatti. Would that I could offer you more than faggots for your warmth, but what the gods have provided must suffice. Permit me to offer you my ancient fleece with which to wrap yourself.

—How were we defeated? It is a matter swift in the telling, Lord. The Greeks struck us under cover of darkness, from the depths of a thin autumn mist that hugged the slopes like the folds of a sea cloak. We never saw them coming; we only heard them at the last possible moment, when they had already come close enough to crush the dried summer leaves that littered the earth. Sentries shouted the alarm then, but their cries died in their throats, stuck there by the sharp spear points of hard Argive bronze, and then the full force of the assault struck us like a sudden Borean frost, chilling each man's sinew to the very core. Like serpents caught before their dens on a cold autumn morning, we were shocked, sluggish in response, too slow to recoil and strike, too easily killed. Even as I sought to bring my warriors into a loose line of battle, the first Greek wave struck us full on the flank and knocked us reeling from beside our campfires. They were infantry, those Greeks—no archers with polished horn bows came against us, no fleet-footed Locrians who wear linen corslets and carry slings into battle—nothing but heavy infantry, armed to the teeth with spear, sword, and axe. They were Athenians, I think: I remember the owl ornaments which adorned their shields, and they showed us no mercy.

—By what means I cannot remember, but somehow the men came together above the camp, and there, across the slope, I gathered them quickly into a closed front. We held the high ground in that moment, for the Greek assault had come from below, from the north, from the direction of Thymbra . . . from the direction of the Plain, and when it came it drove us straight back, up Gargaron's rocky slope toward the frosty mountain passes into Mysia. For such a threat we had been completely unprepared; instead I had thrown out scouting patrols to the west, expecting attack—if an attack developed—from the west bank of Scamander or from the direction of Assus, something seaborne that would put ashore north of Lesbos in an attempt to turn our southern flank. What the Greeks actually accomplished was something altogether different; they brought off the unexpected, our complete surprise.

—We never knew how they had reached us, how they had crossed the Plain to infiltrate behind our lines, but they had and in force, and in that moment the matter seemed moot. Later, much later, I learned that Paris may have had something to do with it, may have failed to fulfill his commitment to guard our flank, but that report, brought to me years ago, remains rumor: facts were scant and remain so, and I refuse to condemn. Regardless, regardless of how they had reached us, regardless of whatever oversight or negligence had allowed them to traverse the Plain and negotiate the valley of Scamander, the Greeks had struck our right flank with the clear intention of destroying us, remaining on Gargaron, and cutting the last Mysian supply route into the Troad by which we might replenish Ilium. Given our position, had we been able to retreat with sufficient arms, we might have been able to make a bitter fight of it, but the Greeks had hit us too hard, too fast. Like so many of our fallen comrades, the majority of our weapons lay hacked, broken, lifeless beside our abandoned campfires, and there in the dark, with a few spears, with a sword here or there, with the occasional axe, but more often than not with stones and fallen tree limbs picked up in the rush, we prepared to make our stand and die fighting.

—The second wave of the Greek attack struck us almost immediately, coming forward on the run but in perfect, disciplined silence, and again we were forced to give ground, leaving many more dead behind us as we fell back. By that time, I think, no more than a third of my command remained on their feet, and many of those who did were already weak from loss of blood. I remember a Cicone who could barely stand, dragging past me with an Argive javelin sticking from his side, and I remember too a dark-haired Maeonian whose right ear had been sheared off, whose blood flowed in streams down the shoulder of his field cloak. But I do not remember any of my men uttering a whimper or a sound. Instead, they withdrew as they could and then turned and readied themselves for the next assault.

—We had only a moment's respite in which to take our breath and regroup, for below us, silhouetted against the flames of our dying campfires, we saw a third Greek wave, more massive than either their first or second, emerging from the mists, forming for attack. Like birds of prey bent on an effortless kill, they flew forward, hugging the earth in perfect, breathless calm until they reached and passed through their own earlier assault groups. In that moment—and I remember it distinctly—the only sound I heard was the sound of a cold Borean wind sweeping new sleet through the pine tops. Then, like crashing thunder the Greeks rolled over us.

—We fought hard, there on Gargaron, with our few swords and spears, with our stones and cold tree limbs, with our hands and feet and teeth, but the issue was never in doubt. All around me veteran Trojan warriors fought and died in silence, giving a good account of themselves, going at the enemy with weapon, tooth, and nail in the depths of that icy night, but without shields, without helms or breastplates or strong ash spears forged in the fires of Trojan smiths, we fought without hope, and the Greeks cut us down like late autumn wheat.

—Yes, I survived . . . to drink clear water from the springs of Zeus. Please you, my Lord of the Hatti, refill your cup and make what libation you will. Would that I could offer you wine, but the gods give what they give, and man—weak creature that he is—accepts with gratitude.

—No, that was not quite the way of it. Indeed, the wine skin had gone around, but I allowed each man only enough to ward off the chill, for the night turned bitter cold in the same hour that we established our camp, and then we began to feel the first painful sting of the sharp Borean sleet. So, yes, by my own order the wine skin passed round. It was not the wine, Lord, but the unexpected that killed us.

—Indeed, I *was* struck on the first pass, by an Argive axe, I think; the blow was painful but glancing, doing only enough damage to rip the flesh from my forearm and leave me bleeding. I killed the Greek who struck me, using a quick, upward thrust with my sword, and in the dark, no man noticed my wound, so the effect was not demoralizing to the command. Moments later, when the second wave came in, I found myself knocked unexpectedly from my feet by one of my own warriors, a topknotted Thracian, who had positioned himself beside me and taken the full weight of a Greek spear against his chest. As the spear went in, he recoiled hard against me, throwing back his head and flattening me beneath the shock of his stiffening, blood-soaked body. Pushing the man from me, I regained my legs in good time, gave ground with the remnants of my command, reformed them farther up the slope beneath a thick stand of pine, and, as the Greeks crashed against us like so many raging ghosts, lashed out with sword and fist into one onrushing form after another. One Greek I know I killed, driving the point of my sword straight through his ox-hide shield. I heard the long, deep death wind crawl from his throat as I drove in my sword, but in the same instant, like a piercing tongue of flame, the dying man's spearhead penetrated deep into my thigh, and I went down hard in mind-searing agony. In truth, I remember nothing after that; I do not even remember striking the ground. For me, you see, the battle ended when that last flaming pain closed over my eyes.

—Lord, draw close to the fire. Here in these deep Mysian breaks, the late autumn dawn is long and cold and chills a man's bones to the marrow, especially now, especially when Ida's passes already lie deep beneath the first lingering snows. So rest yourself and take nourishment, for if, truly, you intend to scale the heights and pass over toward the dark Plain beyond, your way will be filled with hardship, and you will need your strength.

—So it was, indeed, Lord. When I came to at last, deep in the throes of night, light snow had fallen across the slopes of Gargaron. The dead bodies of my warriors lay everywhere around me, and even beneath the cold and the snow and the steady Borean wind, the stench of battle, the stench of the dead, filled my nostrils, suffocating my senses with its sweet, sticky smell. Within seconds it drove me to vomit, and then, as I choked and heaved, I awakened to my pain and, groaning—my own bile streaming down my chin—fainted.

—When I came to again, the wind had died and the snow was falling
in thick, dark flakes; like splinters of flint each one stung my skin
before melting, and I remember that my face was wet beneath them.
Far below, down Gargaron's snow-clad slope, I thought I heard the
muffled voices of the enemy, who seemed to have withdrawn in order
to warm themselves beside our abandoned campfires. Whether I actually heard those men or whether my delirium made me hear them, I
cannot say, for in the moment my pain distracted me. No longer sharp,
the fire in my thigh had dulled to the throbbing intensity of a single
red-hot coal, and as my agony subsided, my leg stiffened and began to
go numb. I felt the wound then and found it clotted, the spear-head still
firmly embedded in my flesh, its hard bronze edges close to the bone. I
remember trying to sit up and failing and trying again and, in my
second attempt, managing to pull myself back a foot or more to bank
myself like a sack of barley against the rough bark of a thick mountain
pine, and then—the sweat gushing from my body, even beneath the
chill of the snow which had frozen in rimes to the face of my tunic—I
thrust my wallet between my teeth to muffle my cries and, clenching
both hands around the shaft of the Greek's spear, wrenched the point
from my thigh. The pain came like a hammer blow from the lame god's
forge—hard, driving, slamming down against me with such terrible
force that I thought my eyeballs would burst. Throughout the whole of
it, I remained conscious, screaming into the folds of my wallet, gnash-
ing my teeth until I had bitten clean through its wadded flap.

—There, in that hour, my Lord, fully awake, fully conscious, racked
by my ordeal, I dreamt my death, and the effect was not unpleasing. I
knew then, I think, the outcome of the whole, the final end of the war.
My wife and child were in Troy—Medesicaste of the lovely eyes and
my little son, Tros, who liked to greet me in the evening at the door to
our house and reach his tiny fingers under the flap of my wallet to find
what tidbits I had brought him from the field—and I knew then as
surely as I know now that I would never see either of them again. In
that hour, Lord, I learned the truth, the truth about myself and my wife
and my son and the stone-cold warriors of my lost command . . . the
truth about Troy . . . the truth about man—that of all the creatures
abiding on the earth, there is none more dismal, nor will there ever be,
nor has there ever been. For me, in that hour, in that place, the war

ended, and the failure was my own, mine alone, for the merciless, life-devouring Greeks had defeated me, slamming shut forever the gates to Mysia, sealing forever the fate of my wife and my child and Troy. No more could horse-taming Trojans, returning from Mysia, replenish Ilium with sweet-flavored grain. No more could Priam's strong-willed allies—Lycians, Carians of the rough speech, Maeonians, or black-bearded Mysians—cross over Ida and descend onto the Plain like madded hawks to bolster our defense. In that hour, Lord, it was done; in that hour I knew that the blood of Troy was destined to manure the earth, and there, then, I made my peace beneath the shadows of the pines and felt my own hot blood gush streaming from my opened thigh. When the time came, I took a coin from my wallet and placed it in my mouth to pay the boatman, and then in silence I waited for the Guide to come for me and lead me down through the tunnels of serpents into the everlasting chambers of decay.

—The snow slackened then, and Borean gusts blew up from the Plain, parting the clouds so that the autumn stars shone in the night, and in that miserable hour Abas emerged from between two pines and lifted me, half-conscious, half-dead, to my feet and, against my will, bore me up over Gargaron toward Ida's heights. In my anguish, in a moment of crazed despair brought on by my shame, I threw my head back, focusing all my senses on invisible, distant Troy; the last things I remember seeing as I looked back over my shoulder were the fires on the Plain. At that height, at that distance, each fire seemed like a dim translucent star. But there were thousands, Lord, thousands, and together, at the heart of the Troad, I knew they formed an unbroken ring of flame around the naked towers of Ilium. At dawn, beneath a thin Aurorean gray that veiled the sky from horizon to horizon, we crossed the heights and passed into Mysia.

—If it please you, Lord, share with me this barley cake. It is beggars' fare, I know, but only three days old, given to me by a muscled Carian smith who passed this way on his march into Phrygia. He spoke of war in the land of the Hatti, my Lord. Can it be true? Are you, in fact, collecting warriors to defend Hattusas? Is the danger . . .

—Abas? —Yes, he was a good squire . . . and a good man. He had barely seventeen winters under his tunic when he first came down to us from the north, and in that year the Greeks had already come against us for seven seasons. We called him Abas of the Kite's Eye in those days, for he was young and fleet, and atop Ilium's wall he could call by nation any Argive ship that came scudding in from the sea to beach itself on Trojan sand. Had he been with us on that long-gone morning when the Greeks first appeared, we might have had more warning and swarmed to a deadlier defense, but in that, the first year of the war, my Abas was yet a boy in his father's house. He was born, I recall, in Percote, the son of an armorer who plied his skill in the frontier barracks of the Lion. The boy too, when he came of age, went into barracks with the Lion, training as a spearman, but by that time the regiment's core had already come down to the Plain, where they formed a mainstay in the command of Asius, son of Hyrtaeus, fighting hard against the probing Greek attack. Later, during Hector's great offensive in the war's ninth year, they came under the command of my Lord Aeneas and gave a good account of themselves in our drive toward the sea, but on the third day, when the Myrmidons struck us on the flank, rolling up our line, the Lion was cut to pieces, fighting as rear guard during our long retreat to Ilium. Abas, assigned as regimental runner, was twice wounded during that withdrawal but still managed to make good his escape, and on the following day, when Polydamas reorganized the army, disbanding the Lion and setting its few bleeding survivors to reinforce the Boar, Aeneas himself assigned Abas to be my aide, and I took him into my home, tending his wounds, seating him at my table with my lady wife and child, and in time I came to value him as a true, close friend. My Lady Medesicaste, too, developed a half-sisterly, half-motherly affection for the boy, for he reminded her, she often told me, of her youngest brothers who had been struck down in their youth, during the war's third year, while fighting upcountry in the Dardanian hills. She honored him then with the same attentions that she had once accorded her brothers, and Tros, sensing the warmth that bound us all, responded in kind, making Abas the unchallenged tutor of his play. In the end, perhaps without conscious intention, Abas became bound to us by hoops of loyalty, and he gave loyal friendship to the bitter end.

—That is how he found me, you see, by the sinew of loyalty, and by the strength of that loyalty, I survived. During that last, lingering year, as Abas's wounds healed, the Greeks pressed us continually, harder and harder, so that each day brought us a new and unforeseen crisis. My primary problem throughout that year was supply, for the food stocks, already low, were growing lower, and a fierce hunger was beginning to gnaw at every belly in Troy. My work then became endless, and as soon as he was able, I set Abas of the Kite's Eye to help me solve the crisis. He showed me his mettle quickly, applying a sharp mind and keen, analytical intelligence to each new problem we faced, and I was much pleased. So impressed had I been with his upright character, so impressed did I become with his native ability that in the same hour that I was given my command, I appointed Abas to be my Master of Scouts, sending him immediately out to the west, in the direction of Assus, to screen our front as we marched into position on Gargaron. In all respects he did his job well, and that is precisely why he could not have foreseen or forewarned us of the impending Greek assault that ultimately annihilated us from the rear, coming up so fast and undetected over ground that we ourselves had covered only hours before.

—He found me then in the dead of night—stiff, still bleeding, covered with crusted snow, on the point of death, waiting to die, wanting to die—and against my will extracted me from beneath the enemy's nose, dragging me up over Ida's highest passes into Mysia. And then, Lord, on the following day—after he had carried me halfway down the reverse slope, found me food and water and shelter and an old Mysian dame to tend my wounds—near nightfall, turning on his heel, he went back, for loyalty, against all my agonized protests, to report our defeat and extract my wife and son from Troy, and in the numberless seasons since I have never seen him again.

—No, my Lord, I can never go back, *never* . . . my shame is too great. I should have died, don't you see . . . on the mountain, on Gargaron, in the snow, with the men of my command. Instead, cheating the gods of a just death, I survived, and now I know well enough that I am doomed to perish here, far from holy Ilium, where no man knows my name. —That the gods are just, I do not deny, for they have made my punishment complete.

—Once, long ago, in that long-gone year, as I lay bleeding in this hut, I would have challenged the Thunderer himself for the chance to go back, but the Fates prevented me—the Fates and my deep, unwholesome wound. Then, mind you, I cursed the Greek who struck me, for he had smeared his spear point with poison, and my wound, festering sore, refused to heal. Slowly then, day by cold day, autumn gave way to winter, and on Ida's heights the snow froze deep, filling the passes until they were open only to dark-beaked eagles in flight, and then, too late, my wound closed and began to heal.

—In the spring, using this same staff that still makes my third leg, I learned to walk again but walked only with great pain. That day is fifty winters gone, but still I walk with pain, the pain of my shame, the pain from the wound that will never heal.

—That is true, Lord. Some, I am told, got out. From time to time, travellers like yourself have brought me glimpses of survivors. My Lord Aeneas, I have heard, escaped to the West, to lands unknown across the wine-dark sea—but without Creusa, carrying only the aging Anchises over his shoulders, leading only his son down from Troy and away from the flames. In the dark evenings, Lord, I thank the gods that he did not pass this way to see me here, alive, a defeated Trojan general without his standard and without his men. —And Helenus, too, I think, escaped. Some forty summers past a Thracian came this way after crossing the Plain, and in a desolate hour he stopped, telling me what he had seen. He spoke to me then of Prince Helenus in ways that made me believe him to be alive in Thrace, but of that report I have never heard more, and the names of others who were mentioned were unknown to me. Many may have survived, but I do not know, for the path here is narrow and my visitors are few.

—So *no,* Lord of the Hatti: return you to your people with my wish for your victory, but I . . . I will remain where I am. In my wallet, know you, I retain a coin for the boatman, the same coin that I placed in my mouth on Gargaron so many years ago. If it please the gods, the long-awaited Guide will come for me before the first winter snow. Then, after a lifetime of sorrow, my wandering spirit may at last rejoin my command, and let no warrior's barrow be raised over my bones, for I am one of the defeated of Ilium who has given glory only to others and have long been dead in my shame.

Medon in Thrace

—Indeed, the wine at this clime is tart, too tart by half to suit my taste, but one drinks what the gods give and makes an end, savoring the memory of better days and better wines in long-gone years. —It is the mountains, don't you see: here in Thrace they rise too high, and in such narrow valleys the growing season is short. Even in high summer the night shadows follow swiftly in Helios's wake, so the dark grapes grow bitter on the vine and small, and after the pressing the bitterness remains. It was not so in the Troad, Lord. There in my youth the grapes grew round and ripe and sweet, and after the pressing and the magic of the jar we did not cut our wine with water even, but drank it straight from the skin with open heart and joy. Just so, I imagine, is your custom at Hattusas?

—No, Lord, I remained in the city to the finish. My family was there—my aging mother, my wife, and my three small sons. We lived in a house just below the citadel, and I resolved to defend. By the hand of Apollo, there was little else that I could do. By that time, you understand, we had been long under siege, and all of us were much weakened by hunger because in the tenth year food supplies had grown intolerably short. Thus we had neither the strength nor the provender to make good our escape. And there was something more: none of us, I think, ever really believed that high-walled Ilium would fall. We had battled the invading Greeks for ten long years, and not once in all that time had a single Argive warrior ever seriously threatened to scale or penetrate the wall. Clearly, Lord, we lived secure, in hope and confidence, and that security proved our undoing.

—Imagine, if you will, our joy on that last bright morning when we rose from our beds to find the Greeks gone, the shores of the Hellespont littered with the debris of their rapid, inexplicable withdrawal. From every housetop hymns of thanksgiving thrilled the air, and in the streets—even unto the avenues of the citadel—men, women, and joyous children began the dance that did not finish until our final, bitter end.

—Know you, Lord, that I did not go down to the beach. On the previous night, from my watch station atop the wall, I thought I had seen Greek beacon fires on Ida's slopes, so with caution I held my command in place, high atop Troy's southeast wall, guarding against the eventuality of a surprise from the southern approaches. Later in the morning, as the celebrations swelled, I heard for the first time about the horse and learned too that a feverish debate was in progress about what to do with it. The citizens, it seemed, were for dragging it into the city so as to offer it to Athene as a memorial for our deliverance. Priam—and Aeneas, who was commanding the defense—seemed disposed to grant the public their wish, and in this the majority of the council backed them, but gray-eyed Polydamas—and to my way of thinking he was always the wisest general amongst us—opposed the plan and argued instead for casting the horse into the sea as a first step in cleansing the Troad of all things Greek. To this plan Laocoön gave eloquent and well-reasoned support, warning us over and over again to be wary of the apparent Greek gift, and as he spoke, he was joined by his sons, who were equally urgent in their protests. But their prophetic warnings fell on deaf ears and worse. Seized by the emotion of the moment, sensing yet another threat to their will, our citizens— warriors, wives, and all, men and women who were normally respectful before the voice of authority and reason—turned on the instant and vented upon those venerated priests the whole of their pent-up passions, screaming insults so venomous that the three diviners seemed stung to silence by the sharpness of a serpent's fang. But even then, Lord, the warnings did not cease, for suddenly, from between the legs of the horse, prescient Cassandra stepped into view, resplendent in her royal robes, and awed by her beauty, the crowd fell silent. She paused then, my wife told me, surveying the warriors of Troy, their wives, their aging parents, the little children at their feet, and then solemnly extended the long fingers of her ivory-white hand and placed them on the foreleg of the horse. "Burn it!" she cried. "This horse is filled with Greeks!" For several seconds no one moved; then somewhere a woman laughed and then another, and within the moment the gathered mob erupted with such thunderous laughter that far away, even atop the towers of Troy, we heard the sound rolling inland across the Plain.

—They required the remainder of the day to drag that cursed horse up across the surface of the Plain to the ramp before the Scaean Gate. Nearly everyone joined in the endeavor; even my lady wife and three small sons took a turn on the ropes, leaning their thin and hungry bodies into the slow, forward progress of the horse, and not once throughout that entire day did the jubilation cease, did the laughter, singing, and dancing stop. By that time the mood had spread, even to our posts atop the wall where gathered stands of sharp, barbed arrows stood, still at the ready, beside our polished, unstrung bows. For myself, I remained tense, alert, scanning the Plain in the direction of Thymbra for any sign of movement, for even the remotest hint of a Greek surprise, but throughout the morning the only motion I saw came from a single black eagle which circled round and round and round, riding the currents of the wind high above Troy's towers. By the time, then, that Helios reached his zenith, even I had started to relax and let down my guard. And then, Lord, Priam finally returned from the Plain, his swift, golden chariot responding gracefully under the skilled hands of Idaeus, and in the same hour he declared a day of celebration and ordered the granaries thrown open for issue of a full ration, and *then*, I tell you, I began to believe for the first time that the war had finally ended, that the hard, blood-hungry Argives had at last sailed for their homes to leave us in peace.

—Like other garrison commanders—acting in concert with several— I objected when our impassioned citizens finally reached the wall and wanted to make a breach in order to bring the horse inside. For ten years, know you, the high, white walls of Ilium had stood glimmering and vast—inviolate, indomitable, impenetrable, secure above the windy Plain, the bulwark of our safety—and few among us who had commanded their defense wished to see them down. But again the mob's cries prevailed, and by royal decree the massive Scaean Gates were lifted from their hinges, carried to the ramp, and thrown aside—an act, Lord, greeted with untold rejoicing by a people who for so many years had been penned inside. Then, even above the protests of Polydamas, myself, and others like us, the arches above the gates were breached, and the great horse was dragged into the city.

—Our relief that night did not even appear. And under cover of darkness one by one—despite my own best efforts to prevent them—my warriors quietly laid down their arms, deserted their stations, and descended into the streets to join in the celebrations, and then, finally accepting the inevitable, I gave in to the euphoria, stacked my spear beside a host of others, hung up my shield, and wearing only my sword slung round my shoulder by a long leather thong, went home to my wife and sons, to my first full ration in many months, to my first untroubled rest in ten long years.

—I will remember passing through the streets that night for the remaining winters of my life. Above every door in Troy a bright torch burned, a sign of thanksgiving lighting the return of men who were at last coming home from the wall or the Plain or the wide precincts beyond to a full ritual meal and the cleansing ceremonies of peace, but how warrior or wife or child could find one another at home, I do not know, for even at that late hour the streets and byways were packed with people, their thin, ghostly forms leaping and dancing beneath a fiery torchlight, their ecstatic shouts and cries and songs filling the air with a whirlwind of cacophonic sound. —Somehow, after long effort, I reached my home and the warm embrace of my family, and there, together, we made our peace, rededicating ourselves to the household gods.

—Later that night, as I lay quietly beside my wife, the weary years of war seemed to roll away from me like spent waves sliding back into the sea, and then at long last I slept the sleep of peace, secure in my unthreatening dreams. —I do not remember when I awakened, but whenever it was, it was sudden, causing me to bolt from the bed, and then I knew instantly that the house was on fire. Shouting orders for my wife to put our sons through a rear window into the courtyard, I sprang toward the street door to sound the alarm and raise the watch, but I never made it out of the room, for at our door, in that dim, eerie light, my wife's screams pounding in my ears, I came face to face with a helmeted Greek, who swung up the butt of his spear, striking me hard in the groin, dashing me instantly onto our packed-earth floor. Stunned, half-senseless in the agonized throes of my pain, the last thing I remember is reaching for my sword. Then with merciless force something struck like a bolt along the back of my head, and night's black wing swept over my eyes.

—Take an almond, Lord. They grow well here in these mountain valleys and soften the edge of our too-bitter wine, and these, particularly, of last year's harvest are ripe with nourishing flavor. Were the harvests of the Hatti equally bountiful in this, a year of mild rains?

—For how long, do you ask? —I cannot say. For hours, for many hours, I know: for perhaps a day. But of what may have happened during the interval, I do not know, for when I awoke—beneath the hammering beams of Helios—I was not upon the hard-packed earth of my home but on the Plain, near the banks of the Simoeis, in a dry, dusty field heaped high with Trojan dead, and I awoke to the sound of flies. I remember turning over then and trying to raise myself, but the moment I did, pain assaulted me with such unremitting fury that I again lost consciousness, coming to only later, only moments before nightfall, to the crackling sound of fire. In the moment I thought myself back in Troy, back in my house listening to the horrifying screams of my wife, but then, sparked by my fear, I opened my eyes and brought them painfully into focus on a wall of flame that without restraint was raging toward me across the field, swept forward by the rushing wind. Whether the Greeks had intentionally fired those dry stands of grass for the purpose of making our pyre or whether some wind-borne spark from the roaring fires of Ilium had ignited the conflagration, I was never to know, but whatever the case, the result was the same: directly before me, I saw hundreds of swollen corpses jerking and writhing beneath the flames.

—I moved then, as quickly as I could, fighting to remain conscious, pushing, crawling, and dragging myself over one corrupted corpse after another until at last, with the fire already licking at my heels, I slithered over the edge of the river bank and fell crashing into the white running waters of the Simoeis. Above and behind me the high flames raged, and then, riding a single gust of wind, they leapt the bank, swirled through the air, and enveloped the fields beyond, racing north toward the Hellespont with all the force and fury of a storm.

—I remained in the river for hours, holding fast to an exposed root with my head barely above the water's surface, and I continued to remain that way, letting the cold, rushing currents revive me, until the surrounding fires had burned themselves out. Even afterward the air remained thick with dense smoke and the creeping stench of burned and rotting flesh, and finally I could stand it no longer. Lunging forward into the river, I forced myself to swim, but even then I found the going difficult, for I found that I could not swim free of the bodies. One after another, they bumped against me, floating face up or face down, moving down toward the sea from whatever tortured point the Greeks had thrown them. That is when I knew for certain that the whole city had been put to the sword, for many were the children's bodies which floated by me in the dark, making their solitary way toward the deep chambers of the sea.

—With painful effort I eventually crossed to the opposite bank, caught an exposed stone, and pulled myself ashore. I tried my legs then and found, with the help of a staff, that I could stand, even beneath the unremitting pounding in my head, and in that moment, for the first time, on the northern bank of Simoeis, I turned to look back on the agony of Troy.

—Even now, my Lord, across all my winter spans, the horrors remain vividly seared on my eye. After what must have been an endless day of fire, Ilium still burned, her once-white towers shooting straight up into the night sky like pillars of angry flame, and above them, across the entire Plain, rose a mountain of smoke so wide, so high, so darkly visible that it extinguished all the stars in the sky. To me, Lord . . . then as now . . . it seemed that the whole world had gone up in fire, leaving me alone in the dark for dead.

—Four nights later, naked, delirious, half-starved, I crawled into the charred precincts of once-blue Abydus-by-the-sea. On the following morning, with kites already perching on the scorched walls around me, I was found in a narrow street, near the ruins of my father's house, by a party of Thracian scouts who had been sent by their king to look for survivors. In answer to your question, to the best of my knowledge, I am the only Trojan they found alive.

—Could it have been prevented? Could we have survived? Could we, yet, be masters of the Plain? —Indeed, Lord, those questions make the bitter wine that I have been forced to drink through all my lingering years, and in truth I do not know. —Perhaps. Perhaps, given some altered critical decisions, we might have held on to prevail.

—No, Lord, not in *that* way: in the matter of the Spartan whore, her return would have been of little consequence. Offers were made, I assure you, more than once and rejected early by the Argive high command; I heard of each on good report. That she was beautiful, there can be no doubt: she *was* beautiful . . . beyond words. I saw her once myself, before lordly Antenor's dwelling in the avenue of the citadel. She had made a visit, I think, to Antenor's wife, and while marching my command to the armory to draw new bundles of arrows for our defense of the wall, we passed that way in the moment when she took her departure. I halted the command immediately, there, in deference to the royal colors worn by a page who was already standing in the street, and then we waited patiently, expecting a glimpse of Hecuba, or lovely Laothoe, or another of Priam's wives, but seconds later, preceded only by her maid, the whore emerged, cast her soft eyes gently over the heads of the crowd, and caught my soul. —Clearly, Lord, she had a beauty that went beyond my powers to describe, but she was not the root cause of the war, and her swift return to Menelaus of Sparta would have brought no end to the fighting, for the Greeks, Warrior Lord of the Hatti, did not invade the Troad merely for the sake of a woman, not even for the sake of Helen, whose ethereal beauty rivalled the gods.

—Know you then that the war was fought for control of the sea, but not *on* the sea as it should have been, and therein Priam had made a fatal decision. Clearly, by my recollection, Priam failed to initiate the kind of naval program that would have given him a fast fleet with which to protect our shores. Bear in mind that the source of all Troy's prestige, wealth, and power, the very foundation of the royal house and the stability of Ilium, rested on our unchallenged control of the Hellespont. Owing to the swift, unpredictable currents that are stirred in that channel by Poseidon's dangerous hand, those white-capped waters always have been and always will be gravely dangerous to seamen who attempt to sail them, and that is particularly true of the race which speeds

through the narrows from a tense northern point near Percote and runs
down with fury toward the fishhook harbor at Dardanos. For leagues
along that course the rocky Trojan shore is littered with the bleached
ribs of the dead and the broad-beamed hulls they sailed. Early in his
reign Priam solved that problem by developing such an efficient system
of overland transport that all could circumvent the danger. Thus—
winter, spring, summer, and fall—he ensured the uninterrupted flow of
commerce from all points west along the blue Aegaean to the remote,
peopled lands of the east and the dark, black sea beyond. And his
accomplishment made Ilium great with wealth and power.

—For all practical purposes the royal house of Priam made good its
ends by shutting the Hellespont to foreign commercial traffic. Instead
of risking the passage, merchant bottoms coming from points west
were invited to put into Besika Bay, offload their cargoes onto the
beach, repack them onto the sturdy backs of Trojan horses, and then,
for a reasonable fee, transport them safely overland to the sheltered
Trojan harbors north of the race. From there, after shipping each load
onto a broad-beamed Trojan hull, the cargoes were sent north into
Thrace or east across wide Propontis toward Phrygia, the dark, black
sea, and the shores of the Hatti beyond. Given the risk in the race,
given its white-capped fury when Poseidon raised his hand, given
Priam's new, secure option, all nations wishing to ply the inland trade
embraced his new arrangement, paying reasonable fees which left all
parties with a clear profit after avoiding the dangers of the race. From
time to time, certainly, some ambitious captain or another wished to
forego the fee and attempt the race on his own, and this Priam permitted, providing that the ship at risk first agreed to take aboard a skilled
Trojan pilot and a set number of fresh Trojan oarsmen who could
bolster the strength of the crew. The fees for this service were less than
for overland transport, but the risks were clearly greater, and the plan
enjoyed only sporadic popularity.

—In time, then, the Troad waxed great in wealth and power, and in
time Ilium became the envy of the world, and that, Lord, was the
beginning of our undoing, for in the thirtieth year of Priam's reign,
when I was yet a boy in my swaddling sheet, the Mysians looked
hungrily upon Priam's wealth and tried to wrest it from him by attacking the Troad after the first spring thaw. Thus began the first of four

Mysian wars fought over a length of twenty years. In truth, the land battles of those wars bled Ilium white; my own father, fighting at the head of the Bear, went down to a Mysian dart in the third of those raging conflicts, but the point I wish to make is that each of those successive wars was brought to its conclusion, not by the battering strength of the hard Trojan line regiments fighting across Ida, but by the Shark, the Trojan naval command that bore down from its base on Tenedos, striking fear into the Mysian coast, bottling up the ports and preventing grain supplies from reaching the enemy from across the wine-dark sea.

—In those days, you see, when Hector and Aeneas were still leading battalions in the Boar and the Kite—before, even, Deiphobus had learned to draw the bow—gray-eyed Polydamas already commanded the Shark, winning by astute intelligence the last two campaigns in those prolonged, bitter wars. Young though he was, he was by far the most able commander then in service, and his use of the sea was brilliant. When the wars ended, then, with our occupation of Mysia and a new treaty of alliance which made Priam the Mysian overlord, Polydamas approached the king and begged him to expand the fleet. Already, even then, plying the dolphin-road in growing numbers, he had seen and measured the increasing strength of the Greek fleet whose narrow, high-beaked hulls heralded such a revolution in ship design that they threatened even the strength of the Troad. Priam should have listened, but he did not, and eventually he rued the day. Polydamas, you see, was a commoner, the son of a smith: he had ability, intelligence, even genius, but not favor—favor, Priam reserved for the nobles. In consequence, the lessons of the Shark went unheeded while Trojan shipwrights went right on building, according to the old plan, ships that were broad-beamed and slow to command.

—That was not the only reason that we were not prepared at sea, but to my thinking the others deserve even less admiration. Clearly, in all matters of policy, Priam favored his sons; in one way or another his bias was borne home to all of us, even the lord Aeneas, in countless unpleasant ways. In this case it is enough to say that during the Fourth Mysian War Hector had at last risen to command the Boar, replacing old Morys, who was dropped in the field by a Mysian spear. Thereafter Hector fought splendidly and not without brilliance, winning a great, perhaps the only *true,* land victory in the campaign when he threw the full weight of the regiment, reserves and all, into a last desperate gamble before Thymbra and turned the Mysian flank. Then, Lord, the slopes of Ida ran red with Mysian blood, and in defense of their accomplishment the Boar fought well, but in the wake of this victory, too much was made of Hector's achievement. In itself, mind you, the victory was real: Hector had taken a great risk and succeeded against all odds, but what the army and what Priam, in particular, failed to take into account was the fact that the Mysians were weak with starvation, already preparing to withdraw. You see, Lord, beyond Ida, Polydamas had put more than five thousand hardened Sharks ashore in Chrysa, cut the Mysian lines of supply, and brought their army—fighting against Hector on the opposite side of Ida—almost to its knees. No matter, *the* great victory in the Fourth Mysian War was accorded to Hector, and in sum, with the council as with the people, his prestige increased immeasurably and, along with it, the army's. Promoted to corps commander during the following year and raised to a seat on the council, Hector proved eloquent on the army's behalf. As a result—only gray-eyed Polydamas dissenting—Ilium's resources were increasingly lavished on the line commands while the Shark, out of mind and sight at its base on Tenedos, found itself forced to scrounge and scavenge for its very existence. In all, swayed by paternal interest, Priam allowed Hector to exercise the guiding hand.

—Five years later, when the Greeks made ready for war, we found that we had no alternative but to fight them on the Plain. Had Polydamas been heard, had the success of the Shark been studied, I think we might have turned the Greek thrust even before it reached our shores, for Polydamas's intention was to fight them at sea, far to the west in the vicinity of Scyros, with a well-seasoned fleet both strong enough and fast enough to give us a decisive victory in the first encounter. As the event turned out, fearful of losing what few naval forces he had—even before the war began—Priam ordered the entire Shark north, up the Hellespont, to bases around Propontis, and then, to Polydamas's shame the regiment was ordered ashore, marched down to the Plain, and integrated into the line. They fought well, of course, throughout the length of the war, but in my view Priam's neglect of the Shark, their commander, and their accomplishments lost us an opportunity, and in the end that opportunity might have made all the difference.

—Bitter wine, indeed, but as you see, the metaphor is apt, for in those last, long days on the Plain we emptied the skin to the dregs, and never . . . before or since . . . has life's wine tasted so sharp. Pray you, Lord, that the Hatti never have to drink its like.

—Pardon? —No, there were other decisions as well that might have made a difference, but in kind they were limited and usually tactical by nature. Nevertheless, some were immensely important. Consider Hector's offensive in the ninth year of the war when he risked all in the attempt to burn the Greek fleet. By the third day it was clear to those of us commanding that the offensive had failed. As before Thymbra some fifteen years earlier, Hector took the supreme gamble, threw in all our reserves—garrison troops and all—and made one last effort to roll up the Greek line. We had realized some early success in the attack, certainly, but at the end of two days' fighting both armies still held their ground—worn, weary, parched by the heat and the dust, covered with clotted gore but still in position, still locked in that implacable, deadly stalemate—and to my thinking, at least, we remained powerless either to break their line or drive them into the sea. We held a council of war then, there on the Plain, and at the close, for the first time in public, gray-eyed Polydamas offered Hector his thoughts. "They are not Mysians," I remember him saying, "but Greeks, well-fed and strong, hungry only for bright Trojan blood and the wealth of the Troad. They have reserves, which we do not, and there is no Trojan army at their backs strangling their line of supply—the advantage you enjoyed so long ago before Thymbra—so let me persuade you, my Lord, to retire on Troy. It is the wise thing to do, to conserve our force so that we may fight on another day." It was the sensible plan, the military plan: conservation of force and men and lives, and, angrily, Hector rejected it.

—On the following day, when the Myrmidons broke our line, turned our left flank, and drove half our army to destruction in the waters of Scamander, Hector died fighting, trying to cover our retreat, but his error in judgement, Lord, had sealed our doom, for in the long months that followed, even with immense help from our allies, we were never again able to muster enough men to threaten seriously the Greeks in the field.

—There was another mistake too, which springs suddenly to my mind, which might have made a difference, but that one, I think, came late in the war, mere months before the event of the horse.

—By that time, I remember, the Greeks were close to encircling us, but in the direction of Mysia we held a single supply corridor that wound down from Ida's passes to Thymbra and from there, by means of sheltered valley trails, worked overland, approaching Ilium from the southeast. With supplies from Thrace, Phrygia, and upper Dardania completely cut off and with all access to the sea denied us, that single corridor had become our lifeline, our only means of replenishing Troy, and in the closing months of the war we lost it through an unparalleled act of negligence.

—For weeks in advance the Greeks had put out probing formations, looking for our line of supply, but owing to the quick reactions of our commanders at Thymbra, the line had held, and the Greeks—in their every attempt to cross Scamander to sever it—had been repulsed and thrown violently back to the west bank. Not once in all that time had our Mysian supplies been interrupted, and while we never received enough to relieve our hunger, we did manage to keep Ilium alive. We knew the upcountry trails far better than the Greeks, of course, so they were never able to cut us off completely. Day after day, however, they applied more and more pressure to the line which ran south from Thymbra along the east bank of Scamander, and by the high command's estimate a sizable penetration and breakthrough might be expected at any time. If or when that happened, the Greeks would be in a position to close off all of our supply, and then Troy would fall as surely as the leaves from the trees.

—Aeneas commanded the army then, and sensing the danger, he resolved to put a veteran fighting force on Gargaron so as to thwart the expected attack from the west. Polydamas acted then as chief of staff, and according to his estimate, the position could not be held by fewer than one thousand men, particularly against aggressive assault. He so advised Aeneas, I think, and Aeneas so advised the council, and when the decision was put before Priam, he balked. You see, Lord, the force Aeneas had designated for this all-important task was the Shark with

Polydamas commanding; all in all, it was the best possible decision, but for reasons that have never been explained, Priam rejected both the plan and the commander. Instead, when the council finally adjourned, we learned with some concern . . . *no,* amazement, I think . . . that Keas, son of Eussoros, had been selected to command. I knew him, Lord, for a good and able warrior experienced with the spear, but for many years his enormous administrative capacities had confined him to the staff and the problems of supply, and his selection seemed to me a poor choice because we needed him desperately where he was, organizing the supply trains and setting their routes. Then we also learned that he was to be given an eagle standard, indicating that he was taking the field in command of an independent regiment numbering more than one thousand men. —In fact, fewer than four hundred were mustered when the unit finally marched—less than half the number thought necessary to hold the position. And then, Lord, we learned why. Less than an hour after Keas had marched, Prince Paris was also promoted to field command, given a standard of his own, and ordered to march toward Gargaron at the head of eight hundred Mysian veterans. Clearly, Priam had created a joint command for the operation with the obvious intention that the second formation support the first by moving rapidly onto Gargaron in order to protect Keas's flank. In sum, that is how I envisioned the disposition, and from between grimly tight lips, flint-eyed Polydamas said that it was so.

—I feared then for Keas, for in my experience no one who had ever depended on Paris for support had survived. And thus it fell out, for in the long, cold night that followed, Keas and his entire command were slaughtered where they stood by a surprise Greek penetration in force that crossed Scamander under cover of the weather and went storming up Gargaron through the precise area where Paris was supposed to have moved into his defensive positions. Had any other Trojan commander been guilty of such a failure, he would have been put to death and his standard burned to blot out his name, but for the son of Priam . . . well, the point is moot.

—No, Lord, such was not the case. In fact, Paris had the temerity to claim that he *had* been in position, that he carried secret orders from his father, instructing him to withdraw toward Thymbra if the Greek advantage became too severe. In fact, by the time we could do anything about it, their advantage had become severe—so severe that we were never again able to turn it. I do not know who commanded the Greeks on Gargaron, but he was astute, for from the moment he discovered our weakness and struck us hard with such deadly force, he continued to pour men and supplies so quickly through the breach that by mid-morning on the following day, when I was sent up to assess the situation, not even a fully strengthened Trojan corps could have thrown the enemy off Gargaron. Then, Lord, we were truly surrounded, our last, thin line of supply cut. —As in the beginning, so in the end: the decision to send Paris had proved fatal.

—No, Lord, I have never gone back . . . and never will. After my rescue and my long, painful recovery—for the Greek, that night, had struck me a glancing blow with his sword, laying bare my skull—I served for some years under the standards of Thrace, campaigning far to the north and, once, along the far shores of the dark, black sea where fortifications are made with logs and the warriors wear skins and fight with the bow. I was wounded again there, many times, and finally, once, so badly with a lance that I developed a limp, and then I returned here, thirty winters past, and made this farm with my own hands. In me, Lord of the Hatti . . . *now* . . . the way of the warrior is cold, for my speararm has lost its strength, and it is as much as I can do to milk my goats and sow my seed in the dark, upturned soil. No, I will fight no more, Lord, but never passes a night in which I do not remember who I was, and then, when the dark hour comes, I still think of my lady wife and my little sons and the high white towers of Ilium and drink my bitter wine.

Merops in Mysia

—Abydus? —No, my birthplace was Percote, blue city at the water's edge. If you go there today, little remains: a few charred timbers, a fallen wall or two, some domestic dogs gone wild. Lordly Thoas and the great Achilles led an assault against it in the sixth year of the war and burned it to the ground. At the time I was away in Mysia, arranging grain shipments to supply our companies at Troy, so weeks passed before I heard what had happened. Today, I suppose, my once-young sisters must be bent like me, old slaves in the houses of some long-forgotten Achaian nobles who carried them away in the holds of their high-prowed ships. I don't know, of course; I can't say. I never saw them again and never will.

—But in my youth, Percote was a noble city: long, broad, drenched by the sun, and washed by the shimmering waves of broad Propontis where it raced its course toward the sea. My grandsire used to call the race Poseidon's finger; if the trope holds, we lived under the crook of the first joint in a high, blue house facing the beach. To the south, near the finger's tip, the tall, white walls of holy Arisbe glistened in the sun, but to the north, across the race, the cliffs of Thynia stood glimmering and vast, and above them—above them—the great blue mountains of Thrace ascended into the clouds. The sight feasted the eye, I tell you, and as a boy I never tired of feeding upon it—upon that and the ships.

—Oh, indeed, my friend, the ships were everywhere. My grandfather and I used to watch them by the hour. Before our own steep beach, the broad-beamed, heavy-laden merchant hulls of Thrace hugged the coast, working upstream under sail and oar toward the wide, open reaches of Propontis. Along the opposite shore, going downstream toward Sestus, Dardanos, and mighty Troy, empty ships rode high in the water, their red prows flashing in the sun. And in between the race was alive with activity: here a bargeman floating with the current; there the ornate craft of a noble making a state visit to the citadel on the Plain, and in between a varied host of smacks and bumboats swarming over the water in multiple directions, each seeking its own course and speed and all resembling ants when, in a field, their hill is disturbed by a plowing ox or a man. And all of them, in one way or another, were carrying the fruit of the land either to or from holy Ilium. It was a grand sight, I tell you. In my youth, to me, it was the whole world. —All of that is gone now, of course—gone like Abydus and Sestus and pretty Percote; gone like Ilium and the House of Priam, Lord of the Plain: gone forever like leaves blown out to sea on the wind.

—Put this cloak around you, my friend. Autumn evenings are cold in these Mysian hills—long and dark and cold, and the embers of age burn but sparingly. Let me offer you a cup of this Lydian wine. Here, when Boreas blows into our hidden valleys between these hills, we like to warm our wine and sprinkle its surface with barley.

—No, good friend, I had not nearly so many years on my back. Even then, when we marched down first to windy Ilium and encamped on the Plain, I carried no more than fourteen winters behind me. Lordly Asius, son of Hyrtacus, commanded our contingent, and my father marched as his lieutenant, commanding the companies from Percote. And I—I marched beside my father and wore light leather armor. While the army was on the move, I carried a bow, but when we finally reached the long, broad Plain of Troy and went into bivouac on a grassy bank beside white-watered Simoeis, my father took my bow away, handed me a short ash dart, and set me to learning the face of the land. At the time, you see, I was much too young to fight; I was much too small, a mere stripling, so I became a runner. And then for four long years I carried messages for our contingent, journeying by both day and night between my Lord Asius, or my father, and the Trojan high command.

—Pardon, Friend? —*Oh.* No, no, when first we reached the Plain, the Argive host existed only in men's minds. It was spring, you see;

Zephyr had just blown in across the tail of Boreas, and everywhere one looked new growth was breaking ground: green grass was up, the trees were budding, and around the bases of all of the little hills blood-red wildflowers bloomed in profusion. To the naked eye, war seemed as foreign, as distant, as completely improbable as the return of winter, and the Achaians were nowhere in sight. They existed, then, only in the mind's eye, only in the calculations of diplomacy, but the air was silent, the Plain in bloom, and the sea empty.

—A moon passed, as I recall, perhaps two. In my own young mind I became convinced that the old king's alarm had been false. Everywhere around us, you see, the land was at peace, the soil in full fruition: in the fields, the grain was already knee-deep, its yield assured, and as I passed to and from the white, high walls of Ilium, carrying messages from my Lord Asius or my father and returning to camp with complex, long replies, I made a point of running through Priam's pastures, where hundreds of new foals were gaining their legs, running free against the western winds. To me then, in the spring of my own new youth, the threat of war seemed a grand illusion, the last hazy fantasy of a tired, old king.

—This error, you understand, was entirely my own. Ah, my friend, how shall I say it? Had I been older, had I been more attentive, had I been through the experience of war before, I might have read the signs more clearly and understood them. But I had not, and I failed utterly to grasp the significance of the moment. No matter to me that the Mysians had marched in to camp their thousands beside Scamander, that Paeonians, Lydians, and Carians were bivouacked along the length of the Wall of Heracles, that Dardanians, Phrygians, and Maeonians were swelling the ranks of the citadel; no matter to me that the whole wide, windy Plain of Ilium had become an armed camp: I did not believe that war could be made for possession of a woman, so for me, when the war came, it came without warning. One fine spring night I went to sleep on a cushion of myrtle, the scent of wildflowers drifting through the air, and the next morning, when an alarm trumpet blasted me awake, I leapt to my feet in shock to find the long, broad beach alive with Achaian ships, their high prows racing in from the sea, one after another, riding up hard onto the sands, issuing swarm after swarm of bronze-clad warriors who darted instantly inland like clouds of angry wasps. Then, my friend, I can tell you, I saw much fighting and much killing. Never before had I been as spent, as utterly worn down as I was then, by nightfall at the end of that first long day. We fought halfway across the Plain that day, giving ground slowly while glorious Hector tried to concentrate our strength, and throughout the day I ran and ran and ran, until I thought my lungs would burst, carrying message after message between our field commanders. By midnight both armies had fought to exhaustion, and when the battle lines stabilized and the formations began to disengage in order to go to their rest, I found myself among the warriors from Sestus and collapsed from fatigue beside one of their campfires.

—Ah, your cup is empty, my friend. Let me pour you more wine, and take, too, this piece of cheese. Presently, I will ask Tripclea to skewer us a piece of meat: with that, we may make a meal.

—Yes. Yes, you are right: I learned much that day, not the least of which was that war could be made for the possession of a woman.

—Pardon? I beg your pardon, friend, but my ears, you see, are no longer what they were in my youth. I have difficulty now hearing the call of the hawk, and when men speak to me I can no longer hear their whispers.

—The woman of Sparta? The wife of Alexandros, the Lady Helen?

—Yes, friend, I saw her once, in the sixth year of the war. I was a field commander by that time. My elder brother fell in the fifth year, and after raising his mound, my father reorganized our command, splitting my brother's company and giving me one third. I commanded about two hundred men then, and when our turn came, we marched up to the citadel, on rotation, to act as a part of the garrison. We were there, I think, only ten weeks: as I recall, that was the usual length of the tour, and in the main we guarded the massive granaries that lined the interior walls. It was dull duty, as I remember, long but not arduous, and if memory serves me, I organized the men into a series of watches, allowing for four hours on guard, four hours on standby, and four hours off. We camped in the streets in makeshift huts thrown up against the walls of houses, and as a rule our food was good although our accommodations were anything but comfortable. The citizens were courte-

ous, a little aloof, perhaps, as was their habit with outlanders, but in
the main I think they were grateful for our presence, even if they did
exhibit a mild superiority toward us. I am told that this attitude became
more pronounced in the ninth year, after the failure of Hector's great
counteroffensive, but I cannot attest to that, owing to the fact that I had
gone upcountry beyond Mysia to recruit Lydian mercenaries.

—Whatever the case, in order to draw grain for my own bronze-
armed warriors, I went each week to the steps of the inner citadel, and
there my Lord Priam's stewards issued each garrison commander a
tally stick showing marks for each man we had brought into the city. At
the moment of this presentation, we took an oath that the tally was
correct, and then later, at our assigned granary, we exchanged the stick
for our weekly rations. The last time I went up, you see—following the
presentation—I lingered for a time to exchange words with the commander of the Carian garrison, and while the two of us stood near the
steps that led directly into the center of Priam's palace, a group of
women appeared on the porch above us. My Lady Andromache I recognized immediately because she had shown herself during a previous
presentation. The other ladies I did not know; the Carian thought one
was sapient Cassandra, and for myself, I thought the eldest amongst
them might have been the queen, but I considered this only in passing,
for on the moment the women turned and parted slightly, and I saw,
issuing from the main portal of the palace, another woman whose
beauty took my breath away and knew her instantly for the Lady Helen.

—No, my friend, I am not able to do that, and in truth I would be
foolish to try. Beauty like that cannot be described. The other women
were also beautiful, mind you—beautiful and elegant and polished: my
Lady Andromache's poise inspired me with thoughts of a goddess, and
her clear, smooth limbs shone with the bloom of a rose, but even my
Lady Andromache, among all of the others, looked like a crow beside
the wife of Alexandros. —No, my friend, beauty like that eludes the
exterior eye; it beggars description: it has to be felt, here, somewhere
inside of a man, perceived with the whole of his being. When faced
with it, one is utterly consumed by it, against all odds, against all self-
restraint. The Lady Helen was more than woman, you see, more than a
voice or a movement or a talent of flesh, more than a man has a right to

comprehend, and yet, as I stood there, I comprehended, or thought I did, the measureless infinity of her beauty, and in that instant—then, there—I knew why we, who possessed her, would risk everything to keep her and why the Achaians, who had lost her, would defy death to have her back. Finally, you see, in that one brief instant I knew for certain the nature of the war, its terrible finality; the realization, coming as it did so unexpectedly, shook me to the core.

—That was the last time I ever saw her, there on the porch of Priam's palace, and that one fleeting vision has lasted me a lifetime. Here, now, with the years on my back already surpassing four full score, I can still see her face, her form, as blinding as the noonday sun before the inner eye of my mind, but she is gone from our world, the Lady Helen—she has been gone a long, long time—and when I think back on my youth in Percote and my manhood on the Plain and my one clear vision of the Lady, the high hills of Mysia, which rise around us like so many walls, seem cold and bleak. One farms, of course, and one eats, but still, something of former wonder has disappeared from light.

—Ah, look, my friend, the quarter of a young porker. Sit you down here, if you please. Tripclea will attend us while her daughter prepares for us some barley cakes.

—Indeed, my friend, the tales you have heard are true. —No, they are entirely true. The Lady Helen's husband, the prince . . . Alexandros . . . was not respected among us. Oh, yes, he did take his place in the front rank from time to time, and his ready wit and charm did make him popular with some, but for myself I never liked him. And among the contingents with which I served, my attitude was the norm.

—I was not his friend, of course, nor wished to be. He was older, you see, by some ten years or more and ran with a pack of Mysian bloods who were far more skilled in carousing than in the long, hard work of war. As I say this, mind you, I do not mean to suggest that he did not have his moments. Many's the time that I watched him wade into the press of battle with sword or bow to accomplish hard destruction among the Achaians: he brought down the great Achilles, you know, with a single, well-aimed arrow, and scores of lesser nobles through ten years of war, and once, against the Greek wall, I thought he rivalled his brother as a tower of strength. But to my way of thinking, those instances in which he showed courage were more exceptions than the rule.

—We of Percote, holy Arisbe, and Abydus thought the man unreliable. Thrice in the first year of the war, as we led our bronze-armed warriors to the attack, Prince Alexandros promised that he would lead his Dardanians in our support, and thrice he failed us. In each case we were badly mauled by the enemy's superior numbers—once by the Athenian infantry under Menestheus and twice by bronze-armed Spartans under King Menelaus. In each instance, had the support that Paris promised been forthcoming, I think we might have prevailed. My Lord Asius, who lost his son to a Spartan spearman during our last retreat, never forgave the prince for his negligence and publicly rebuked him for breach of trust, and this before Priam. But lordly Priam, wise and true as he was . . . lordly Priam had a blind spot where his sons were concerned, and my lord's words fell on closed ears.

—The great king was strange in that way. He misjudged, I think, believing that in time all of his sons would grow in character to match Hector, but he was wrong about that. You see . . . Hector was the best: none, not even one of his brothers ever approached him in strength of character or practical ability. And he was generous, too, generous to a fault and as reliable as the hard rock walls of Troy. We learned that quickly in the early days of the war and respected him for it because once the man committed himself, he moved heaven and earth and the gods themselves to make good on his promises, and in battle that kind of reliability inspires a faith that can move armies.

—I am not saying, mind you, that Hector was perfect, faultless, sublime because, of course, he was not. He was, after all, mortal—a man like you and me: he ate, slept, fought, made love, defecated, felt heat and cold—blood flowed in his veins. And he made mistakes, too, as men do. Early in the war they were minor and occurred but seldom. Usually the man was a cautious fighter, cool and calculating, but year after year, as the war dragged on, the tension, the strain, the awful responsibility of command slowly wore him down. And in the ninth year, in the midst of his last great counteroffensive, he made the one major mistake of his life, and it cost him his army, his life, and his city—in fact, it cost us the war.

—At the time, you see, for a reason that none of us ever fully com-

prehended, the Myrmidons had been withdrawn from battle, and the
fierce Achilles had disappeared into the isolation of his encampment.
For myself, I know that I suspected a ruse: given the time, the place,
the situation . . . well, all conditions seemed perfect for a grand de-
ception, and I assumed that King Agamemnon was doing what I would
have done in a similar circumstance—holding the great Achilles and his
long-haired Myrmidons in reserve, waiting for just the right moment
before again committing them to battle. Because I was temporarily in
command of our contingents—my Lord Asius was killed early in the
offensive and my father wounded—I had the opportunity to put my
views before our prince during a hasty staff conference called on the
field. To my lasting regret, I failed to carry the argument. My Lord
Hector, setting aside my reasoned advice, attributed the Myrmidon
withdrawal to a political difference that had arisen between the great
Achilles and the sons of Atreus. And rather than exercise caution in the
face of uncertainty, he seized upon the moment to commit us to a final
grand assault.

—We fought then as we had never fought before, rolling across the
Plain like black thunder, driving the entire Achaian army before us,
down toward their wall, down toward their ships, down toward the dark,
deep sea that waited to swallow them. And in the moment of our triumph, in the very instant when we at last brought fire to their ships, the
threat that I had feared materialized, and the Myrmidons struck us on
the flank, rolling up our entire line. Lordly Patroclus led their attack,
but even without the great Achilles in their van the Myrmidons were
highly effective. They were rested, you see, full in their strength while
we, who had been fighting for two long days, were nearing the point of
exhaustion: given the time and the place, we could not withstand them,
and we gave ground rapidly before them until we once again found
ourselves beneath the high, white walls of Ilium. In that hour, owing to
a twist of fortune that I shall never understand—perhaps a god had
intervened—my Lord Hector killed the noble Patroclus, and in the
wake of this victory the army became wildly exhilarated, driving the
Achaians steadily backwards until nightfall, when we found that we had
regained almost all of the ground we had lost during the Myrmidon
counterattack. But we had spent ourselves in doing it, and our ranks

were horribly thinned. The Plain itself, seething with fire and smoke, was stained with the blood of thousands; many . . . many Trojans had died, and that is when we should have withdrawn into the safety of the citadel.

—That last black night was endless, my friend . . . long and hard and cold. My Lord Hector, sensing victory within his grasp, was adamant in his resolve to renew our attack at dawn while we, his lesser nobles, attempted in every way to persuade him to withdraw. By far the most intelligent among us, the wise Polydamas warned again and again of the dangers we would face if the fiery Achilles returned to battle, but my Lord Hector would hear none of it, and the army held its ground. And in the morning, when Aurora's cheeks blushed blood-red and the burning sun squatted on the horizon like a blazing forge fire, the great Achilles took the field, struck us like a blinding sheet of flame, and split our army in half. Those of us who could made a fighting retreat toward the city, but the others, those pitiful thousands trapped against the banks of Scamander, were consumed, their life threads burned away like dry barley stalks in the heat of summer fires.

—My Lord Hector had the opportunity to escape, but he refused to take it. In the end, you see, he had staked everything on a single throw of the dice and lost. And rather than live under a cloud like that, he resolved to kill Achilles or die, and he died, fighting bravely beneath the shadow of the wall.

—I fault him, of course; he made a mistake, and it cost us the war, but at the same time I cannot say that the same mistake, the tendency to make a mistake like that, is not a part of every man. The war had gone through nine long years by that time, the Trojan treasure was spent, the granaries were running low, and our army was worn down to its last quivering nerve. And then suddenly victory was within our grasp. Who can determine where bold becomes overbold? Who can judge the moment when clear thinking turns to rash? I fault my Lord Hector because the responsibility was his, but faced with the same conditions, I am fairly certain that I would have made the same decision that he made . . . there, then, beneath the shadow of the wall. But only Zeus in his wisdom can know.

—Tripclea, fill my friend's cup with wine, and if you please, bring us some of Euclea's barley cakes, hot from the oven. And friend, help yourself to a portion of brown honey; it remains from the summer hives, and its sweetness is the breath of spring.

—No, friend . . . no, I was not there at the finish. —I do not know how to describe to you my feelings, my reactions to my . . . survival. In one sense, truly, I am grateful to be alive, but in another less explicable way I feel an enduring hollowness, an emptiness, a lingering sense of guilt. All of my men died beneath the shadow of Ilium: my family at Percote, my men at Troy, my friends on the Plain, and all of my youth and strength and home burned with the city, but I survived, a single leaf without a tree. Since then the winds have blown me where they would until, finally, they have dropped me—tired, stooped, and gray—into the depths of this narrow valley, where I edge my way toward the chambers of Hades.

—No, I was not there at the finish; I was upcountry, deep in the hinterlands of Phrygia, conducting an embassy for royal Priam.

—Five, perhaps six months after the death of lordly Hector and long after even the swift Achilles had been slain, I found myself summoned into the inner citadel in the midst of the night, and there, in a narrow, blue-tinted room furnished with a worn throne, I finally came face to face with royal Priam. He was an old man by that time, gray as the sky on a winter day, but his eyes were ice blue and clear, and when he spoke, his voice was firm. "Welcome, my Lord Merops," he said to me in greeting. "I am told that you are a reliable man, and I mean to send you on an embassy. Look about you, my Lord: my people are wasting away. Even the dogs in our streets are starving, yet soon they must make meals for men. Hie you hence, my Lord, into the mountain fastness of Phrygia, to a remote but mighty people called the Hatti who live far to the east beyond the rocky shores of broad Propontis. Take them my sword as proof of your identity and tell them *Priam needs men and grain to stem his troubles.* Be fleet, my Lord; recall your youth and run for me now as once you ran across my windy Plain, carrying words between the far-flung camps of the army and these, my noble walls. Be fleet, my Lord. Be fleet or the dogs of war will surely gnaw our bones."

—I went then in silence, exiting secretly from the city at a dark hour.

I needed five days to outstrip the Achaian lines, to elude their sentries, foragers, and raiding companies, and after that I used four more, running from dawn to dust, before I reached the first unburned human habitation, but I found that deserted, abandoned, and I ran on. I judged I had travelled upwards of fifty leagues by that time, but in all that distance I had yet to meet a living, friendly face. You see, my friend, the Achaians had raided deep into western Phrygia, and all that remained was the blackened, burned-out earth.

—At dawn on the tenth day I swam the broad, sky-blue waters of Sangarius and found myself once more among men. These bronzed horsemen were vassals of the Hatti, and after hearing my embassy and seeing me both rested and refreshed, they put me to horse and sent their swiftest heralds to guide me into the mountain fastness to the east. I had hard riding then, day after long day, as one herald passed me to the next, but on the evening of the sixteenth day, as lordly Helios sank beneath the horizon and lather from our horses foamed into the wind, the last herald and I raced through a narrow gorge to emerge onto a broad, windswept plain, and there in the distance, for the first time, I saw the citadel of Hattusas and knew my journey's end.

—Friend, the hour is late, but here in the bowl enough wine yet remains for two more cups. Will you join me?

—I would not test your patience, friend, to relate details of the Hatti's preparations for the long march that followed. Let me say only that in the high, walled citadel of Hattusas I found the Hatti king, a young, hard man of bronze who heard my embassy with quiet courtesy and then sent out his call to arms. Two moons later, after his army had been assembled and provisioned and well after the march had begun, we were back on the banks of Sangarius. There, the Hatti dispatched me to hasten forward and carry his greetings to royal Priam.

—And then again, my friend, as before, I left both horse and men behind, swam the river, and ran through a blackened land, through one dark valley after another until at last I struck white-flowing Simoeis and quickened my pace toward the Plain. By that time, indeed, I had already grown wary: Achaian pickets were nowhere to be seen, and where I should have cut the tracks of their raiders and foragers, nothing remained but cold signs. And then, you see, as I ran faster and faster down the long banks of white-watered Simoeis, through league after league of endless silence, I began to know the terrors of despair, and in the end, I think, I *knew*. And still, my friend, I kept the faith and ran, ran harder *then* than I had ever run before.

—When I finally reached the foot of the valley, when—finally—I left the river's bank behind and ascended to the Plain, my only vision was desolation; my only greeting, the sound of the wind. A league distant, where once in my youth the white-walled towers of Troy had risen high into the blue sky, their glimmering crowns extending almost to the clouds, there then all that remained was rubble and smoke. Across the wide expanse of the Plain I could not see a single living man, but the dead lay everywhere and the kites and the fierce, full-bellied dogs, and then, when I looked down toward the sea and saw that the high-beaked ships were gone and that long, white waves were breaking up high over the beach, washing away the stumps of the Achaian wall . . . then I knew that it was finished and knew, too, that I was alone.

—And so, friend, as I say, I have lived since like a leaf blown from its tree. Here in this narrow valley where my flight has ended, I merely await the coming of my Lord Hermes and contemplate my descent into the chambers of decay. But I ask you, my friend, is it not thus with all men? Is it not our function to win glory for ourselves or yield it to others? In my time, I think, I have done both and lived fully, but in the days that remain to me and in the long, cold nights of these Mysian hills, I know too that I will wear out my thread in the shadow of Ilium. That is a fact, a destiny that I can never escape.

—My friend, our wine cups are empty, and the embers of this dying fire glow low. Let us to bed, and in the morning when Aurora blushes, I will show you the path toward the land of the Hatti and send you on your way with cheese and olives and enough barley cakes to satisfy your hunger from here to the banks of Sangarius.

Pyracchmes beneath Laurion

—Sometimes—even here, even this close to the sea—snows crust so deep over Maronea that the field stubble no longer stands to view. In such times, with my own eyes, I have seen kites fall frozen from the limbs of dying pines that rise like so many glistening spears across the upland slopes of Laurion. Then the hard march up from the slave barracks becomes endless long against a sharp, bitter wind. And even here, even deep within the bowels of this mountain, the thin, blue fingers of Boreas twist between the faults and fissures, and there is much danger.

—Hold your torch high, friend, and learn to listen for the dulled reverberation of a quick, flat crack, and then pray you to the Shaker of the Earth that he does not make the shaft's roof fall, dashing us all into the chambers of decay. —I have slaved in these mines now full fifty years: that crack, when it comes, sounds inevitably the crack of doom, striking harder and faster than the fall of a swift Achaian sword; for those in its wake there is no escape. Then, know you, the veins sweat— and those thin trickles that drip silently from the roof to fill these pools—both slow and harden into ice, filling every jagged rock seam and fault with a widening Borean wedge. When the wedge drives deep enough, like the blade of a sharp, bronze axe sinking into oak, it splits the rock with a sudden crack, and then the stone falls, crushing everything beneath it. In the dead of winter, when the snow lies deep above ground, these tallowed torches serve for more than light, for then, friend, large numbers of us are forced to move quickly through these darkened tunnels, searching for faults, holding our torch shafts high up toward the room, lightly heating the seams so as to prevent the ice. Thus sometimes we survive. Thus the hard-bitten Greeks extract yet another talent of silver from the mines of Laurion.

—No, friend, indeed I was not always so, for once in my youth, far away on the distant Plain of Troy, I carried a spear and fought beside Hector and Sarpedon of Lycia and the great Aeneas and commanded the Paeonians when first we marched down from Amydon to bolster Priam's defense. My men were bowmen all, and I was strong in the knowledge of their use and gifted, particularly, in the way of hill fighting, and thus, following Polydamas's sage advice, my Lord Hector put us into the line on the western flank, across that long, low line of hills that men call the Wall of Heracles. There, massed either for attack or defense, we fought for nine long years, giving a good account of ourselves in the war against the Greeks, but then the situation changed: in the summer of the ninth year, after holding the Greeks so long at bay, Hector, against all sound advice, made ready an offensive to destroy the ships that stood like sharp-beaked kites across the wide sands of the Trojan beach.

—Why Hector chose that precise moment in the war to call for a maximum effort, I do not know, and for me, always, the matter will remain as shrouded in mystery as the heights of Ida, where Father Zeus makes the home of the gods. As an outlander, you see, commanding no more than one thousand warriors, I was never fully privy to Priam's grand design nor to the high deliberations of the royal council; throughout the war then, for as long as I was a part of it, my Paeonians acted a tactical role, being too few in number to command large voice in the conduct of the campaign. Even so, I had my place on the military council, and there, some days before Lord Hector launched his final offensive, I heard flint-eyed Polydamas speak, putting forward what seemed to me a sounder, alternative plan. Sage Polydamas, you see, warned in advance against making the great offensive, calling it a gamble, calling—instead—for the unexpected: a surprise naval assault, using Mysian and Carian hulls, that would race forward over the beaches of Tenedos to recapture the island. This plan, which promised to reduce casualties while destroying forever the main Greek base of supply, enjoyed immediate popularity with many of the army's commanders, but Hector, exhibiting a rooted disdain for any undertaking at sea, heaped scorn on the plan, eventually evoking a royal decree to ensure its utter and complete defeat. Thus, under cover of night the army began shifting its dispositions in preparation for Hector's grand assault, and that is when finally, after long years in the hills, my hard Paeonians moved down from the Wall of Heracles and out into the midst of the Plain to take up a position at the forefront of the Trojan line. We carried spears then, leaving our bows to our squires, and went forward into the press armed like heavy infantry. Three days later, when the Myrmidons struck us like thunder from the depths of their camp, treacherous Paris withdrew suddenly, exposing the whole of the Paeonian flank; I remember whirling to meet the Greek attack, only to be instantly struck down by the spearhand of Patroclus, whose eyes blazed like the sun. I fell then, almost onto the porches of Hades, while the hot, dry dust of battle settled slowly over me there in the midst of the Plain.

—No, friend, fill now your water bags and ascend again to the mine's entrance, and move quickly or you may feel the whip, which at these depths—with indifferent attention to Achaian law—will be applied swiftly with repeated strokes. These are cisterns, you see, cut into the floor of the shaft at distances of thirty paces, not for the purpose of drinking or long storage, but solely to collect the water that seeps down from above. Thus, during spring, summer, and fall, using the ant-like toil of many slaves, the Greeks keep the mines of Laurion drained and dry. —You have a kinsman working in the depths, you say? —Work faster, friend, so that his stronger, younger arm may mine bright silver from the shafts below, unthreatened by an unexpected flood.

—No, for that was not the way of it: I *was* left for dead, my dusty body stripped of all but the bloody linen of my loincloth. I recall nothing of that time, of course—and not much after for several days—until I suddenly came awake beneath a molten fist of sweat. I had little understanding of where I was then, but my assumption has always been that I had been dragged into one or another of the Argive compounds and chained to a slave stake, for in the moments before I again lost consciousness, I heard other voices around me, bewailing their fate in Carian and Thracian. Someone . . . someone perhaps sent to me directly by the hand of Apollo . . . must have tended my wounds, spreading cobwebs over their surfaces, for when I awoke at last and knew that I remained alive, I recognized that I was cool and dry, and I knew immediately that my wounds had begun to heal. I remember trying to sit up then and failing, and that was the moment in which I fully became a slave, for in that hour I first felt my chains and this worn collar that I still wear bitterly around my neck. That was an hour of deep grief for me, for in no more time than it takes a strong, armed Paeonian to draw and release an arrow, I knew my fate, my broken life, and closed these eyes over my own salt tears.

—Slowly, then, feeling the weight of this collar around my neck, I turned my head, opened my eyes, and looked reality in the face. —Reality, for me, friend, was the foul, open hold of a Phoenician slave hull, and there, chained to a thwart, I found myself held, side by side, with other Trojan wounded. I called out then, finding my voice and body weak, shrunken, barely alive, but even so, I was answered immediately by a dirty Phoenician boy in rags who gave me water to drink and then examined my eyes. When he had gone—to tell his captain, I think, that I would survive—the topknotted Thracian chained beside me lifted his hand and pushed it into my mouth, giving me to eat the last crumbs of a stale barley cake that he had saved in order to give me strength. He could not speak, that Thracian, for he had been wounded in the throat by a sharp, barbed arrow which had severed his vocal cords. Regardless, he showed me a kindness on that voyage, for the Phoenicians were niggardly even with the watery soup by which they kept us alive, and the Thracian, thin with hunger, might easily have eaten the remains of that cake himself without ever passing me so much as a crumb. —As I say, friend, he showed me an act of kindness there, under that weather-beaten sail, and in all of my winters I have never forgotten him. I saw him last on rocky Lemnos, in a corner of the slave market, chained by his feet to a stone post with others of his countrymen who were being bartered by lot to a party of armed Cypriots. He gave me a smile then, and a friendly nod with his brow, knowing already, I think, that he was destined for a life of toil in the blue-veined copper mines above Soli. —As I say, I have never forgotten him, for in my most dismal hour, with no more than a simple human act, he redeemed me and taught me—again—how to live.

—We were at sea for five more days on that voyage, even after I regained consciousness. That old Phoenician hull was broad and slow, and the sea—greatly stirred by Poseidon's hand—thwarted our progress with an ever-rising swell. In the end, with Myrina already in sight, we began taking salt green water over the bow, and then for the first time we were released from our chains so that no man might drown. Phoenician sailors with swords stood over us, guarding against any attempt to seize the ship, but so worn and weakened were most of us that we struggled merely to remain alive, holding ourselves upright through each successive roll while the hull, twisting and popping its seams, shipped more and more water into the hold.

—We entered then, on the fifth day, hull down deep in a treacherous sea that threatened to sink us within sight of the beach. Those who had the strength bailed frantically with leathern bags thrown down by the crew and with stone gray Phoenician pottery that had been used by the crew for carrying food and drinking water. In the end, as Helios sank from view across the low stern, the long pine oars went out, and pulling away together, the crew's oarsmen beached the hull before Myrina beneath the last faint rays of a dying sun.

—We were beached then, but in deep water with the hull riding low. Without regard to any man's safety, the Phoenician captain forced all of us over the side across the beak of the bow, and from there, where the sea was chest deep, the hard-driving surf washed us ashore under the watchful eye of the Lemnian beach guard that collected and chained each man as he rose dripping from the surf. From there, under guard, we were moved slowly up the beach and on through the streets of Myrina toward the dark base of her citadel, and there, beneath the south wall where Lemnian slave dealers are wont to set their posts, the Phoenician entered into negotiations with a one-eyed Locrian and struck a bargain that ended the first leg of our journey when we were chained en masse to the Locrian's posts.

—I do not remember the precise length of my stay at Myrina, but by the time I was herded onto ship again—this time in an Athenian bottom—my wound had closed and something of my former strength had returned after daily nourishment on a thick barley soup laced with fatty lumps of goat cheese. The Locrian was shrewd, knowing full well that thin, gaunt slaves sell cheap while men, full and whole for work, command always an impressive price. In the end, as one man after another regained his strength, the Locrian gathered them together in groups of ten, selling one and all for the same high price. My group—made up of four Carians, a Dardanian, three Mysians, a Lycian, and myself—was the last to be sold, to a party of thick-maned Athenians who bought us, specifically, for toil in the Laurion mines. Of the group I am the only man left alive, and I have survived here, year in, year out, on much less fare than that old, one-eyed Locrian ever dished out.

—And so, friend, in my twenty-eighth year, in an Athenian bottom sailing full before the wind, I came here to Maronea, to the slave barracks of Laurion to live out my days in toil.

—*There,* friend, and remember the spot, for in winters past the ice has always formed thick athwart that fault, and once, no more than fifteen years ago, some twenty men were crushed there when the roof beams gave way. We shore here, now, with rough-hewn pine taken from Laurion's slopes, but even so, the element of uncertainty persists. So let caution be your guide, and mark the place for strong avoidance. Beyond, by the distance of a stone's throw, stands the overseer; make good haste, friend, looking sharp and nimble, or both of us will taste the bite of the whip.

—On the Wall of Heracles? —Just so, my friend, for the fighting was bitter hard, but as I said in passing, my Paeonian archers were skilled bowmen all, and I had particular knowledge for maneuvering them across those thick, brush hills. —Say you again? —Even so, for the tactic was not entirely my own. As I told you, sage Polydamas urged my disposition toward those hills, and following the council in which the matter was decided, following the hour in which Hector assigned me to the position, gray-eyed Polydamas drew me aside. "Pyracchmes," he said, pointing toward the Wall, "with one thousand archers, you should be able to hold those ridges for a hundred years. Combine mobility with defense in depth, and the Greeks will never get around you or through you, for the ground is too rough." He was right, you see; he seemed always right to me, and had he commanded at Troy . . . well, the matter is closed. —But about the Wall of Heracles, he was dead right: the secret, friend, was mobility.

—Those hills of the Wall, you see, are narrow and long, separating the wine-dark sea from the deep blue valley of Scamander and the dusty Plain beyond. To the north, the Wall ends at the Hellespont, high above that corner of the beach where once, long ago in my youth, the full might of Achaian Greece anchored its strong right flank. From there, rising due south, running parallel to the coast, the Wall stretches back toward Besika Bay like the ribbed curve of a bow worked by a craftsman from the horns of an ibex. Never more than a mile wide at any given point, the length of those hills exceeds a distance of two full leagues, and in that space—given the ground—a competent commander can find more than ample room for defense.

—The ground? —It consisted of low, steep hills, separated by deep ravines, all water courses running either west toward the sea or east into the valley of Scamander. The ravines were thick with willow, ash, and yew interspersed with myrtle, but across the slopes stands of scrub oak grew thickly toward the sky, sheltering shaded grass and small white flowers that bloomed in clumps between the rock-gray fissures. It was excellent defensive country, for the enemy could never move through it in an unbroken line.

—Weeks before the Greeks made their first grand assault across the beaches of Tenedos, Hector had already ordered us into position along the Wall, and that is when, after a preliminary reconnaissance, I moved my Paeonians into a strong base camp atop the heights, midway between the Hellespont and the long, arching beach at Besika Bay. We made no attempt to fortify the position, for to my mind, considering the limited number of men under my command, our best defense was the ability to melt away swiftly down any number of game trails that converged on the camp, and in order to ensure future success with the tactic, I set my men immediately to learning the ground. Within the following weeks, then, we came to know the Wall's terrain, its nooks and crannies and hidden recesses, like the muscled backs of our hands, and to that end I apportioned the regiment into ten distinct companies numbering one hundred archers each. Once we knew the ground, once we had studied every pitfall and advantage the terrain provided, I began putting my subordinate commands through a long series of tactical exercises designed to teach them how to coordinate their efforts both in attack and defense; thus during those early, pre-war weeks we devel-

oped a precision of movement as well as a tactical competence that
served us unswervingly throughout the remainder of the war.

—My lords Aeneas and Hector inspected us on the Wall, mere days
before the Greeks struck, and they were well pleased with what they
saw, saying so publicly at the conclusion of their tour. Later, after the
battle had joined, flint-eyed Polydamas came amongst us, observing
closely our methods of attack, withdrawal, and defense, and after going
into battle three or four times himself—fighting directly beside me at
the head of my swift command—he offered refinements on my tactics
that saved me countless casualties in the years to come. "Conserve
life," he told me. "This war is destined to be long and bitter and hard
for all of us; for holy Ilium itself, success or failure will rest with our
ability to outlast even the most ambitious Greek attacks while maintaining an unbroken front. Strike and fade away, my Lord. Rely on your
bows and the long-distance killing power of your slings, and for the
time you are on the Wall, discard the way of the spear for its skilled
employment will take you too close into the press. Kill Greeks, Pyracchmes, but do it from a distance, keeping your own command intact."
That was wise advice and sound military thinking, and as a result I
altered one element in my methods and saved many lives.

—When the Greeks had first stormed ashore, swarming over the
beach like so many angry ants kicked loose from their mounds, we had
met a number of their flanking units on the northern tip of the Wall and
successfully defended against them, combining archers with spearmen
for mutual support. Clearly, during those first days we had denied the
Wall to the Greeks, killing many outright and wounding far more as
they boiled up the slopes against us. We made good use of the high
ground there, withdrawing as necessary across each successive ridge so
as always to keep some distance between ourselves and the main thrust
of the Greek advance, but in seeking to use the spear as a main pillar of
our defense, I had erred because such tactics brought my own men well
within range of Greek javelins, and thus more than forty of my warriors
had gone down in agony. Clearly—though we had killed and wounded
far more Greeks over the course of that first, three-day battle—we
could ill afford to lose half so many men, and I knew immediately that
my methods for engagement would have to be changed. Wise Polydamas showed me the way, the only way that my bright-eyed Paeonians

could accept battle, do serious damage to the enemy, and survive.

—As you say, my friend, our way of the bow was the Greek's undoing, at least in so far as the fighting along the Wall of Heracles was concerned. Know you, then, that following the Greek invasion and those first prolonged days of battle in which both armies fought to complete exhaustion, a lull ensued that went on for many days, even weeks. And then, early on a morning when the sea breezes shifted to blow in a squall, the Greeks made their first serious attempt to outflank the main Trojan defenses on the Plain. The axis of their attack came straight down the brush-covered spine of the Wall.

—Without question, the Greeks failed to achieve even the mildest element of surprise. Indeed, the Trojan high command—myself included—had anticipated their move, and my scouts—lightly armed runners who were skilled in the arts of reconnaissance—had been schooled by me about what signs would most quickly forewarn us of an impending attack. In consequence, on the night before, I knew that large numbers of Boeotian spearmen were massing beneath the Wall's northern rim, just inside the confines of their darkened camps. I made my dispositions accordingly, establishing archers in depth across a length of seven successive ridges, and then we waited alertly, watching for the first advancing line of Boeotian infantry.

—Dripping with rain, their hard bronze arms glistening with moisture, they came at us that morning from beneath the cover of the squall. I still remember the water streaming from their black Boeotian beards and the sense of purpose in their fast advance. We looked down on them there, from the summit of the Wall's second ridge, from the depths of a gnarled stand of oak that seemed stunted by the wind. Not realizing that one of the Wall's narrow, brush-filled defiles interposed between us, the first Boeotian company caught sight of us, uttered a fearsome war cry, and broke instantly into a run, its hard bronze spear points glistening at the ready even from beneath that morning rain. —I still remember those men, the icy hatred in their eyes, all of them charging forward like so many wet and ravenous lions eager for the kill, and I remember too their screams of anguished frustration as they burst from the scrub against the edge of that impassible ravine, for in that instant, as all of them drew up shocked, short of their goal, I gave command, and my hawk-eyed Paeonians loosed their arrows. —We

killed many with that first sharp volley and wounded more, dropping
some into the depths of the defile while others, taking barbed points
through their necks or eyes, staggered backwards over the scrub, their
long, agonized death rattles lingering in their throats. I made a second volley then, but before it had struck its mark, I sounded the ram's
horn, and my men—moving with the stealth of foxes—melted up the
game trails, moving back up the spine of the Wall toward the next
forested rib.

—As I look back, friend, I remember that the entire evolution took
place exactly as planned. Struck down unexpectedly and with killing
force, the Boeotians required some length of time to recover and regroup, and in truth I think we so hurt their first assault company that it
was permanently withdrawn from the battle: throughout the remainder
of the war, I do not remember ever again seeing the three white boars
which marked that unit's shields. Whatever the case, the Boeotian commander was slow to react, slow to bring up his second company and
throw it into action, and during the interval I passed my own warriors
back along the spine, down through the succeeding ravine, and up
through my next line of archers, who were already in position, already
threading shafts to their bows.

—Again we waited, and again the Greeks came at us from beneath
the rain, and again we caught them along the edge of the interposing
deep defile. And again, friend, many Boeotians went down beneath
sharp Paeonian arrows. The Boeotian commander had thrown two
massed companies into this, his second assault, and fully half brought
their slings into play, trying vainly to provide cover for their spearmen
who ranged along the ravine's lip, searching desperately for paths
which would lead them down across that defile and up onto the opposite heights, where they might finally come to grips with my archers.
Rather than withdraw in the face of this second attack, I held my men
in place, and within a short time we made the air so hot with our
arrows that the Greeks were again forced to withdraw beyond our
range. Then, in the dim, rain-drenched distance, across the ridge top
from which we had only recently retired, the Boeotians began massing
even more of their companies, bringing up one after another and halting them in full view, well beyond the range of my eager, quick-eyed
archers. In less time than it takes a deep-winded runner to pace a

league, the Greeks had assembled as many, perhaps, as one thousand warriors across the rocky northern ridge. And then, friend, the Boeotian commander gave himself away, for thus assembled, those heavily armed warriors stood their ground without making so much as a single aggressive move. Instead, there in the rain with the water streaming from their shields, they broke as one into the low, hollow chant of their sea hymn, lifting it toward the sky. With the speed of a hunting hawk taking a white-winged partridge in flight, I knew then what my opposite was up to, knew to the marrow of my bones that somewhere—out along the sea's wide beach where the Wall's ravines empty across the sands, where their every menacing movement would be well masked from the alert eyes of our regiments on the Plain—a Boeotian flanking force of considerable size must already be trying to work around behind us while the larger, stationary demonstration to our front tried, by its provocative immobility, to hold us in place. I acted swiftly then, sending back runners to my subordinate commands, and in less than an hour, no more than five hundred strides to the rear, my rain-drenched warriors fought that battle's decisive engagement by annihilating from above the Greek flanking force that had tried to work its way up the ravine behind us.

—Indeed, friend, we had foreseen the enemy's move and planned for it—not on the day of his assault but weeks before while studying the ground. I mentioned this to sage Polydamas when he first came up, and to this hour I remember the light that blazed from his eyes. "*See* that it is so," he said sharply. "*Force* the enemy to attack you in the way that will make him most easy to defeat. Defend the second ridge," he said, pointing north with his spear, "but give way quickly after the first brief engagement. Then, my Pyracchmes, you must hold on the third rib, and *that* will force the Greeks to make an assault on your flank. When it comes, it must make its way up this gorge, for the first two defiles end in bluffs that not even a Greek could scale. Defend the ridges in depth, but along the lip of this ravine concentrate the remainder of your warriors and annihilate the enemy when he tries to work in behind you." Thus, on a warless afternoon that gleamed bright beneath Helios's beams, Polydamas and I planned a battle that I later fought in the rain against four hundred climbing Boeotians and won on the strength of the strong Paeonian bow.

—Precisely. As we had predicted, the Boeotians, marching under cover of the rain, worked quickly around our seaward flank and began climbing up toward the Wall's spine by means of that first passable defile. During the interval, leaving a trusted subordinate to command those of my archers still facing the Boeotians to our front, I worked my way back to the edge of that gorge through which I knew the Greek flanking attack must come, and there I took command of those of my archers who had retired after inflicting our first hard blow on the enemy. Across the ravine, under the command of another of my subordinates, fully three hundred more of my warriors had assembled, taking up their positions, watching in silence for any movement along the floor of the watercourse below. Not long after, Greeks began appearing, clawing their way up the gorge like files of well-armed ants, their muffled weapons held at the ready. They were apprehensive; that much was clear, for they all moved forward in jerks and starts, the kind men make when they are trying to elude well-aimed arrows in war. Even so, even before they reached our positions, they had started to climb the ravine's walls by means of the narrow game trails that they readily found below. I waited then, until their leaders were only a few paces away, until their entire command—some four hundred and more—was fully exposed, mired in the mud across the steep sides of the slope, and then, like an eagle on the wing, I pierced the rain-swollen air with a loud Paeonian war cry and stood forward, listening to our sharp arrows sing. And then, friend, was much and terrible killing, for not a single Greek climbed out of that ravine. Instead, all along the break's northern face, fully exposed, stricken Boeotians went down hard, felled like thick mountain timbers under woodsmen's blades—rolling, crashing, falling like dead, heavy wood amidst a clatter of cascading arms into the narrow watercourse below, and for the remainder of the morning those waters ran red to the sea. —Not a single Greek survived; not a single prisoner was taken.

—By noon the squall line had passed inland, and then, in plain view of the Boeotian main body, I withdrew my warriors from the third rib, all two hundred of them, running them quickly down through the bloody gorge and up again onto the opposite heights to station themselves beside my three hundred other archers, who had done so much of that morning's deadly work. Not long after, hugging the earth like ferrets, small parties of lightly armed Boeotian scouts made their way forward to the lip of the gorge, and there, after first allowing them to take full stock of the carnage we had wrought, we emerged from the woods and showed ourselves—all five hundred—walking slowly forward from between the trees, our bows at the ready. —Thus, displaying our might, the battle ended, and never again through the course of the war did the strong-armed Boeotians try to come against us across the ridges of the Wall.

—Just so, friend, for where one man fails, another is compelled to try. Thus, in the war's second year the Arcadians tried us, pressing a hard attack across the ribs, using tactics that were similar to those employed by the Boeotians but with this difference: their flanking assault, when it came, was both larger and faster, and well coordinated with the striking pressure put on our front. In the Arcadian's case, then, I found myself forced to throw the entire Paeonian regiment into a battle which prolonged itself over a period of two bitter days. Still, in the end we handed the Greeks a decisive defeat; they lost many, many lives and never came against us again, leaving us undisputed masters of the Wall of Heracles throughout the remainder of the war as we Paeonians knew it. Only in the ninth year, when my Lord Hector ordered us down to the Plain, did the Trojan left flank go unsecured, and for what followed I can speak no word. But for my Paeonians, I have only praise, for in Troy's defense they were the strongest of the strong, ever unswerving in their courageous defense of the Wall.

—Even so, friend, for the torch in your hand burns thin. We have not far to go now before we return to the face of Laurion. There, beyond the entrance to the shaft, we must unyoke these water bags from our shoulders and spill them over into the stone trough that channels the mine's waste waters down into the deep Maronean valleys below. We return then, moving always quickly beneath the overseer's eye, to the tunnel of the torchmen who wind these willow wands and dip them into the tallow that burns so bright in the shaft's depths. Inside the tallow chamber, while the torchmen pack our bags, we take a moment's rest and break the rationed barley cake, and then, we begin again the long, sharp descent into the mine.

—No, friend, in truth, I have never adjusted. Rather, I have survived, pitting my strength each day against the unknown dangers of the mine. But late at night, when Athene's owl passes, just as I did so many years ago as I hunkered in my winter hut on the snowbound Wall of Heracles, I still think long and hard on my father's citadel in Amydon and recognize the fact that now—at this great distance, in this late year—no man lives who recalls my name. —How otherwise should it be, I ask myself, but as surely as we are here, friend, I know in the deep depths of my mind that defeated warriors are like leaves on the wind, fallen into the sear, blown loose from time and borne by the whirling currents into the last state of decay, and yet, in the long, dark hours, when the Earth Mother at last falls silent, I still think back to my father's hall on the wide, green banks of the Axius. Then, friend, I can almost see the pale, yellow flowers of spring and the dancing feet of my sisters as they chased summer butterflies and the strong right arms of my brothers as they learned with skill how to pull their bright Paeonian bows. The Guide, I think, will come soon enough for me now, on some dark night in the dead of the coming winter, but even so, in the last fleeting moments before he leads me finally onto the cold porches of Hades, my thoughts, I know, will flow back across time like rivers running down to the sea, and then, there, in my last lingering dreams, I will once more go home to Amydon.

—Turn to the right, for the tallowing chamber is not far beyond, and my old bones are much in need of rest.

—So tell me, friend, you say you are a Dorian? With your pardon, I know not the name. Were your cities, too, overrun and your people defeated by the relentless Achaian Greeks?

Diator beyond Olympus

—Patience, Dorian, *patience*. Thy eagerness is understandable, even admirable, but overbold; at these altitudes the snows on Olympus are destined to melt as slowly as those over mist-covered Ida above the Plain. Even so, fleet-winged Zephyr will blow in soon enough, strong from the west, breathing a new spring over this frozen, northern land, and *then*, Dorian, when the snows have melted to ankle depth, we will move hard and fast through the passes before us and down across Thessalia beyond, striking dark iron against the Argive heart of Phthia. Then, Dorian, the Achaian Greeks will go down before us like new-mown fields of hay, and may sharp-beaked kites feed greedily on their limbs.

—Trust me, Dorian . . . I know it will be so, for the Greeks believe us to be massed in Dolopia. Over and over again that fact has been confirmed by Argive captives taken by your raiding columns along the ridges of the Pindus. No longer can there be even the slightest doubt: the Argive high command thinks us poised like eagles ready to sweep down over Aetolia in a drive toward the sea. —Trust me, Dorian. You have paid me dearly in hard-won gold, and now, by making the Dolopian demonstration that I advised, the Greeks believe you to be where you, in truth, are not—where only your holding forces demonstrate daily to their ignorant, blind-eyed view. Your holding force is like your anvil only, but when the snows melt and the frosted Borean rimes begin to drip from the trees, then, like a bolt the iron mass of your hammer will hurl itself down from these Olympian heights to crush the Achaian flank. Then the Argive alliance will know their error, but *then* it will be too late.

—Yes, I know well the price of failure. Indeed, mighty Dorian, I know it better than you, so think not to shake my beard with your threatening admonitions. Command in battle is *your* responsibility, not mine, for I advise here only, taking my payment in your hard barbarian coin. If you would make my life forfeit for your success or failure, give over your standard. Then, Dorian, I myself will lead your warriors into bronze-bright battle, striking the merciless Greeks as once, long ago in my youth, I did across the windswept Plain of Troy.

—Nay, Dorian, if you intended no insult, none is taken, but my advice remains the same. Wait, and when the hour is ripe, strike them with the unexpected, hard on their flank, and the whole eastern might of Greece will fall before you. Trust me, Dorian, the plan is sound.

—Indeed, I lost all: father, sister, wife, and son . . . house and home . . . friends, neighbors, relations, my identity, all . . . all of them lost long ago in the war at Ilium. We were Trojans, you see, not outlanders, not Mysians or Carians or Lycians, but Trojans born and bred, connected by marriage to the royal house of Priam. —Yes, by marriage: my blue-eyed sister had married young, to Isus, son of Priam, he who went down to an Argive spear in the ninth year of the war. A son of Atreus killed him in open battle on the Plain, stripping him of his arms, and in the same hour my grief-stricken sister ran wildly from the house and threw herself screaming from the heights of the Trojan wall.

—Nay, it was even so with my father, for he died on the same day. In that, the ninth year of the war, my father commanded west of Scamander, on the broad Trojan flank near Besika Bay. —Observe, Dorian, on the sand table before us, I will draw in the positions, thus.

—He was in his sixty-eighth year by that time, my father—gaunt, lean, and gray—but he could still hurl a strong spear in company with younger men, so when Lord Hector mounted his last great offensive on the Plain, my father was given a new standard, placed in command of other aging warriors grown long in years—nearly two thousand in all— and ordered into the field. He did not, of course, move into a position from which he could be expected to join in the main thrust; instead, he marched that graying regiment across Scamander, onto the rocky, wooded heights overlooking Besika Bay. There, deploying toward the west, he took up a blocking position so as to secure Hector's deep left flank against the remote possibility of a seaborne Greek assault from their island base on Tenedos. It was quiet on those heights, almost serene. My father's command, you see, was largely honorary, a mark of respect for a grand old general who had served well in his time and for other warriors like him, and their placement in the line was a mere precaution during a critical hour. The commoner, Polydamas, I remember, did not favor the assignment, claiming that it invited Achaian attack from the high, ribbed Wall of Heracles. For the nine previous years, you see, Paeonians had held the Wall, but they were young men, all of them, still strong in the integrity of their spear arms, and needing their strength on the Plain, Hector called them down, arguing before the high council that the Argives would be too hard pressed by his attack to mount any serious threat along the Wall. Even so, in the event that some unexpected threat to my father did develop, Paris was designated to go to his relief, and there the matter stood on the day we opened the offensive.

—Myself? —No. Even before Hector attacked, I was already fighting east of Simoeis, attempting to extricate a green regiment of topknotted Thracians who had lost their way during the long march down from Colonae. Under the very noses of the Argive fleet, which then controlled Propontis, Thracian hulls had slipped in to put that regiment ashore under the cover of darkness. Then, moving only at night, those Thracians had been working down toward the Plain under Artemis's darkened eye. On the third night, while threading their way through the shadows of the Dardanian hills, they had accidentally bumped the Argive left flank. Immediately, the Thracians found themselves surrounded on three sides but in good position along the spine of a ridge, and up that, back toward the east, gold-armed Rhesus, King of Thrace, withdrew his entire command. Within a short space, finding ground that he was certain he could hold, he took his stand, and the engagement stabilized. The position was waterless, so he quickly sent runners toward Troy to report his situation, and eventually two found their way to the Plain, bringing us Rhesus's request for help. The high command turned the matter over to Polydamas, and Polydamas called up my battalions—the Talons of the Hawk—and sent us forward at the run into those steep Dardanian hills. We fought then for two days in succession, striking hard-fighting battalions of Corinthians who only gave way slowly before the pressure of our assault. We might have had far more help from the Thracians, I think, had they been better trained and war-wise in the way of battle, but they were not, and in the end the Hawk's Talons, fighting largely alone, forced a Corinthian withdrawal. Then, conducting a bitterly fought withdrawal of their own against the Argive forces still pressing them from the north and west, the Thracians pulled back through our lines, reaching the Plain only late in the day. By that time Hector's offensive had already opened, and there, on that first, dark night, Rhesus and twelve of his staff were treacherously murdered in their sleep by Argive raiders who slipped past the pickets. —So, as you see, on the day that my father died I was still fighting east of Simoeis, pushing my command forward toward the Argive camp along Hector's far right flank.

—No, Dorian, that was not quite the way of it—not quite, and even now the recollection makes me shudder, for my father's squire—a sharp-eyed lad of fifteen and a fine sprinter, the son of Acamas— brought me the report in clear detail. He reached me, I remember, late that night, waking me from a sound sleep somewhere beside a campfire on Simoeis's dark, northeastern bank. How he found me, I will never know, but the measure of his merit is that he tried at all: under cover of darkness the wide Plain was crawling with wandering warriors, their long ash spears at the ready, each of them searching with owl's eyes for one more quick-blooded victim. He found me, then—the son of Aca-mas, my father's squire—and woke me and delivered into my hands my father's eagle-crested standard, the symbol of his command. The lad was wet, shivering with cold, for he had crossed the swollen Simoeis only moments before, taking his bearings from the glow of our fire. How he avoided my sentries along the river bank, I do not know, for they were good men all, alert and keen-eyed, and would have put a spear through his back without a moment's hesitation on that night, for it was clear to me that he had no knowledge of the password but had braved the danger regardless. —He was an admirable warrior, that Tro-jan boy. On the following day, without so much as a whisper, he went down hard into the lightless chambers of decay, taking an Argive arrow just beneath his armpit.

—My father's death, I think, had been equally hard, and that too had been made without so much as a whisper, by his own decision, on the southern ribs of the Wall of Heracles, for know you, Dorian, that without regard to Trojan expectations, the Greeks had, indeed, attacked along the Wall, rolling down its abandoned spine like an unstoppable wave in the same hour that Hector attacked on the Plain. According to the son of Acamas, the attacking force consisted of lightly armed Boeotian infantry well supported by close-cropped Euboean archers, whose feathered arrows filled the sky like darting flocks of birds when a stooping kite wings suddenly into their midst. Considering the matter now, here, across these lean, long years, I think the Greeks must have taken the entire night to move up into position across those deep, rocky defiles on the Wall, for when their assault struck from beneath Aurora's first flush, it struck in force with the single purpose of annihilating my father's regiment with its first sharp blow.

—The Greeks came then, upwards of five thousand of them, sweeping across the ridges north of Besika Bay, moving silently like the wind while the sky above filled almost to a point of darkness with flint-sharp Euboean arrows. My father gave no ground, Dorian. —Old, gray, and lean those aging Trojans might have been, but they were also—all of them—scarred veterans of our long-past Mysian wars, and they knew well how to defend their standard against a surprise attack borne down to them from the high ground. They stood then like the dark, lichen-covered boulders around them—hoary with years, gray with granite time—waiting for the swift Boeotian attack to shatter against them, and it did, once, leaving hundreds of dead Greeks and Trojans mingling their blood across the rocky, broken ridge. —Given the numbers involved, considering the odds, the tactical situation called for a rapid, fighting withdrawal. My father knew that, knew it as surely as I stand here now beneath this iron-gray sky, and knew, too, to the center of his being, that his worn command was no longer young enough, no longer physically capable of making a hard-fought retreat to the Plain. Down to less than twelve hundred men after the first Boeotian impact—wounded all, bleeding—they had neither the wind, Dorian, nor the speed nor the strength to make a fast-paced withdrawal and knew it, knowing too that only their will sustained them. My father made a warrior's decision then and called forward the son of Acamas. "Take this, my standard," he told the lad, "and run like the wind to the high citadel at Ilium, even unto the royal throne of Priam, and tell my king these words: *Even beneath Helios's mid-morning beams, Diator and the loyal Grays died fighting in defense of Troy.*"

—The lad ran then, as my father commanded, like a fleet wind skimming across the Plain, but on the crest of the succeeding rib, he turned once more, looking north from whence he'd come. The last Acamas's son saw of him, my father had formed his regiment into two mutually supporting lines; at the slow march, with my father at the forefront, the Grays were moving silently forward up the spine of the Wall, holding their antique arms at the ready, thrusting the bronze point of battle into the Greeks' very teeth.

—How say you, Dorian? —No, that much is true: royal Paris did not move up to support my father in the moment of crisis. But neither Paris nor my father, I think, can be faulted for the fact. Know you, for one, that the Boeotian assault developed too swiftly and in too much strength for rapid, supportive reaction. In fact, only by means of my father's last, doomed attack were the Boeotians in their numbers prevented from sweeping down onto the Plain and rolling up Hector's line. The Boeotians paid dearly for annihilating the Grays, both in blood and in time. That was the price of my father's death—time . . . a precious hour, perhaps more. In the interval, as soon as Acamas's son had reported the threat, Hector withdrew not one but two Carian regiments from the Plain and sent them running hard, back on the sprint, skimming across the knee-high grass like swarms of wasps, to check and defeat the Boeotians along the banks of Scamander. The Carians stopped the enemy just as they descended from the Wall, and thus my father's delaying action served its purpose. I honor his memory, Dorian, as a warrior of Troy.

—Just so, for royal Paris was already heavily engaged at that hour, at the dead center of the Trojan line in Hector's main battle before the high-beaked ships. The fighting there was savage, both by night and day: he could not have disengaged and cannot, I think, be faulted for failing to support my father.

—Did I know him, do you say? —Yes, I did. He was much blamed, of course, for the troubles of Troy, and in the matter of the Spartan whore, certainly, the blame was just. Without regard to the woman's wishes—and that she wished to remain at Troy, I have no doubt—but regardless, the stain of wife-rape tainted us all. Still, the Greeks made war against us for something more than the Spartan bitch, and for that, Paris bore no blame.

—The man? —Handsome, blue-eyed, strong. He was a fine archer, an even better boxer, and he could run like a lion. I watched him compete once with the Lydian champion, and Paris outdistanced the man by the length of a spear-cast. He ran bare-footed, I remember, with a relaxed mien, and bested the Lydian by the length of his stride. He trained daily, I think, even during the war, for he took pride in his body and kept his skin well oiled with the dew of the olive.

—As you say, he was vain, of both his strength and his appearance. And that, more than anything, I think, tended to set him apart from the rest of his family and from other, less noble men. I knew him, certainly—after a manner of speaking, we were related by means of my sister's marriage—but I did not call him friend and knew few Trojans who did. He was a man capable of immense charm, but he was erratic too and moody, and without warning, on the slightest provocation, his moods were apt to shift, so swiftly and so unexpectedly that even the members of his family found him difficult and aloof. For reasons that defy my ability to explain, he often found his closest companions among the young Mysian bloods that garrisoned Thymbra. Those warriors—nobles all—were as wild as the savage winds that blow down from Ida across their own broken and erratic lands, and then, in Troy— although grateful for the military help that the Mysian alliance brought us—we disliked their uncivilized behavior, treating them with diplo- matic warmth only. At this distance . . . I do not know . . . perhaps wise Priam sensed our dislike for the Mysians and sent Alexandros to make amends, to keep the fires of friendship burning brightly between us, but on the whole, on the evidence of his character, I rather think that royal Paris found in the Mysians something that accorded well with his own temperament, and thus the bonds between them. —As you say, Dorian, for the sons of kings, men make allowances.

—No, for Lord Hector, no man made allowances; the need never arose, for he was as unlike Alexandros as the almond from the grape. Both had grown from the same loin, but there the similarity ended, for Hector was a man among men, strong in deliberation and deliberate in command. He was a head taller, I always thought, than any of his brothers, but at this dim distance, I sometimes wonder if *that*—my recollected perception—hasn't more to do with the matter of his character than anything in his physical stature. He lived modestly, I remember, in a bachelor corner of the royal apartments that was wholly without opulence, but in the war's third year, after her father and brothers had been wantonly cut down by that savage, Achilles, he took beautiful Andromache to wife and made her a home. In their fourth year together, she bore him a son, and later, honoring the boy's father, the army named the boy Scamandros.

—In so far as the times allowed, I think Hector was happy in his life and settled—in ways that few of his brothers ever were—but at the same time, as those long, bitter years went by, the mark of care creased his brow more and more deeply. Even at this distance, Dorian, the strain he felt exceeded your own, for he was besieged in his own land, commanding Ilium's entire defense against impossible odds. Nevertheless, Hector remained firm, directing our efforts with hard determination, husbanding with his father the failing resources of Troy, and waiting—always waiting—for a Greek mistake, and in the ninth year, when he thought at last that he saw a fighting chance, he went boldly over to the attack, striking the long Greek line like a wind-whipped sheet of flame.

—Even to this day, Dorian, the matter remains unclear. Given the time, the place, the enemy—given the same hard choice—I would still favor Hector's plan. —You have heard it said, you say, that Polydamas was wise beyond his years in the way of battle? —Indeed, the remark is just. Sapient Polydamas was a field commander for Priam during both the Third and Fourth Mysian Wars, and his tactics were nothing if not brilliant, but remember, he won those victories at sea, in command of the Shark. I need not remind you, I think, that the Greek War was fought ashore, on the Plain, not at sea, and there, Priam rightly placed

Hector in command, making Polydamas his sometimes chief of staff. Remember, too, that Polydamas was a commoner, not privy—like members of the royal family—to each political nuance of the war, and that, to my way of thinking, was exactly as it should have been.

—About the Wall of Heracles and my father's regiment, Polydamas was right: I admit as much. But remember, too, that he had opposed Hector's grand offensive, arguing instead for a seaborne attack on the Greek lines of supply. At the time most of us suspected his motives, for in truth I believe that he was not above envying Hector, even after Hector had done him the honor to make him chief of staff. It is true, I think, that Polydamas's plan had both merit and a chance for success, but consider, Dorian . . . the results would have been long in coming, requiring more than a year of shortened supply before the Greeks could have been forced to their knees whereas Hector's design—the plan to burn their high-beaked ships—promised immediate, decisive results, particularly in light of the political rift that was just then showing itself in the heart of the Argive command. *That* was the root of Hector's strategy—to strike so swiftly, so forcefully, so unexpectedly that, even in the event of a repulse, the Argive alliance would collapse in disarray under the combined weight of our blow. Hector's was a good plan; given the same chance again, I would support it even now and pray to the gods for bright-winged victory.

—Yes, the third day was decisive. On the third day, without warning, roaring like howling thunder, the Myrmidon butcher, Achilles, burst from the Argive camp with such penetrating force that he drove a sharp wedge deep into the army's center. For Troy it seemed the beginning of the end: within a single hour hordes of Greeks had poured through the breach in our line, moving southwest with all the speed and power they could muster. By noon they had trapped fully half of our army against swift-flowing Scamander, and then, with our army split, the real slaughter began.

—I knew this only by report, you understand, for throughout, pressing forward on my own along Hector's far right flank, my command—some six hundred bronze-armed Trojans of the Hawk's Talon—had remained well to the east of white-watered Simoeis, driving steadily north against the few Greek companies that came out to meet us along the base of the Dardanian hills. By mid-morning, I recall, with only half a company of Arcadians still facing us, we were well within sight of our objective—the wave-washed beach east of the Greek camp. In that moment, even as I raised my father's standard to signal for our final assault, a winded runner reached me from the depths of the Plain, from Polydamas, bringing me word of the Trojan disaster along the banks of Scamander. And then the runner merely heightened my perceptions of disaster by reporting, too, that Greeks on my left—forces which should have been on my left—had already fanned out across the Plain, far to my rear, penetrating with speed and resolution into the upper valley of the Simoeis, where they had seized the undefended fords. Thus, with success in sight I suddenly found myself cut off, nearly surrounded and trapped by the unseen enemy advance.

—I suspected then that the Arcadians to our front were a ruse, a mere bait thrown out to lure us closer to the Greek camp, and in that moment I blew the ram's horn twice, recalled my attack line, and began turning the regiment toward the east. My plan, Dorian, was to force march the Talon as swiftly as possible into the safety of the Dardanian hills; from there, by means of circuitous routes, I hoped to skirt the main Argive threat to my rear and return to Troy by using a variety of well-marked Phrygian trails to the east. Even then I remember thinking that our escape would prove difficult, for the retreat I envisioned would require a five-day march on the one-day's rations that remained in our wallets. At that moment, with my warriors' bellies at the root of my concern, in the midst of our turning evolution, the massed might of a hard Corinthian hammer came hurling down against us from a concealed position on the same slope that we were preparing to climb. In the same instant, no more than four hundred strides to our rear, an entire Arcadian regiment rose suddenly from concealment along the steep banks of Simoeis and stood, silently, holding their long ash spears at the ready. —A Corinthian hammer, Dorian, against a massive Arcadian anvil, and it smashed the Hawk's Talons as surely as you, in the spring, are destined to smash the Argive Greeks. —Trust me, Dorian, the way to beat them is by shrewd use of their own tactics.

—Yes, I survived, but on that day, the third day of the offensive, I was struck down in my prime by the hard, bronze edge of a Corinthian mace. Like the Grays, Dorian, the Hawk's Talons refused to stand and wait, preferring instead to go instantly over to the attack, and many were the Corinthian dead that we left bleeding on the hill, even as we, the outnumbered, went down beneath their weight.

—That was the last I ever saw of the Dardanian hills, of white-watered Simoeis, of the windy Plain, of towering, holy Ilium . . . of my wife and my son, and I have never returned, for when I came awake suddenly and with much pain on the following day, I found myself chained in the leaking hold of a Phoenician slave hull bound for Samothrace.

—Nay. Look you with eagle eyes as long as you like, but on my neck the slave collar has never made its bite. —By the hand of Apollo I escaped the Greeks an independent man, for fever struck that hull, striking down captain, guard, and crew, and many Trojan captives, even within sight of Samothrace. Aeolus must have released all winds together in that hour, for across the span of two days following, such a tempest blew up that the sky went black with thunder. Then Poseidon turned his hand, tossing that leaking hull like a wood chip loosed from an oak by a bright Trojan axe. For three days the sea boiled with unparalleled fury, and then, on the fourth, later in the morning, the Father of gods struck our mast with a blinding bolt, and the hull came apart at the seams. In that hour silent death took one after another, Phoenician and Trojan alike, beneath the deep, night-dark swells. For myself, I remember lunging suddenly for an oar and locking myself to its long pine shaft by the sheer strength of my will. I rode for hours then, across those waves, fighting fatigue, fighting the dull throb of my pain, until the last hour of daylight when, by the hand of the sea-god, I found myself thrown quickly through the surf up a steep pebble beach. I had no strength left with which to crawl so much as a single pace inland, so there, across those hard stones, I fell mercifully to sleep and slept the sleep of the dead.

—On the following morning I came awake suddenly to find myself surrounded by hook-nosed warriors, one of whom was prodding me with the butt of his spear, a spear I recognized instantly by means of its markings to be the killing tool of the warlike Cicones. I spoke then the name of Euphemus, son of King Troezenus, son of Ceas, who had often wielded his battalions beside my own across the Plain, and in that hour I was delivered from danger on the strength of a name and on the strength of the Trojan alliance.

—I intended to go back, Dorian, to return to my home and the fighting and the windswept Plain, but in the weeks and months which followed there was hard fighting enough before the Cicone citadel at Zone as one Greek raid after another came in strong across the deep salt sea. The Greeks, seamen all, raided the Cicones time after time, bringing bitter war to that blue Aegaean shore, intending that no Cicone grain or reinforcements ever reach the Troad. In the end the Argive Greeks blackened the land, burning orchards and fields and every Ciconean hull still capable of putting to sea with either men or rations. —Those were hard times, deep in the shadow of Mount Ismarus, for there once more I lifted my long ash spear against the invading Greeks and took my place at the forefront. And then—early one morning, quietly and without fanfare—it ended.

—As I recall, I was guarding Zone's eastern approaches. Lordly Troezenus, old but just, had recognized my worth and experience and given me a small command, and there, athwart the road that led up from lower Thrace, we held a blocking position on some heights overlooking the sea. As I scanned the horizon that morning, searching for Greeks who might have put ashore to our south, I spied only a lone figure approaching along the coastal path at a steady pace. I went down then to the lip of the path and waited, and when the man again came into my view, I saw that he was a topknotted Thracian courier. Upon seeing me, he neither slowed his pace nor hurried it but came straight on until he stood before me, his long ash spear cradled easily against his shoulder. "The war is ended," he said simply, plainly. "Tell all you see that Troy has fallen. The Achaian Greeks have put all Ilium to the sword; the alliance is broken. Priam lives no more." And then, Dorian, he moved on, taking the word deep into northern Thrace. As the sound of his stride faded away, I remember being suddenly aware that cicadas had begun to chirp in the trees, and looking around me at the buds and new grass, I realized for the first time that the end had come in the spring of the war's tenth year.

—Nay, Dorian, you need have no doubts: the plan is sound. Trust me, when the spring thaw comes, *then* is surely the moment of my revenge, for I have waited full fifty years to make the Argive doer suffer. With my plan and your strong force, the Achaian Greeks will be no more, disappearing from the earth like my long-dead comrades at Troy into the ageless chambers of decay.

Odios at Alybe

—Handsome Alexandros? Had he been my son, Outlander, I should have put him to the sword the moment he came ashore with that beautiful Spartan whore.

—Nay, I was there at the time, down from the citadel of Alybe on an embassy to royal Priam who ruled in those days over the high, white walls of Ilium. We were allied, you see, the bright-eyed Alizones and the civilized Dardanians who raised horses on the Plain, allied in politics and commerce—allied, Outlander, in much the same way that your masters at Hattusas seek to link with us today. Know you, then, that thrice annually guarded pack trains from Troy worked upland into these high mountain valleys to bring us sweet-smelling, lowland grain and wide blue bolts of Trojan wool caught fresh from the loom and pale Dardanian pottery and new stores of bronze weapons with which to defend ourselves against the harsh barbarian hinterlands. They unloaded there, before our strong west gate where narrow fields trail away gradually into the valleys below. Much excitement filled those long-gone days when the Trojans finally mounted the rim to unpack before the citadel, and while the accounting went forward in the hands of Priam's able clerks, we poured libations to Zeus, feasting the Trojan guard on broiled kine. Then in public ceremony—after exchanging salt, and bread, and wine—Priam's chief clerk and the officer commanding made their accounting known, handing over the tally sticks into my father's hands, for know you, Outlander, that in those days Epistrophus the Strong ruled this land at the head of the hardened Alizones while I, Odios, his eldest son, trained at his side.

—Even as you say. With the Trojan accounting complete, my father passed the tally sticks to his own sharp clerks, and they made verification; not once, Outlander, in the twenty-two bright years that I witnessed the count, did Priam's agents ever make so much as a single error. Then, with the count confirmed, my father sounded the ram's horn, and on the instant, like a whisper of winds, his hard, skin-clad warriors rose from the depths of the fields and moved forward, their ash spears and ox-hide shields at their sides, bringing in the ingots from our secret silver mines in the valleys below. Before my father, they massed in their hundreds, standing tall like live oaks in the shadow of the citadel, and then, on command, after first being saluted by the Trojans, they lifted high the shrill chant of our war hymn, honoring our guests. Then, Outlander, the prearranged numbers of ingots were dropped on the ground by warriors of my father's first rank, and these, collected in leathern bags by my father's clerks, were presented to the Trojans in return for the goods received. The moment the exchange ended, cheers filled the air, and the bright-eyed Alizones broke ranks, treating the Trojan guard to fresh honey cakes and bunches of our deep purple grapes brought ripe from the vine. Thus, Outlander, the exchange. And after a long night of feasting and fellowship, when Aurora at last blushed faint across the far, eastern horizon, Ilium's skilled packers demonstrated their craft and departed for the Troad, carrying bales of our matchless wool, soft-tanned hides, and sealed, leathern sacks that were crammed to overflowing with our precious Alizonian silver.

—Help thyself, Outlander. Thy cup is nearly empty, and this, our sweetest mountain wine, comes fresh from the best skins where they hang from the rafters in the depths of our citadel. And partake too of the figs which have been placed before us. They arrived only this morning from the plains of Lydia.

—Just so, for like an antique hull at sea, I have allowed myself to drift uncertainly. —As I said, I had first marched down to the Plain on an embassy to royal Priam, and as I also said, had pretty Alexandros been my son, I would have put his devious, treacherous neck to the sword.

—Know you, my guest from Hattusas, that I liked not Priam's

sons . . . with the qualified exception of Hector. I did not know him, of course, before the war. At the time of my embassy lordly Hector was away at Dardanos, in camp, commanding the regiment of the Boar, but later, before Ilium, I fought often beside his standard, learning to respect him as a warrior and as a man. Toward me, I can tell you, Hector maintained always a bearing that was correct, forthright, even noble, but it was also without warmth and often cold. Still, one always knew where one stood with Hector, for in no uncertain language he gave his thoughts forcefully, and that is a fine thing in a field commander and in a man. Clearly, Hector was a man of plain speech and forthright dealing—a man like the father who sired him, and that, more than all else, drew the army's commanders to him and retained their support. But in so far as the remainder of Priam's breed . . . they were soft and spoiled, young men of well-oiled countenance and dripping tongues who had wallowed long, I think, in the untold luxury of Troy, and such, according to my thought, was the source of their ultimate undoing.

—Yes, Outlander, spoiled. As spoiled and slippery as the slime that one finds coating peeled figs left too long in the sun. To illustrate, the reason for my embassy to Troy was, in part, rooted to the shifting eye and slippery tongue of one of Priam's sons—Pammon—who came up amongst us with the twenty-third pack train, and then, for the first time in our long winters of alliance—in full view and to the complete astonishment of Priam's red-faced clerks and guard commander—attempted to falsify the Trojan tally. Immediately, the cheat was known—by my father, by our clerks, and by all the Alizone warriors at hand. Willowy Pammon had no rightful place in the proceeding; clearly, he had accompanied the caravan for sport and diversion only. Nevertheless, he had usurped the royal prerogatives that Priam had entrusted to his clerks, and this foolhardy act, in a matter of moments, threatened to wreck the exchange. In deference to the young man's rank, my father addressed him in careful, diplomatic language, making clear to Pammon the full measure of Alizone displeasure. For any reasonable man, my father's speech would have been enough, but in Pammon's case it was not. So unmoved was Priam's son by courteous civility, so blinded by his own rank and name, that he turned imperiously on my father and scornfully insulted him, suggesting that our long-standing exchange was mere Alizone tribute to "The Great Lord of the Plain, Priam,

Father of Royal Pammon!" Pammon's proud words died on the wind, Outlander, for in the same moment that he uttered them, on my father's command, our narrow fields, our town, our citadel, our whole land, fell silent, and then, like a single quickened heartbeat, five thousand long ash spears crashed down hard against Alizone shield rims, and the sound echoed like thunder across the high ridges of Alybe. Then the blond hair stood stiff along the back of Pammon's neck, for he was gripped by fear and never came again into the high mountain valleys of the Alizone.

—As you say, my embassy was made to repair any untoward bitterness that might be lingering in Troy following Pammon's return. We valued the Trojan alliance, you see, and sought no breach in our lasting, good relations. Thus, on a warm spring morning, while our high mountain wildflowers danced in the wind, I took up my ash spear and a handsome silver gift for royal Priam—a bright mixing bowl, I remember—and made my way to Troy at the head of fifty of our skin-clad warriors.

—Indeed, by Priam and his royal court, my embassy was accorded the highest marks of respect. Pammon's affront to us, his immense discourtesy, was altogether unknown at Troy. Later, by paying close attention to an informant, I learned that Pammon had first threatened and then bribed the pack train commander in order to ensure his silence; this too characterized his approach to the royal clerks, and in the end, his shame was not revealed. Thus, my embassy was greeted with warmth and friendship and renewed pledges of aid in times of trouble or famine. Clearly, Priam was plain in his dealings with my father and good to his word, and the council behind him responded in kind.

—Just so, Outlander, for if the court was forthright, Priam's sons were not. Instead, as recollections serve me, each in his own way showed himself to be thoroughly of Pammon's kind. I did not then meet all of Priam's sons, but those who did pass before me showed invariably some weakness of character, some flaw, some shortcoming that I later learned to recognize as a clear forewarning of their behavior in battle. Hooknosed Agathon, for example, was an impetuous braggart, but his limbs were soft from the sweetmeats of the palace, and when he finally confronted a Greek on the open Plain, he took a bronze spear through his vaunting mouth, and death closed coldly over his eyes.

Hippothous—younger than Pammon by some two winters—practiced a cruelty in public that I have never again seen in a man. Once, I recall, while walking in Ilium's open market, I chanced to see Hippothous emerge drunk from a wine shop in the same moment that a street urchin lunged forward to avoid the wheels of a chariot. Striking unexpectedly at his royal senior's knees, the urchin looked up swiftly to plead apology, but before he could utter a single word, Hippothous lifted the boy by his groin and dashed him with such force against the nearest wall that the boy's ears ran bright blood. Four winters later, while putting a Greek to torture in the midst of the Plain, Hippothous and his entire command were overrun by an enraged battalion of Myrmidons: I saw the action from a distance and saw too that the infuriated Achilles hacked off Hippothous's limbs and left him shrieking in the dust where he slowly bled to death. Clearly, Outlander, beneath Zeus's hand, a balancing, rough justice prevails amongst both gods and men.

—No. No, I do not assert that Priam's sons lacked courage—lordly Hector was brave, sapient Helenus had courage enough to lead, Deiphobus fought well against the Greeks, and each man commanded in battle with some precision—but even so, we Alizones thought the most of Priam's sons unreliable, too easily turned from the war's aim by irrelevant whims. Greed or sloth or petty envy too often prevailed amongst them. —Oh yes, their envy of one another was legend amongst us. Priam had so many, you see . . . so many sons . . . and all of them were vying with one another for precedence in their father's eyes. Too frequently, their all-consuming envy of one another so distorted the clear aim of the war that anything like the achievement of a common purpose became utterly impossible.

—Yes, Outlander, I can make the case more plain. In the sixth year, at the height of the spring flood when white-watered Simoeis ran raging across the Plain, word reached the council that holy Arisbe was under attack by a combined force, some three thousand allied Greeks who had stormed ashore on the previous morning from more than sixty of their high-prowed ships. Abydus, holy Arisbe, Percote, even distant Colonae—all of the upland Trojan citadels—had been raided before by sharp Greek assaults that struck like lightning and then withdrew down the safety of the Hellespont, taking whatever spoil they were able to carry away. Those raids, all of them conducted with limited objectives, had rarely numbered more than a thousand Argive warriors, and in each case the Dardanian garrisons in place—the sharp-pawed Lion at Percote, the slumbering Bear at Arisbe, or the bronze-shod Mustang at Abydus-by-the-sea—had proved sufficient to repel the threat and hold in check all serious Argive incursions into Priam's northern domains. But in the sixth year the situation changed. By then Greek pressure on the Plain had become intense, and in order to meet and turn it, Hector had reduced the northern garrisons to a single battalion each, ordering the other two battalions in each upland regiment down to the Plain and into the line. Without regard to our well-fortified citadels at Dardanos or at distant Colonae, Trojan strength along the central sector of the upland front was low, as low, perhaps, as three thousand warriors divided evenly amongst the various garrison commands. Thus, when the immensity of the Greek assault became known, flinty Polydamas rose immediately before the military council and took the speaker's staff. "Thus," I still remember him saying, "the Argive attack against the upland flank begins. In such numbers, the Greeks intend to stay, and in such numbers, they are capable of overrunning each of our distant, upland garrisons. We must send immediate help, or our link with Thrace may be irrevocably severed and our whole northern flank may cave in."

—As you say, my guest, flinty Polydamas made a shrewd assessment of the situation. The course of action he recommended was equally sound, and on this occasion, I remember, Hector agreed with him in principle, for the threat was profound, but then, concerning tactical operations, those two preeminent generals fell out. Wise in the way of war, Polydamas urged Hector to return to the upland front—at the quick march—the borrowed battalions of the Bear, the Mustang, and the Lion, arguing that they knew the terrain and would fight harder in defense of their farms, homes, and families than they would on the Plain. Hector accepted this argument but refused to turn the upland battalions loose, reasoning that their freshness and hard fighting ability was presently giving the army its only edge against the main Greek line on the Plain. Hector's assumption, if I remember it rightly, was that the Greeks had made the northern attack for the clear purpose of demoralizing the outlanders—to such an extent that Hector would have no other choice than to take them out of the line and start them marching north in order to defend their homes. This Hector stoutly refused to do, and then, curiously, as he rolled the idea in his mind, he began to conceive of the attack on Arisbe as nothing more than a Greek feint. Polydamas argued hard against this notion, citing again and again the critical value of our northern flank, but as the moments passed, Hector clung to his conception, and in the end the idea hardened into adamant. In Hector's mind, to the dismay of Polydamas, the Greek assault against Arisbe was nothing more than a raid in depth—a prolonged attempt to draw Trojan strength away from the Plain. Set thus, Hector made a fatal decision. The Lion, the Bear, and the Mustang would remain before Troy while smaller, more readily available units would be rushed north to relieve the pressure against Arisbe.

—I heard this news with misgiving, for know you, Outlander, that on the same day the exhausted Alizones were being rested inside the walls after spending more than five weeks fighting on the line. Even with the replacements then arriving from Alybe, our strength, at best, numbered no more than twelve hundred spears, and the only other available units were Guards battalions commanded by Priam's sons. "Lord Odios," Hector said to me in low tones, beneath a deep-set pair of eyes, "move the Alizones east, up the valley of the Simoeis, on the quick march, to a distance of six leagues. From there move north swiftly and attack the Greeks before Arisbe. Do not stop until you have driven the Greeks into the sea. Lycaon, my brother, and five hundred Guards will support your eastern flank while Antiphorus, son of Priam and Laothoe, will cover your western flank with five hundred more. Once you join with the garrisons defending, you will be strong enough to drive the entire Argive raid howling into the halls of Hades."

—Moments later, after the call had already gone out to rouse my tired command, flint-eyed Polydamas caught up with me in the street before the main Trojan armory, where I had gone seeking an issue of slings for my warriors. Taking me quickly aside, Polydamas spoke to me in flat, sharp tones. "You will be on your own," I remember him saying. "Antiphorus has the capacity to fight and may support you, if he likes the odds, but even so, guard both of your flanks well. Know you, Odios, that even as Hector labors to give Antiphorus independent command, Antiphorus envies Hector his place on the Plain and would hold his battalions back to make his brother's plan seem more unsound. With Lycaon, the matter is worse, for he is young, inexperienced, and unsure of himself, and he has fought not often across the length of the Plain. Even so, he shares his brother's envy, and in that lies real danger, for both may desert you in the crisis. Fight hard, then, but trust to yourself, and above all, conserve your men." "And the garrisons?" I asked, "Firm as rock," came the unqualified reply. —I think I decided then how I would fight my battle, but I did not yet know that the mere getting there would be quite so difficult.

—We marched at dusk, moving down from the Scaean Gate and out across the Plain at the double pace. We had a good moon, I recall, and stars, and in the distance, wide across the horizon, Greek and Trojan campfires flickered in the night like a multitude of fireflies. We moved silently, with muffled arms, hearing only the rapid tramp of our feet and, overhead, the occasional cry of a nighthawk streaking up from its kill. Within an hour we reached the banks of flooding Simoeis; there, passing swiftly through our lines, we turned east to begin working upcountry beside the swirling white river.

—We moved then like the spring wind, blowing strong up the valley of the Simoeis. I do not know how hard we ran, for the telling sound of our footfalls was silenced by the onrush of the water where it crashed down from the mountain fastness of Phrygia over rocks and boulders and stones, driving hard with force toward the Plain. Whatever the case, our pace was strong, bringing us full up to the high mountain fords before dawn. There, causing the army to halt and rest, I brought forward my most brawny warriors and, with them, light grappling lines, and in less time than it takes a sprinter to race half a league, we bridged the ford by means of horsehair hawsers. I put Lycaon's Guards over first, causing them to fan out to the east so as to cover the remainder of the crossing, and then in quick order I put over my own men, running them forward in groups of ten into the waist-deep water. Hand over hand, without firm footing, they breasted those swirling waters on the mere strength of Trojan horsehair, and then it was done. Antiphorus's Guards came last, and as they climbed dripping up the banks, I sent them west, one by one, into the scrub oak woods on my left flank. And then, with each formation in position, we began to climb up across the heights of the Dardanian hills, moving quickly forward over a variety of well-travelled trails that took us steadily north toward Priam's embattled dominions by the sea.

—After dawn we began to meet fleeing outlanders—women, mostly, with small, wide-eyed children held tightly in their arms while others, older girls and boys, hurried along behind. Some carried bundles, others only food and water. Most, I remember, were from the farms and hamlets surrounding Arisbe, but later in the morning we began seeing parties from Arisbe itself—old men, women, and children who had been sent from the town during the night, without guard, owing to the size and intensity of the Greek threat to the front. Firm intelligence was scant, but from all we heard that fighting before Arisbe was severe, that the Greeks had already advanced to the citadel's north wall. Finally, as Helios reached his zenith, we bumped a party of old men carrying antique spears; these numbered the Greeks at more than four thousand and reported more incoming hulls on the horizon even as they had escaped from the citadel by means of a ravine which skirted Arisbe's far south wall. All of the able-bodied men in the town, they reported, had taken up arms to defend the walls, and combined with the garrison, those five old men estimated Arisbe's defensive strength at slightly more than a thousand. The Trojan bow, they reported, was much in use as was the sling, which had proved particularly effective from the heights of the wall. Still, all were of the opinion that the Argive assault was neither raid nor feint, and to those old minds, the Greek objective seemed clear: the Greek command had landed in force with the intent of reducing the citadel and thus splitting the northern flank. "You will have more than you can handle," said one old warrior whose ancient battle scars shone bright across his cheek. "Where is the Bear? Where the strength of the Lion? It will take more than a regiment to throw those Greeks into the sea; Priam should have sent a corps."

—We moved on, quickening our pace, running hard through the breaks toward the last, low line of hills that separated us from the sea and holy Arisbe on the Hellespont. I sent out runners then, to both Antiphorus and Lycaon, ordering Antiphorus to combine with the garrison at Abydus in order to march on Arisbe from the southwest while Lycaon, after joining his Guards to the Lion battalion at Percote, marched down on Arisbe from the opposite direction, from the high northeast. The Alizones, I planned, would mount a direct assault from the inland heights, distracting the Greeks from our threats to their flanks by striking them head-on with the shock of close combat. —It was a good plan, the battle order I sent out to Priam's sons, but then, Outlander, envy reared her head, and as a result the high, blue walls of Arisbe came tumbling to the ground.

—Disregarding my orders for the coordination of our attack, Antiphorus sent my runners packing, throwing back word that he was taking independent command of his formation and going over to the offensive. He went in then, alone, without the strength of the Mustang, not on the flank as I had ordered but closer to the left center of the Greek perimeter. There he bumped a rock-hard battalion of Athenians, engaged them in close combat for perhaps a quarter of an hour, and then withdrew, claiming a major victory. He had acted impulsively, to be sure, employing less than half of the western strength he might have marshaled, and in all respects his attack was a dismal failure. It became an even greater failure when he withdrew toward Abydus, vaunting the glory of his Guards, rather than retiring on me, for as quickly as an eagle winks, he uncovered my western flank after alerting the enemy to a new Trojan presence on the field. This alone would have been enough to destroy our chance for victory before Arisbe, but not content to withdraw and crow, Antiphorus made one more self-serving move that ensured our failure: he taunted Lycaon for cowardly reticence.

—Indeed, Lycaon *was* carrying out my orders. Already in that hour he had skillfully positioned himself midway between Arisbe and Percote and sent runners north to call out the garrison of the Lion, and elements of the Lion had armed and started south to join their strength to the Guards. Then, suddenly, Antiphorus's runners reached him, boasting about their general's victory to the west and carrying, too, his scorn for Lycaon's *overcautious* attitude toward the battle. A more seasoned commander would have laughed in the courier's face, but stung red with envy, Lycaon gave himself over to rage, and in the passion of the moment—without logic, foresight, or reason—he threw his entire command immediately into action, without first warning me or waiting for the strength of the Lion to come to his support. Clearly, the presence of the Lion was the only thing that saved Lycaon from disaster, for within a few hundred strides from his starting point, he ran

up against the alerted Greeks, and well-integrated companies of Locrians and Spartans sent him reeling with heavy losses. Only the Lion,
coming up quickly from behind, gave him enough defensive cover for a
withdrawal, and then both the Lion and the remnants of Lycaon's
Guards were hard pressed all along their line as they made a fighting
retreat toward Percote.

—Just so, Outlander, and in that moment I saw my chance. I reasoned that the Greeks, distracted by the Trojan pinpricks to their east
and west, hotly engaged before the face of Arisbe, might be temporarily unprepared for a quick, sharp thrust from the Dardanian hills. The
old men had been right: the Greeks were ashore in force, and judging
from the strength spread before me in the distance, I thought their
number closer to five thousand spears with still more of the black-
beaked hulls working north up the race from their strong camp on the
Plain. Clearly, with the collapse of Priam's sons, we had no hopes of
either rolling up the Greek flanks or throwing them back from Arisbe
into the sea. There were too many Greeks, and they were far too
strong. Acting together, the Mustang, Bear, and Lion might have made
the difference, but my twelve hundred Alizones were doomed to failure
in any such undertaking, and, wisely, I sought to conserve my men.
What did seem within our grasp was a temporary breakthrough to
Arisbe's south gate, a quick thrust that would strike like lightning,
shocking and parting the inland Greek perimeter just long enough to
allow Arisbe's defenders to escape into the cover of our line. I would
have preferred to attack after dark, but with large numbers of the
Greeks drawn off in pursuit of Antiphorus and Lycaon, I seized the
moment and struck, after having first moved the Alizones forward using the concealment of a wood.

—The Argives facing us were Rhodians, three companies of them,
and we did not roll over them with ease, but we did penetrate their line,
warping the edges of the gap backwards in both directions, and then we
fought like angry boars for more than a quarter of an hour until my
runners reached the citadel and the desperate defenders began streaming out to join us in battle while making good their unexpected, quick
escape. With the defenders' strength added to our own, we proved too
much for the hard-fighting Rhodians, who were trying to close the gap
behind us, and then they really did give way, opening wider the escape

corridor that our shocking thrust had created. I sounded twice then my ram's horn, and like slow-moving bees awakened suddenly from slumber, the battle-worn defenders of Arisbe—men, boys, and elements of the Bear—retired rapidly through our lines, working back onto the lower slopes of the Dardanian hills.

—Argive reinforcements began to come up then, Corinthians and Spartans, seeking to trap us within their folds, but with the same energy as before I sounded my ram's horn again, and on the instant my bright-eyed Alizones turned the concentrated focus of our withdrawal toward the southeast, overrunning an extended company of Corinthians, leaving some one or two hundred of them dead in our wake. We got out then in good order, with small losses in numbers killed, but with many troublesome wounds. The defenders of Arisbe covered our retreat for as long as necessary, but then, having eluded the Greeks who had not the strength at hand to pursue us in numbers, we made good our withdrawal into the hills. The last thing I remember as I looked back over my shoulder was the smoke, for by that time the Greeks had fired both the town and the citadel, and immense black plumes fluttered into the sky above the flames.

—As a military evolution, the expedition to relieve Arisbe was a strategic and tactical failure; forever after, the Trojan uplands remained split—a hopeless contingency brought on, I submit, by the sibling envy of Priam's two sons. During the years that followed, we were never able to close that breach in our far northern flank, and slowly the Greeks widened and deepened it until first Percote fell and then Colonae and finally blue Abydus-by-the-sea, and thus our links with Thrace were cut, reducing considerably Priam's ability to make hard war. Still, on that long-gone morning when the Alizone marched up from Troy, we did succeed in saving the garrison, extracting the defenders through hot battle to fight another day, and the glory we earned remains high in the minds of men.

—Sup you, my Outlander from Hattusas, on the viands placed before us. The lamb has been seasoned with garlic and wine, but beware the olives, for they are tart this year throughout the valley of Alybe.

—That is even so, my guest, for as the waves of memory toss hard across my eye, I have drifted yet again from my oft-promised subject.

—So, as I say, had he been my son, I should have struck off his head
with a silver-studded sword and never looked back. The justice of the
hour required it: pretty Paris had violated another man's wife. Is that
not the law that binds men? Must not the doer be made to suffer for the
commission of his crime? Justice begins at the top, Outlander; if callous disregard prevails there, what recourse for the rest of men?

—No, in fairness, Priam cast not a callous eye on the matter—rather,
an eye too fond for a much-beloved son. I was there on the beach, you
see; I saw it all. There was concern in the meeting but not outrage, as
there should have been. Rather, the old king set his heart above his
head, uncorking, thereby, a wineskin of disaster, and in the end, all
Troy drank from the bitter cup. Clearly, Paris should have been put to
death, immediately and on the spot, in obedience to the law. The Spartan whore should have been sent back and the Spartan treasure with
her, and had it been my responsibility, I would have sent gifts as well
and copious apologies for such a deep transgression against the law.

—For the woman, my guest? —No, I think not, for to my mind the
Greeks made the war to preserve the law. —How say you? —Yes, beautiful . . . beautiful . . . *beautiful* beyond my powers to describe. I
never spoke with her, but I saw her, there on the beach, on the day
Paris brought her to Troy, and in the instant of her first, sudden appearance, she stunned the crowd to silence. Part of the effect, no doubt, was
shock, for Troy was totally unprepared for Alexandros's transgression,
but even so, as I reflect calmly, I still believe that silence to have been
the effect of the whore's beauty, for, indeed, she stole men's breath
away and women's, too. It was always so and always remained so, even
in the darkest days of the war. Here in a wine shop, there on the Plain,
in the midst of a Trojan street or home or market, men, women, and
children would rail at her presence within the city, screaming obsceni-
ties toward the palace, calling her the Curse of the Gods, and then,
somewhere, she would appear, suddenly and without warning, before
one or more of her accusers, and all would fall silent in the immediate
adoration of her beauty. She wore often, I remember, a pained expres-
sion about her features, for she well knew how the feeling ran against
her, but even so, the strength of her beauty was ever beyond compare,
and all Troy went down fighting to keep her.

—Yes, my guest, and still I say to you that Priam should have exacted a rough justice for his own son's treachery. Some matters, Outlander, are beyond dispute; the matter of wife-rape must never be condoned. I have put men to death for the same crime here in Alybe—even one of my own sons—and as a result the law has remained firm, preserving marriage, home, and family. That was a part of the problem at Troy, do you not see: too many princes disregarded the law, and Priam condoned their transgressions. In view of what happened there, I resolved never to make the same mistake.

—Paris? —Upon landing? —Giddy, and far too proud of his own strength as he leapt from the hull onto the beach. Even as I sit here beside you, I remember him still, his blond locks falling about his ears, pacing tall across the sands—his bronzed chest affectedly puffed out— to salute his father and the bright queen, and then, without so much as a word, he tossed his hand in the direction of the hull's beak, and Helen appeared. He was unsure of himself with Helen, I thought, but with the rest of us he was all too sure, exhibiting an offhand, haughty demeanor that was at once intensely indifferent and flippant. Clearly, the citizens were of no more importance to him than the numberless grains of sand on the beach. He was a study, I tell you, in selfishness, and to my thinking he remained so throughout the many years that I knew him. I would no more have gone to war for *his* sake than I would have sought to preserve a serpent lurking coiled beside a path, for to me that image always defined the man: he was a serpent, clearly, coiled against the bosom of Troy.

—What say you, my guest? —*Why* did we fight? —Your pardon, my gray ears are thin with age, and now I no longer hear in the night the hoot of Athene's owl, nor by day the cry of the Cloud Gatherer's eagle. —Yes . . . *why?*

—Know you, then, that grim necessity beckons many a man toward death. In those days we had not, as we do now, an alliance with your noble master at Hattusas, nor did we have the outlets to the dark, black sea which the Lords of the Hatti have afforded us. No, in *those* long-forgotten days, high-walled Ilium accorded us our only link to the sea and the far-flung nations of the earth, and in time of barbarian war their once-bold alliance was the foundation of our strength. So when the

Greek war came, we gave our lives to protect Trojan strength, believing as we did that we secured our own. In that place, at that time, it was fight or die, for high Alybe just as much as for holy Ilium. Thus, as soon as I returned from my embassy and informed my father about the way things were, he divined the consequence, placed me in command of fifteen hundred hard Alizone warriors, and sent me doubling back to the Plain. And within eleven moons, the whole world erupted into bloody war.

—I fought hard then, for nine dark years, even through Hector's great offensive. My brother joined me in that last great battle, at the head of nine hundred spears, and on the morning of the third day, retreating hard across the Plain, he was trapped against Scamander by an entire Greek corps and went down fighting with his entire command. For myself, I was badly wounded in the thigh, by a sling-thrown Locrian dart. The surgeons who saw to my wound were Mysians— many such were practicing in Troy about that time—and their methods were unsavory. First my wound refused to close; then it festered; finally it began to smell. Thinking that I was about to die, Priam finally ordered me returned to my father along with the bones of my brother, which had been packed inside a honey-filled urn and sealed with the wax of the bee. Thus, in the midst of a delirium-darkened night, during the last days of the war, the remnants of my bright-eyed Alizones took me up, on the same litter as my brother's bones, and carried me into the night. —Nine days later, I am told, even as we outstripped the Greek lines, even before we reached Alybe and this hard, stone valley around us, Troy fell. —No more than twelve armed warriors accompanied me home: in so far as I know, they are the only spearmen, as I am the only general, to survive. Small wonder, then, Outlander, that I am able to say to you that had Alexandros been *my* son I should have put him to the sword in the same moment that he stepped ashore. —More wine?

Antiphus on Tmolus

—Nay, my Lord of the Hatti, we went down then, swiftly into Lydia—no waiting, no hesitation—four thousand strong, bronze-faced Maeonians all, armed hard for war on the Plain. With the eyes of my mind I still remember the day.

—My father's heralds woke us early that morning, indeed, at Aurora's first blush. Upland battalions had marched in on the afternoon before to camp en masse across those fields to our north—there, where I point my dart, where now the barley sways tall before the wind, and even so many as those stalks of grain seemed the linen-clad warriors of the Uplands. And even so many more seemed my brother's command marching out from the citadel, joining their long, Lowland files to the upper might of Maeonia. Then, my Lord, we were many indeed, spreading beneath the fleet clouds like wave after wave of harvest-ripe grain.

—My father came out then—noble Talaemenes, whose mother was the Gygaen Lake—and there, standing straight and tall and gray, he uttered the words of war, dedicating us all to the service of royal Priam, his faraway kinsman who ruled over the windswept Plain of Troy. Then, in full view of his assembled battalions and with appropriate ceremonies of sacrifice, my father thrice struck the Lowland standard against the face of Mother Earth and gave it over into Mesthles' hands, sanctifying my brother's office of command. Shouts and cheers went up immediately from the ranks of the Lowlands as all ash spears rose in salute to my brother and the noble father who sired him, and in the next moment the air filled with the deep, low chant of our war hymn. Great was my brother's glory in that hour and great too the gleam in my father's eye as the massed Lowlands applauded him. And even in the same moment that the war chant ended, it began again—with the shouting and the cheering and the upraised spears in salute—for my father, know you . . . without waiting, without hesitation . . . had thrice lifted the Upland standard in the direction of snowcapped Tmolus and handed *me* my office of command.

—We lingered then no longer, for in the same moment that the Uplands ceased to sing, Mesthles and the Lowlands marched off, swiftly taking the lead, moving down like eagles toward the plains of Lydia. There were no lingering farewells, no final prayers in the shadows of Tmolus's slopes, and the last I ever saw of my father, wise Talaemenes, he was standing dry-eyed but gray, tall in his chariot, as the Uplands passed him in review, moving quickly down from the heights past our summer villa at the headwaters of the Cayster. How he reached that spot before us, or why, I have never known, but in my old age as the years crawl hard up the slope of my spine, it still pleases me that he did, for that is how I have always remembered him, standing tall in his chariot, every inch a king.

—That is so, Lord of the Hatti, for the march down to Smyrna was long and hard, and we were nine dusty days on the road, making the Lydian plains thunder beneath our feet. For as long as we remained in the mountains, we marched in column, one battalion after another, curving through our high Maeonian valleys like a thick serpent secure in its own strength, but when we finally struck the plains on the morning of the third day, then—in order to hold down the dust—we reordered the army into a loose line abreast, broadening our front across more than a league. Even now I recall the sight, for together we moved like bronzed autumn leaves blown forward on a wind, our long ash spears stretching away endlessly toward the limits of either horizon, and in those hours we were mighty in our strength.

—Our advance was well planned, by both my father's staff and the clerks of the Lydian King; throughout the length of the march no man went hungry. Instead, for five days we ate a grain ration that we carried in our wallets and a substance of dried goat's meat that had been prepared in advance and issued to each warrior by the clerks of my father's stores. On the morning of the sixth day, near groves of oak that rose like giants from the midst of the plain, we met pack trains sent out from Smyrna, and from those we replenished both regiments with enough cheese, barley, and dried fish to complete the journey with strength. On the ninth day, as Helios dipped his purple beams, we shot at last the low mountain passes above Smyrna and caught our first sight of the wine-dark sea. From there we descended quickly to a prepared camp along the white sands of the beach, where the warriors of Lydia greeted us warmly, feasting us on kine and fresh-baked barley bread and not a little wine.

—Even thus, my Lord, if my bronzed Maeonian warriors are to march east in order to join our strength with the might of the Hatti, so must the provision be made, for the march is hard, and long after the melt the way to Hattusas remains bitter cold. Let there be a pact between us—between myself and your right royal king—that Hatti provisions be prepared for our replenishment athwart the plain at Zippasla. I will put an army in the field and provision it for ten-days' march. They are quick, my warriors, and march like the wind: I will guarantee their pace for eight leagues each day—a rate which, at the end of Helios's tenth circuit, will place them along the banks of white-watered Sangarius. Guarantee me that you will resupply my warriors there, before Zippasla, and in return I will put five thousand bronzed Maeonians in the field to fight beside the Hatti against the barbarians to the east. And let Hatti clerks be sent to me in order to sort out the details.

—As you say, the voyage to Troy was fraught with wonder, for none of us had ever before ridden the rolling pathways of the sea. We sailed together, Lydians and Maeonians, on the morning after our arrival at Smyrna. Royal Priam had sent more than eighty broad-beamed Trojan hulls to take aboard the Maeonian regiments, but the Lydians, wearing their leather corslets, took ship in their own fine hulls, sleek craft built to the Greek design that leapt across the waves like dolphins. There were also Carian hulls amongst us and some Mysian craft, for the fleet of Smyrna—though well built—was small, and many were the warriors who went forward to Troy.

—We sailed then like winged seafowl, coursing above the waves, our sharp beaks dripping with the foam that lordly Poseidon sweeps from his beard. Then, my Lord, one felt the power of man, for with each stroke of the mallet swinger, all my strong-armed warriors learned to pull away together, chanting the taught rhythms of the Trojan sea hymn, and our long, pine oars flashed mightily beneath the sun. —How may I describe it to you, for even in these, my gray and waning years, I can still feel the blood shoot sharply through my veins in the moment of my recollection. —First the sound of the mallet, striking hard against the hull with a firm flat crack, and then the shudder as all my fine, young warriors pulled away together, dipping their bright oars deeply into the surface of the sea. One sensed the power then, the forward lunge of the hull, the unified strength of fifty hard Maeonians straining their backs against the tranquil might of the sea. And then the mallet and the stroke and the first low chant of the sea hymn and across the face the first sting of salt as wisps of foam flecked upward over the beak and back onto the rowing benches to wet the beards of my men, and then, like an arrow loosed in flight, the hull shuddered once more to send us scudding across the waves, picking up speed as the rhythms of the mallet swinger increased. High in the stern where I took my place beside the steering oar, the roar of the sea made music to my ears.

—We beached that night before Mysian Pitane, consuming our rations in the shadows of our hulls. Mysian vendors came down to us there, selling dried figs and olives and a moist, yellow cheese that was as tart as their wine, and after sunset elements of the Mysian beach guard came amongst us, and the talk was of Troy and of royal Priam and of what life might be like on the wide, windswept Plain of Ilium. It was the Mysian opinion, I remember, that slings and hunting bows would come into their own before Troy, owing to the height of the walls and the immensity of the field. We Maeonians took a dim view of the Mysians for making that remark, eschewing men who spoke openly of setting aside their spears in order to fight at a distance, but in that, as events proved, we were wrong, for the Mysians fought well before Troy, and in the end both sling and bow proved their value in the ten-years' fighting on the Plain.

—We were one more day at sea before finally putting ashore in the Troad, but our second day upon the waters proved as unlike our first as a javelin placed beside an axe. Gone, on the second day, was the gentle lapping of the waves. And gone too were the clear, bright skies and

Helios's beams. In their place, from the moment of our first rising, Aurora blushed a deep, dark red, and then, I remember, the brows of our pilots knotted with concern. —We were away then like the wind, the entire fleet pulling hard for the lee of Lesbos, which we reached in good time by mid-morning but not before the first gray squall had blown coldly over us, soaking us to our skins. Within the following hour the wind came up hard, the sea rose, and our tortured pilots steered as close to the Lesbian coast as they dared, seeking to avoid and survive the higher, more dangerous seas to the east, for there, truly, Poseidon made rage with his hands.

—We spent all day beating up the coast, under both sail and oar. Throughout, the sea remained rough, and not a few, myself included, became sick with the relentless pounding. No libations served to quell Poseidon's anger, and one after another, squall after squall rolled over us, blowing down like hard thunder from the Lesbian heights, forcing wind and rain into nostrils, eyes, and ears, and then in late afternoon we emerged from the protection of the coast to brave the wide, open sea as we struck directly for Assus, the high Trojan citadel which stood like a dark sentinel above the southernmost cape of the Troad. Our original intention had been to beach the fleet at Besika Bay so as to approach Ilium from the west by means of a short march, but once we emerged into the open channel north of Lesbos, the futility of such an undertaking became immediately apparent. There in those unprotected waters the full fury of the wave-path struck us so intensely that we dared not venture west into the Aegaean. Instead, with one mind the Trojan pilots made straight for the sheltered beach at Assus, and even then our survival remained in doubt, for the green, boiling sea rose like Hades before us, gaping dark and deep through mountains of swirling foam.

—Indeed, Lord, in the end we made the voyage safely, putting all ships ashore before Assus. —As you say, the immensity of the event beggars description, for what man with words can capture Poseidon's fury. The whole sea shook with his anger, and now, here, in my darkest dreams, I wonder still at the omen he there gave us of the future to come and at the obscure vision of our priests, who failed utterly to divine it. Surely, in that hour the three sisters had already measured our threads, and Poseidon was merely showing us the knife.

—That is so, my Lord. We sheltered that night within the walls of Assus, taking barley soup for our supper in order to settle our stomachs, and on the morrow, wrapped in our sea cloaks so as to ward off the sharp, driving rains which still hurled in against us from the sea, we marched north in files, bending our backs to the earth like hunched white beetles. Then, beside a multitude of swollen watercourses, we moved swiftly inland. We moved, I remember, over what might have been described as the lowest, westernmost slopes of Ida, but we saw little of the mountain's heights, for throughout the morning the rains poured thick about us, and the going became ever harder as my slogging Uplanders ground the flowering earth into thick, dark mud. We climbed then throughout the morning and throughout most of the afternoon, and as the watercourses narrowed to trickles, the realization came over me that we had reached the crest, the summit of that long ridge separating the southern reaches of the Troad from the long valleys which drain toward Scamander and the distant Hellespont beyond. There beneath a hard, rock rim our Trojan guides halted the column, recommending that we make, for the night, what camp we could.

—Throughout the night the rain continued, driving in hard from the sea, and on the following morning, after breakfasting on nothing more substantial than a few dry figs, we marched off, still cold from our camp and soaked to the skin. From the crest we descended quickly toward the valley of Scamander, and about mid-morning the rain began to let up, although it continued to drop plentifully from the trees which were then in full leaf and heavy with collected moisture. We struck Scamander at noon, and there, beside that high, white-watered river, the rains finally stopped altogether, leaving our ears tingling with the sounds of the wind as it rushed through the trees above the gushing torrents of the river. There, to warm my men and wring the cold from their bones, I ordered the Uplanders into a quick march and sent them loping forward to the chant of our war hymn.

—Gradually, as we descended, Scamander's valley widened. Pastures came first into view, where black-maned Trojan horses ran before the wind, and then fields of sea-green barley borne drooping beneath the dew, and then farms, and finally sky-blue Trojan villas arranged like sleeping Titans amidst cultured groves of cypress, oak, and poplar. There, too, we saw our first Trojans, detachments of the Wolf and the

Leopard, who rose as one man from before their bivouac fires and cheered us as we hurtled by, moving down hard in the direction of the Plain. That, I think, more than anything, brought my men to themselves, washed the fatigue from their veins, and warmed their pride, for clearly in that hour we heard Troy's joy in our coming and rejoiced in our strength. Not long after that, far to the east we saw the Trojan fortress of Thymbra perched on a crag like the black body of a vulture, and then suddenly we found ourselves truly in amongst them, for there, where the forks of Scamander converge, we struck the main road into Ilium and found her citizens making their way to and from the city with a variety of provender, and these too cheered my Uplanders, offering wine and bread and warm salutes, lifting their tiny babes and little, curly-headed children high into the air to watch and remember our passing. And then, my Lord, with a suddenness that I still recall with shock, we rounded the base of a long, sloping ridge and saw for the first time the broad, windswept Plain of Troy, stretching away toward the white-capped Hellespont, and in the distance, atop a promontory that jutted out from the east, glistening white beneath a late afternoon sun that had only then broken free through the clouds, the high, rain-washed towers of holy Ilium outlined against the sky. Thus our arrival before Troy in the spring preceding the war.

—On that matter I harbor no doubts, for the royal Hatti are known for their generosity, and loyal victors are always accorded their share of the spoils. —No, my Lord, the question to which I seek an answer concerns the length of the Hatti campaign, whether or not you will want to hold my Maeonians should Hattusas require a defense. I seek no prior right of approval as to *how* my warriors are deployed; rather, I seek to send you well-trained men who are ready and able to fulfill their intended role. —Just so. When the Hatti heralds return, bearing the terms of our treaty, let one amongst them bring clear indications of whether your king wishes me to send archers or spearmen, for on that decision much may depend in their time of preparation.

—Royal Sarpedon, King of the Lycians? —Yes, I knew him . . . not as well, perhaps, as noble Glaucus, his second-in-command, but yes, I spoke to him often and enjoyed his company more than once, both on the field and in the staff precincts of the citadel.

—That is correct: his physique was matchless among the Lycians, for he trained daily with all weapons and exercised his bronzed body so as to be ever ready for the demands of the war. Know you that many reputed him to be the son of Zeus, divine in his lineage, and his mother, whose beauty was famous amongst the Lycians, was lovely Laodameia, the bright-eyed daughter of Bellerophon. I swam beside him once, contending in exercise along the upper reaches of Scamander where pools in the river are both wide and deep, and there, on an afternoon, he outdistanced me from one bank to the other by the length of a man. He did not boast, I remember, in the strength of his victory; rather, he encouraged me—in a way that was almost paternal, for he was my elder by some ten years or more—showing me methods by which to improve my stroke, and when we swam again, he seemed to take sincere pleasure in my quickened form even though it brought me to within a head of overtaking him.

—One might so think, my Lord, but no; that report of him is unfounded and untrue. To my recollection, he was in no way vain. He expected, certainly, the utmost deference from the men around him, but remember too that Sarpedon was peerless, a right royal king who deferred by choice, at Troy, only to Priam and to Lord Hector, who exercised unquestioned command of the army. Had Sarpedon wished to press the point, I think he might have outranked Hector on the field; by precedence, certainly, the nobility of his birth and station gave him the right. Instead, in order to achieve and ensure a unified command, he deferred to Hector, and great was Sarpedon's support, for all the lesser kings and princes followed his wise example. I knew this to be so, for once, early in the war, in the temerity of my youth, I broached the subject with Glaucus. I remember still the smile that played about his eyes when he made me an answer. "Antiphus," he said to me, placing the broad palm of his hand athwart my back, "in this enterprise, the unity of the army is everything, and in this venture, we fight for the integrity of the Trojan, not the Lycian, homeland; thus, my master's decision is just." I saw it then as clearly as I see it now, and it was so, and in the offing, I learned to admire Sarpedon's wisdom and grieved deep when he went down fighting in the ninth year of the war.

—On the Plain? —Yes, throughout the fourth and fifth years, I served directly under Sarpedon's command at the very heart of the Trojan

line, and there my Uplanders went to the forefront many times along-
side the Lycians. Mesthles and the Lowlanders were then integrated
into Aeneas's corps, where they saw bloody engagements across the
north bank of Simoeis, for during those years the Greeks were still
probing to the east, looking for a weak point in our line where their
shock battalions might break through to envelop our flank. But on the
Plain, in the midst of that high swirling dust, we fought according to
the old style, wearing ox-hide body shields and marching forward into
combat armed only with sword and spear, and in that evolution Sarpedon proved himself the master in battle after battle. The trick, you see,
was to present the Greeks with a solid, unbroken front—a wall of body-
shielded warriors armed with long ash spears—and then to wait and
react. —Yes, Lord of the Hatti, *react.* As you say, it is not the way to
win, nor was it then, but the key is in the tactic that was put forward.
At the center, I must tell you, we were never expected to win; instead,
our function was to *hold,* to attract as much of the Greek strength from
the right and the left as possible and hold them in place. Then, it was
hoped, Hector, Aeneas, Paris, or another of the army's independent
commanders, fighting to either side of center, would—eventually—be
able to exploit a Greek weakness and break through, off center, to
penetrate and roll up their line. But at the center, across the broad
length of the front, we held and held and held, absorbing one Greek
blow after another.

   —Indeed, Lord, that *was* the tactic Sarpedon developed. At the forefront, you see, he maintained an unbroken front to a depth of some four
heavily armed ranks, but three hundred strides to the rear, no fewer
than three highly mobile regiments—all of them armed with light ox-
hide targets rather than cumbersome shields and throwing javelins
rather than spears—were always ready, waiting to be thrown into the
line. Then, as a Greek thrust developed, Sarpedon appraised its
strength, watching and waiting, determining with fine military judgement whether the Argive field commander was merely demonstrating
to draw our strength or intended, in fact, to force a breakthrough.
Sarpedon waited, then, until all doubt had cleared from his mind, and
at the critical moment, at the moment when the Argive thrust actually
broke our front, *then* he made a sweep with his standard, sending a
fully rested Trojan regiment hurtling down the axis of the main Greek

thrust. Invariably, so much concentrated force brought grief to the Greeks, turning the point of their attack and strewing the earth with their dead. And as our reinforced ranks closed behind the Argive retreat, great was the booty and the glory they left us. I led my Uplanders thirty times in such attacks, and such was Sarpedon's judgement in appointing the precise moment for our assaults that we never lost more than one or two warriors from the mass of our counterattacks, although without question many sustained wounds, particularly where point met point, and there, thrice, I was deeply pinked across the thigh, and twice more I was brought down by mace blows to the helm. Indeed, my last attack under Sarpedon's command was fought with such fury that my Uplanders were six weeks out of the line recovering their strength, for, fleet of foot, we were ever in reserve, waiting to shock the unsuspecting Greek. We had losses then, but the line held, our center always remaining firm. And then in the sixth year Sarpedon took a sharp, barbed arrow between the plates of his corslet, and in that hour he temporarily relinquished command to Glaucus and went out of the line to recover. Not long after, both the Lycians and my bright-eyed Maeonian Uplanders were withdrawn, and in that hour, heralding a change in Hector's strategy, the Trojan regiments of the Leopard and the Wolf were thrown against the Argive center in force and very nearly succeeded in breaking the enemy's front. By that time, however, we were out of it, performing our garrison duties while resting and recovering our strength behind the high walls of the citadel. When we went back again into close combat some three months later, we moved to a different front, and then the war was much changed.

—As you say, my Lord, across the years tactics have altered. Be assured that when my bronzed Maeonians march at last toward widewalled Hattusas, not one of all their swift-moving number will bear the body shield. Rather, my warriors will march with targets and throwing darts and stout Maeonian bows fashioned with craft from the finest horn.

—Indeed, such was the case. I had known Glaucus well, of course, during the two long years that my Uplanders lent weight to Sarpedon's command, but it was during the seventh year of the war that I came to appreciate him most, for in that year, far to the north before Abydus, upright Glaucus saved my life and the lives of my command, and high-ridged Maeonia remains forever in his debt.

—By that time, know you, the Greeks had moved in force up the Hellespont, struck and seized Arisbe, and worked their way inland in such numbers that the northern Troad had been split. Pretty Percote and distant Colonae still held, but effective communication with either Trojan citadel was long and difficult because the Greeks had placed themselves directly athwart the royal highway to the north. In the sixth year, after consolidating their gains, they tried to take Abydus from the sea and failed, so in the war's seventh spring they put additional regiments ashore in the vicinity of Arisbe, concentrated their mass, and attempted to envelop Abydus from the south and east. In order to do so, the Greeks had first to march their regiments straight down the royal road from Arisbe, bumping one after another of the defensive battalions that Hector had placed in their way. The alarm was sounded, then—as soon as the Greeks moved—all the way down to Troy, where couriers on horseback brought Priam the news, and within hours my Uplanders—then bolstering the garrison defenses at Dardanos—were ordered to march immediately to protect Abydus's inland flanks and shore up the defensive battalions that were already coming under heavy pressure from the Greeks. Prince Deiphobus, Hector's younger brother who commanded elements of the Leopard at the time, was also ordered upcountry with the expressed purpose of buttressing our right, inland flank so as to prevent the Greeks from slipping around us to the southeast, and thus things stood in the hour that we marched.

—From the beginning, it seemed, our countermeasures went awry. In Abydus, strong battalions of the Mustang gave the walls a sturdy defense, but fighting beside them was a reduced regiment of Priam's Household Guard under the command of one of his younger sons, Antiphorus by name. According to Hector's orders for the operation, the defensive battalions, which were giving way before the Greek advance down the royal road from Arisbe, were to fall back on Antiphorus, who would combine their might with his own and counterattack in such a way as to give my Uplanders a strong left flank. Thus when the main Greek thrust finally descended on Abydus, the Argives would find themselves facing an unbroken line of Mustangs, Household Guards, my Uplanders—the line's main strength—and Leopards. That was the plan, certainly, but owing to a variety of failures, a disaster developed.

—To begin, Deiphobus did not come forward quickly enough from his bivouac in the Dardanian hills. The Leopards were well trained, mind you, and fleet of foot, but on this occasion they proved slow in moving into position, arriving several hours too late. To my mind, firmer leadership might have made the difference. It is fruitless, of course, to make the point now, for that was long ago when the light in my eye still burned strongly, and in that hour I cursed Deiphobus with the vermin of the earth, for when the Greeks struck us in greater force than expected, they immediately overlapped my exposed right flank, and our line began to collapse. We fell rapidly back then, across more than a league, leaving many dead and wounded in our wake, and then, with fear and fury, we discovered that the promised support on our left and rear was non-existant: Antiphorus and the Household Guard had failed to come out from Abydus, leaving the exhausted defensive battalions, all of them withdrawing under pressure, to be cut to pieces by the leading prong of the Greek advance. There, for the first time, I realized that the Greeks had outwitted us, that their assault had come forward in *two* attack streams, the weaker maintaining pressure on our retreating defense battalions while the stronger, larger force had left the road, worked inland, and struck my Uplanders hard from the east.

—In the instant, my Lord, I saw the pattern of our disaster, for even then, even within sight of Abydus, my bright-eyed Maeonian Uplanders were cut off, surrounded, holding an impossible position across the crests of a low series of hills just up from the sea. By that time too I sensed that I was facing more than a single Greek corps, for during our retreat word had reached me that we were up against Boeotians, Athenians, Mycenaians, Locrians, and Pylians, and from past experience I knew well enough that those particular Argives invariably fought as independent regiments, whenever and wherever they took the field. In the wake of this conclusion, I did the only thing left to me; I drew in my Uplanders, concentrated them on a single ridge overlooking Abydus, and prepared to receive a death blow from the Greeks. —Yes, in that hour, my Lord, I fully expected to die, and so did all my noble men, for our position on that ridge was hopeless, the Greeks pressing hard from every side. And in that hour, without warning, we were suddenly saved by swift-moving Glaucus and two fine regiments of Lycians that struck the Greeks from the rear, offering us a safe pathway to escape.

—No, that is not entirely true, for at the time Sarpedon—commanding the Lycian main body—was fighting on the Plain. He gave his sanction to the order, certainly, for Glaucus said as much in the hour that we reached safety, but the impetus for our relief came from gray-eyed Polydamas, Marshal of Troy, who had apparently continued to urge the dispatch of a larger force to the north, even after my Uplanders had already received their orders and started to march. In such a way, not long after our departure from Dardanos, Glaucus received orders of his own, direct from Polydamas: their overriding concern was that the Lycians make all possible haste to join in the defense of Abydus-by-the-sea. The Lycians ran then, from the fires of their bivouac east of Dardanos, moving swiftly north at a fleet pace, and struck the Boeotian rear in the hour of our greatest danger. Taken by surprise, by two of our best regiments, the Boeotians peeled away before Glaucus, retiring both east and north, and thus a corridor of escape was thrown open, allowing my threatened Uplanders to withdraw with grace.

—Once amongst the Lycians, we turned and stood our ground, presenting the Greeks with an unbroken front across the strength of a corps. We counterattacked, then, and continued to do so throughout the following three days, but we were so outnumbered before Abydus that we were continually forced to slip to the east so as to prevent being again surrounded. Finally, at sunset on the fourth day we were forced to give up all belief that we could drive in through the Greeks in order to relieve Abydus. We withdrew then, falling back on Dardanos, carrying our dead and wounded with us, knowing full well that the northern Troad had not only been split but lost. Abydus held firm for several months, as I recall, owing largely to the determination of the Mustang, of men who were fighting for their homes and wives and children . . . indeed, for their lives, and the stories of their courageous defense were legion in Troy. Relief was twice more attempted, and in strength, but by that time the Greeks had concentrated such enormous numbers around the position that our own best efforts, both of which were commanded by Aeneas, were doomed to failure. Thus, in the eighth winter Abydus fell, and the Greeks burned the citadel black with their fury, and across the Troad one heard nothing beyond a low, dismal moan.

—In retrospect? —My Lord, who can know the ways of the gods? Had Deiphobus moved with more speed, had Antiphorus fought with more courage, had Hector sent a larger relief force, had Polydamas argued his case with more persuasiveness . . . had I made war with deadlier effect . . . all, or each by itself, might have turned the Greek tide before blue Abydus-by-the-sea, but now the point is silent. For me, all that remains is the glory of Glaucus breaking through to us on that warm spring day so many long years ago, for in that hour I learned profoundly the sweetness of life, and the memory has remained with me and will do so until the end of my days.

—Take, my Lord of the Hatti, some of the kine that my cooks have prepared. Here, across the slopes of Tmolus, it is the custom amongst us to braise the meat in oil before soaking it with wine in preparation for the spit. Then we like to see it, fresh from the fire, salted and served hot with olives, bread, and wine.

—As you say, let the language of our treaty be simple but clear, and let no less than five Hatti heralds bring me swift reply, for as you well know from the rigors of your embassy, the way from Hattusas is long and frought with danger according to the perils of the road.

—Yes, I *do* know something of escapes, something more than I have already told you. —*When?* —Know you, Lord, that I was captured in the war's ninth year, on the third day of Hector's great counteroffensive. The beautiful Cassandra once told me that it would be so, but I paid her no heed; yet, at the very hour she named, in the very place that her words had described, I was struck down as she had warned by the furious passage of a Locrian chariot, and there, before that long Greek wall in the very shadow of their ships, I was captured in my prime by a bitter host whose spearheads went immediately to my throat. Four days later, on short rations and less water, I found myself chained to the ribs of a Rhodian hull that in quick time put into Antissa on Lesbos's northern coast. There, without delay, I was sold to slavers from Chios who were collecting men for the copper mines on Rhodes, and in those darkened mines I might have ended my days had not Poseidon come to my aid. In my youth my father and I had sacrificed many bulls in honor of the Earthshaker, and thus, in the hour of my need, he stirred his sea-girt hand, overthrowing my enemies in the height of their pride.

—We had sailed nine days in hard stages after leaving Antissa, running short before a bitter wind to Icaria, Patmos, Cos, and finally Nisyros, where twenty of our number were sold to King Thessalus for hard labor in the construction of a citadel. I was chained throughout the voyage to the thwart of a rowing bench—chained, in fact, beside one of Agenor's sons who had been captured before me on the offensive's first day and who was dying in stages owing to the severity of a mace blow which had crushed his chest. For days—indeed, since the moment of our departure from Chios—the skies to the west threatened, and then, north of Telos at the southern tip of the Sporades, the Thunderer showed us his bolt, causing the entire sky to blacken and erupt. The hull we were riding was old, something the Greeks had captured from Troy and sold as war booty to the slavers of Chios, and in that hour I knew that the rotting timbers beneath us would never withstand Poseidon's pounding. And indeed, they did not, for in a short time, no matter how hard we all pulled away at the oars, the mountainous green seas so cracked and wrenched the hull that the frame came apart at its seams, shipping tons of water with more speed than the stoop of a kite. We went down then, in sight of the Rhodian coast, and there where the dolphins dive, I might have drowned in the chambers of the sea save for the chance accident that, as the ship broke up beneath me, the thwart to which I was chained suddenly snapped, throwing me—chain and body—into the sea. I clawed then for a piece of the wreckage and came up riding a part of the yard or the mast, and in that condition, stung by the salt sea foam and blasted by the might of the waves, I drifted helplessly for two long days . . . still within sight of Telos, still within sight of Rhodes, but unable in any way to do ought but fulfill Poseidon's will.

—On the third morning, my face swollen from exposure, worn with fatigue, half-delirious, I was pulled from the water by the bow-hook of a Lycian merchantman. The Lycians had themselves been blown from their course by the storm, and to the best of my recollection, through the dazed delirium of my memory, they were anxious to put on sail, for those Rhodian waters were hostile owing to the spreading effects of the

war. They headed then for the open sea, preferring to skirt Rhodes to
the south rather than attempt a passage between Caria and Rhodes's
northern coast: in that channel, they later told me, Argive war hulls
were much in evidence, seeking to intercept at their point of departure
any Carian grain shipments destined for our armies at Troy. Too overcome by fever to be much aware, I cannot account for the remainder of
the voyage, but apparently the worst of my trials ended with the wreck;
three days later, on a calm morning, we struck the mouth of Xanthus,
crossed the bar, and making our slow way up the river, beached before
noon in full view of Lycia's royal citadel.

—As soon as my identity became known, on the strength of my
relationship with Glaucus, I was taken immediately into the citadel,
and there, under the watchful eye of Hippolochus, the chains were
struck from my hands, and I was set free to make my recovery. I was a
long time, my Lord, in regaining my strength, and throughout the
whole, lordly Hippolochus, Glaucus's aged father, accorded me the
greatest courtesies, supervising my recovery with a paternal eye.

—On the whole, my stay in Lycia passed without incident, except for
one curious moment not long after I had regained my senses. I was
resting then on a fleece, recounting to Hippolochus his son's achieve-
ments at Troy, and in the course of our conversation, I made some
passing reference to Sarpedon. Immediately, with obvious marks of
respect, noble Hippolochus bowed his head as though the king were
dead. Struck by this impression, I raised upright, and then in halting
tones and low, gray Hippolochus—lonely for his own son—reported
that it was so—that in fact royal Sarpedon's body had reached Xanthus
some twenty days before, that *in fact* the king's mortal bones already
rested beneath a high, earth mound. In my disbelief I feared renewed
delirium. By my calculations, you see, on the precise day that Sarpedon's body had returned to Xanthus, he and I had fought side by side
before the Argive ships, far to the north at the foot of the dusty Plain. I
questioned Hippolochus then, anxiously and at length, and in the end
the answer he made me was plain. "The ways of the gods," he told me,
"remain always hidden to men; wise is the warrior who refuses to
question them. Sarpedon was the son of Zeus. What more need a man
know? Clearly, all things are possible to the gods, and the gods are
forever, but man—man is but for a season, and then, like the cicada,

his dust blows onto the wind." He spoke the truth to me that day, there in the royal citadel at Xanthus, and now, as my long winters gather numberlessly in my wake, I hearken to the strength of his word.

—I required four moons to regain my strength, and throughout that time, no guest was ever better served by his host than I was by the father of Glaucus, but when the first leaves began to fall, I knew that the time had come for me to return to the war, and then, taking only what I could carry—a sea cloak, a wallet of grain, and a stout Lycian spear—I made my farewells and struck inland, marching hard up the valley of swift-flowing Xanthus, heading north toward the Maeonian homeland of my father on the slopes of Tmolus.

—I was thirty days on the road, for the trail was long and the way unknown to me, and not infrequent were the dangers I faced from both man and beast. But then, on a cold morning with Borean frosts already crunching beneath my feet, I crossed finally through a steep mountain pass to see the valley of the Cayster laid out before me, the smoke from a thousand Maeonian cooking fires drifting skyward through the clear, chilled air, wreathing Tmolus like a crown. My heart thrilled then as it had never thrilled before, as it has never thrilled again, and with a single, bounding leap, I plunged down the mountain's side, riding the currents of the wind, racing for home.

—Know, noble Hatti, that I never returned to Troy—never led my Uplanders again in sharp, bright battle across the Plain, never saw the Uplanders again . . . never again embraced my brother, and never again looked upon the face of a single warrior—Maeonian or Outlander—who had fought beside me before Troy, for in the valley of the Cayster, beneath the shadowed, snowcapped slopes of Tmolus, the king, my father, was dead, and in his place, I had to rule. Of all the fine, bronzed warriors who went down with me swiftly into Lydia those ten long years before, only I, my Lord, lived to return.

—Speak, then, to the King of the Hatti. Tell him that the stouthearted Maeonians know well the ways of war and that we fully support him against the barbarians from the east. Tell him that, and let be the will of the gods.

Heptaporos in Phrygia

—The Spider? —No, my friend, in that assumption you are wrong: the Trojan Spider never functioned as an integral part of the army. Rather, the Spider was an independent force created secretly by flint-eyed Polydamas . . . and the elder, Ucalegon, . . . and the wise Antenor whose noble son, Polybus, commanded, and in all the long-gone days of my youth to speak so much as the unit's name brought instant, painful death. Officially, you see, we did not exist, so from whom, friend, did you hear of us?

—May the cold hand of Hermes close over me, for I had no knowledge that *he* remained alive. In fact, until this very moment I believed that all but myself had long ago entered deep into the chambers of decay, paying Charon the boatman with the single copper coin that we wore ever about our necks in token of our readiness. The name you speak astounds me; the news you bring makes fast the pulse of my blood, and yet why should my reaction be so? Has not the whole known world turned inside out? Has not the very earth itself turned, and turned again? In the West, I am told, even the relentless Argive Greeks give way in haste before barbarians, while to the east, straining his resources to make himself secure, the right royal Lord of the Hatti sits uneasy on his throne, assailed in strength across his once-tranquil borders. Where, then, the long, stable season? Where a land in which the blood of men serves other than to manure the ground? And even so knowing, the name you speak unsettles my mind, for long ago in our youth we saw hard toil together in the service of Troy, and he was always my stalwart friend. My ancient heart sings to hear that he lives, and thus I lift my cup in his honor.

—As you say, my friend, with the fall of Troy all need for secrecy ended. And yet, through sixty dark winters the web of the Spider has remained well hidden and remains so still, for I can read through your words that *he,* my long lost companion at arms, revealed nothing to you beyond the unit's name. Clearly, he kept the faith, for as the last to command the Spider, its web is mine to reveal or withhold, as I will. —Nay, friend, put thyself at ease, for in the moment that you came to me, I saw at a glance that you were more than you seemed, more by far than a mere Phrygian grain merchant overtaken by night on the high road into Mysia, and yet I kept you by me, offering you food and drink and the warmth of my hut against this high mountain cold that surrounds us, and even now you are welcome to stay, for you have come to me, I think, from the Halls of the Hatti, seeking to know from me the way of the Spider, seeking to learn from me something that will help your king to preserve his throne. Speak to me, my friend. Have I not divined the truth about you? —Yes, that *is* as I thought. Know you, then, that I will reveal to you as much of the secret as will be wise and useful for you to know. And I will instruct you willingly, friend, for to my mind the lords of Hattusas and the right royal Hatti remain man's one clear hope for stability in the east, and like other men I am not anxious to see chaos come again as it did so long ago after the collapse of Troy. Mark well, then, the words that I speak to you, for mine is the voice of the Spider.

—Know you, friend, before I embark on more complex matters, that in the mastery of disguise you remain deficient. Many are the years that color my beard, but in all of the time that I have walked the life-path, I have no recollection of a single grain merchant—within these Phrygian mountains—who wears so hard and lean a look as you. Clearly, you, or your masters, selected the wrong identity for these regions, for here, where the price of grain is dear, grain sellers are known for their girth and the fat weights of their purses, and all alike travel in the company of armed guards whom they pay for security. That much you should have known in advance, before you ever forded deep-watered Sangarius

to come amongst these hills. In future, should you ever again seek to
veil your true nature, study well in advance and *become*, in all respects, the man you would be. Judging now by the strength of your
arm, I would name you an axe man from the Hatti's front rank. Tell
me, friend, do I strike the mark?

—Only occasionally, Warrior—and that *is* what I will call you, for an
axe wielder you must certainly be, whether you deny the fact or not.
Only occasionally, then, did I go into disguise, but in those instances
when I did hide my identity in order to act as the eyes of the Spider, I
chose my role with great care, studied the part, and then played it with
my life.

—The proof, you ask? —Consider, Warrior, while I make the matter
plain.

—Know you, then, that within weeks after the Greek War began we
knew the fate of many of our warriors who had been captured in open
battle on the Plain. From the heights, on the Wall of Heracles, sharp-
eyed Paeonian scouts had seen one Phoenician slave hull after another
scud empty through Hellespont's wide mouth, beach before the Greek
camp, take aboard in chains our captive brothers, and depart again,
hull down, in the direction of Lemnos and the massive slave markets of
Myrina. In time word of these shipments reached us high in the Spider's upcountry encampment, and in short time a ruse made itself clear
to me by which, given Apollo's protection, we might reclaim many of
our warriors to fight another day across the windswept Plain of Troy.
I spoke then to Polybus, who heard me out before questioning me
in detail, and when I satisfied him with the particulars of my idea,
we took chariot and journeyed together to wise Antenor's villa on the
Simoeis. There we set our plan before the Three—Ucalegon, Antenor, and flint-eyed Polydamas—repeating each detail, and in the
early morning, even before Aurora's first blush, I found myself already
moving overland toward Ida's whitecapped peaks into Mysia beyond.

—I was nine days working south to Pitane, and from there, by taking
ship in a Carian bottom, I made my way to Xanthus, home of our
bronze-armed Lycian allies. In Xanthus, by means of a ring given into
my keeping from the hand of Antenor, I made myself known to lordly
Hippolochus, who ruled in Sarpedon's absence, and he in turn passed
me through Lycian agents deep into Cilicia where I held up for some

weeks on the estate of a Cilician noble. From there, after learning the rudiments of the Phoenician tongue from a tutor who was sent to me and with my hair and beard cut in the Phoenician fashion, I assumed the guise of a mute and bought a land passage with a horse caravan that was moving south toward Sidon, and in that city, after three moons on the road, I arrived before the first Borean winds.

—By that time, I recall, much of the Phoenician merchant fleet had returned home from its far-flung summer trading voyages so that everywhere along the shore dark, broad-beamed hulls were drawn up on the beach for scraping and repair. I found a room for myself there in a waterfront inn and, still passing myself publicly for a mute, made even greater efforts to learn the language by employing a prostitute whom I suborned to my purpose, and in keeping my secret she remained entirely loyal. After some weeks, when I felt that I had sufficiently mastered the tongue so as to meet my need, I bought the woman a passage into Egypt, saw her on her way, and then changed both my appearance and my residence so as to bury my former identity beneath an impenetrable cloak of obscurity, for know you, Warrior, that Argive agents had also appeared in Sidon and to have been known to them would have meant my sudden, painful death and the failure of all my designs.

—I waited then close by the sea, and when the hard hand of Boreas finally descended from the north onto the dark, inland heights, sometimes individually and sometimes sailing in twos and threes, the high-riding Phoenician slave hulls began returning to port in order to scrape down and winter within sight of Sidon. In that year and the next, you see, main battle on the Plain slowed in the late fall, with Greek and Trojan alike taking shelter from ice, wind, and snow until the first melt of spring. Later, as the war hardened, embittering both sides, the old ways of campaigning died quick deaths so that the fighting extended on a large scale throughout all twelve moons of the year. But that was not quite the case during those first two years, and in consequence the Phoenician slave fleet, finding no Greek cargoes either to buy or sell, returned to its home ports in order to ride out the winter while preparing itself to go north again early in the spring, so as to profit quickly from the first resumption of battle.

—I made a survey then of the entire slave fleet, ascertaining which hulls were fit and seaworthy and which were not, informing myself, thereby, which owners and captains were making a profit by their ventures and which were not. In fact, owing to the immensity of the war, almost all had profited by carrying Trojan captives into bitter slavery on Lemnos, but after a lengthy search I found one—the owner of two leaking hulls, a half-breed Egyptian with a blue trailing scar across his chin—who was prepared to sell his ships at a profit, for he had made almost nothing by them during the previous summer, owing to their slow and rotten condition. Passing myself for a merchant of Tyre, I bought both hulls, using sums that were transmitted to me through agents in Cilicia, and then I had both hulls drawn up on the beach to be scraped, caulked, and repaired as best they might be.

—I waited then, through the long moons of winter, biding my time, fitting out both ships for sea, cleansing them as well as I might of the reeking slave stench which had seeped deep into their timbers, and then, when I perceived Boreas's first faint wane, I put to sea in command of a hard lot of Phoenician sailors who liked the glitter of my coin. We were away some days before the remainder of the fleet was willing to put to sea, for it was my intention to beat up into the Hellespont well in advance of the pack, and thus I gambled on the weather and won, and in twelve days—with Lord Poseidon's help and a following wind—rounded Tenedos's western cape and set a firm course for the mouth of Hellespont and the foot of the Plain.

—Indeed, from the moment my hulls passed first between Rhodes and Crete, I found myself in constant danger—not from sea or weather but from Argive war hulls which appeared suddenly and without warning, sailing singly or in pairs, seeking to prevent all commerce from the south—Phoenician, Egyptian, or Cilician—with Priam or his royal allies. In consequence, we were nine times stopped dead in the water and boarded, but our high, empty hulls and the reeking stench of former cargoes served to answer all that any Greek sought to know, and, too, I had by that time so well schooled myself in the Phoenician tongue and custom that not even the hardest of my sailors had penetrated my disguise.

—Thus, on the twentieth morning out from Sidon, we made the Hellespont, working up the race under sail and oar to beach before the slave stakes which were arranged in rows near Scamander's wide mouth at the western edge of the Greek camp. There, tense with apprehension but sensing success, I leapt ashore on my own native soil under the contemptuous, watchful eye of the Greek beach guard and made my way inland toward the hut of the slave stake commander. Immediately, I became acquainted with the suffering of my brothers at arms, for the captives then chained to those posts had been taken in skirmishes across the three moons of winter, and huddled like helpless dogs before a hard northern winter, they were in frightful condition. Many were sick; some were dying; and some—not yet cut free by their captors after nights of misery—were already dead. All were wasted, wan, and thin, and in total I estimated the numbers of the living not to exceed six hundred. My gorge rose then, and in the instant, my most pressing impulse was to draw my sword and strike off the head of the slave stake commander for the extent of his uncivilized inhumanity, and yet the moment the impulse arose, I buried it beneath a smile, knowing full well that only the gods can ever see fully into the minds of men.

—We bargained then, the slave stake commander and I, over the price of men. Marshalling all of my energies and all of my resources, I cast myself as a haggler, whining and wheedling with the feigned skill of a fishwife, and in time, after first corrupting the Greek with a propitious bribe, I struck a bargain which allowed me to carry away fully one third of the captives who were then held prisoner beside those stakes. I would be remiss to suggest to you that the triumph was all mine; clearly the Greeks were preparing to open the spring offensive, and the Argive kings had ordered the stakes to be cleared in preparation to receive new prisoners, healthy men who could be expected to bring far higher prices than the miserable wretches presently behind the enclosure. I bargained then with acumen, but the Greek, torn between the orders from his kings and his own responsibility for setting the price, scattered his force, and in the end he let go the lot to me for much less than they were worth. Later that summer when the fighting raged on the Plain, the price per captive doubled and then trebled, for the warriors captured—mostly Mysians who were then blunting the point of the Greek attack—were fit and strong, even after their wounds, which . . . owing to their youth . . . healed swiftly and with good bone.

—The bargain struck, I paid the Greek price—in gold—and then, some three hours later, having taken more than two hundred of the most able-bodied captives into my ships, I gave command, and all hands pulled away together, backing those wide-beamed hulls laboriously into the race. The current was swift enough so that once well adrift we were able to ship oars, hoist sail, and look to the open sea, for we rode the race directly into it, and there, finally, we picked up the land breeze which carried us strongly in the direction of Lemnos.

—For as long as Helios raised high his beams, I continued to sail due west, toward Lemnos and the hard slave markets of Myrina, but then, well to the west of Tenedos, as the day began to wane, I hailed the captain of our sister ship, bade him follow in my wake, and turned south. And there night overtook us; on a southerly course, sailing hull down before the wind, well beyond sight of land, in the midst of the wine-dark sea, we sailed on through utter darkness, navigating only by the dim light of the stars. It was then, Warrior, that I made my secret known, ordering the captives in both ships released and paying both my Phoenician crews in double coin beyond what any legitimate voyage might have brought them. As I said, they were a hard lot who knew the color of gold, and with gold I bought both silence and loyalty. On short order then the Phoenicians set all my long-suffering brothers-in-arms free, and those worn, exhausted men—heedless of their wounds, their sickness, or their pain—swarmed to the oars like the warriors that they were, pulling away together with more spirit than strength until both heavily laden hulls went lumbering through the seas with the grim, shuddering power of whales. Even so, I found it necessary to restrain the men, for their euphoria in being delivered from captivity threatened to sap the last vestiges of their strength—a strength I wanted to conserve in the event that we were sighted by Greek war hulls and given chase.

—In all events, Apollo's protection remained with us, so much so that I aborted my original intention and stood straight into Assus rather that sailing further south so as to put in at Pitane. This, however, necessitated pulling both hulls ashore and covering them with brush so that blockading Greeks might not see and identify them on the following morning, and this we did in the earliest hour of the dawn by means of our own strong backs but with considerable help from the garrison command at Assus. In retrospect, as events proved, the gods must have guided my hands, for in the broad light of day it became clear to me that the captives I had brought out were in far worse condition than I had thought. Two, Carians both, died in the night, and on the following morning three more warriors—a gaunt Cicone and two thin Mysians—made the sound of the death rattle in their throats and went down deep into the chambers of decay. With the remainder, conditions were grim. Healers came amongst them almost immediately, sent down by the garrison commander, and these prescribed long rest and a sustained intake of barley gruel and light bread. Even so, throughout the remainder of our stay—some seven or eight days, as I recall—at least one man went down daily with the setting of the sun.

—We were fortunate, for another reason, in putting into Assus, but this only became plain to us after a lapse of five or six days. On the same night, apparently during the same hours in which we had sailed east toward the Trojan coast and safety, somewhere out ahead of us a fleet of Greek raiders must have crossed our bow. These, as we were to learn, struck Pitane in the first brisk hours after dawn, setting fire to several Mysian ships and burning a part of the town. Their withdrawal, which they conducted with great order and spirit, was well disciplined, and once at sea they headed apparently due west. Had I continued, as I had planned, to seek safe harbor at Pitane, I believe those same Greeks would have caught me in the open sea south of Lesbos. From all reports they were warriors from Crete under the direct command of gray-haired Idomeneus, their king; trained sea warriors all, they would have swarmed over the decks of my slow hulls like flights of wasps, and we would have been destroyed to the last man.

—We sailed again with the new moon and then thrice more before the end of the Greeks' spring offensive. The Greeks were hardly so successful as they had hoped they would be, and the count of their captives dwindled accordingly. Thus the price that we paid became high in weight of gold, but still we paid it gladly, snatching back our battle-tried warriors from beneath the greedy noses of their captors. Throughout, my luck held, and I was neither betrayed by my Phoenician crews nor detected by the Greek war hulls which pillaged our coast. In the end, I think, I succeeded in recovering some seven hundred of our warriors by means of my ruse, but then on my sixth voyage Apollo deserted me, and I found myself suddenly forced to flee for my life.

—Let this be a lesson to you, Warrior: never attempt the same ruse more than twice, for with each successive attempt the chances for success dwindle by half. That is the rule of the Spider, a child of the gods which seldom relies on a single strand of silk but rather upon an interlocking grid whereby one strand supports another. In my venture to buy back Trojan prisoners from under the very noses of the Greeks, I relied too long on one strand of security and on one strand only, and that strand was myself. I was successful but only in the short term, and when the end came, it came suddenly and without warning, and in that hour my scheme was irrevocably broken.

—No, Warrior, not at sea but in the midst of the Greek camp. That is where I was detected first, immediately beside the slave stakes, by a shrewd Ithacan king who knew the Phoenician tongue and heard in my words a trace of a Trojan accent. I laughed the matter off, protesting that I had traded for years in Trojan waters before the war's commencement, but he was not put off by the ease of my manner, pointing out to me that the bribes which I had offered to the former slave stake commander were excessive to my purpose. Clearly, he seemed to know everything about me by that time: how often I had beached before the camp, to whom I had spoken while ashore, even the particulars of the bargains I had struck and the secondary bribes I had paid to the slave stake commander's aide, a hump-backed minion named Thersites, whose oily manner had made my flesh crawl but whose greed I had carefully cultivated. On former voyages, I had dealt only with those two, but on this, my sixth time to enter the Greek camp, neither man appeared to view, so I faced only the Ithacan, whose shrewd, commanding eyes seemed to plumb the depths of my mind.

—I fended off his queries as best I might, attempting throughout our interview to strike a bargain for more than half of the captives then chained to his stakes, but in this I was singularly unsuccessful; all he would sell to me were the diseased and badly wounded whose chances for recovery seemed slim. —I knew then that he knew, that in his own mind he had penetrated my ruse, and in that precise moment I saw him smile almost as though he admired my stratagem: I feared then for my life, but in that emotion I was mistaken, for apparently he had no intention of killing me, and instead, with a grim smile, he let me go.

—Remember, Warrior, this was early in the war, and by any man's measure the Ithacan was a man of honor: he *knew,* you see, but without putting us to torture, he could not *prove,* and that he seemed unwilling to do. Thus, with some thirty dying Trojans to divide between the ships, I found myself delivered. But still, Warrior, I feared, for far down the beach, near the center of the Greek camp, I spotted two Ithacan war hulls making ready for sea.

—We backed then and caught the race, and in the same moment that the current took us, I made my decision, and my decision was to strike for the open sea, swing sharply south, and run my hulls as hard as their timbers would bear, under full oar and sail, straight for Besika Bay, where I could beach under the protection of our well-guarded shore.

—In the end the Argive war hulls were too swift for us, their oars too well manned. The moment I turned south, of course, I showed my hand, and upon that apparent signal Greek oars flashed in the sun. As much as a league behind me to start, they had shortened the distance between us to half that space by the time they scudded from the Helles-pont, and that was the moment when I knew for certain that I could not make Besika Bay. I gave signal to the captain of the second hull, and both ships turned together, and in no more time than is required for an arrow's flight, we ran both hulls hard aground across the rocky, sea-ward flank of the Wall of Heracles.

—Even then, I think, we would not have escaped had not a company of sharp-eyed Paeonian archers spotted us from the heights and moved swiftly down to hold off the Greeks. Moving inland, up the Wall's steep slopes, dragging or carrying those Trojan captives who were fit enough to go with us, we made good our escape while clouds of Paeonian arrows streaked seaward above our heads. So thwarted, the Greeks did not pursue, contenting themselves instead with firing our hulls by means of pine knots and pitch. The last thing I remember of our escape—before reaching the Paeonians—was looking back over my shoulder from the heights to find the air below dense with thick, black smoke.

—Learn, then, my Warrior of Hattusas, that an effective disguise must be well and carefully planned. But even so, there is no illusion, no matter how successful, that can long elude penetration. —Come, Wielder of the Axe, the night is bitter cold. Help thyself to the wine and wrap thy shoulders in one of the fleeces that hang from the pegs on my wall.

—No, Warrior, the case was otherwise, for we of the Spider were not recruited until we had already proved ourselves in the field. Know you that in the years before the Greek War began, I had trained up north of Percote in the ranks of a hard frontier regiment that often went into battle against the wild barbarians to the east. There I had grown to manhood, and there too, by means of demonstrated merit, I had risen swiftly from runner to warrior and finally to standard-bearer for the entire command. Twice in close combat I saved my general's life, and twice more I led shock battalions to penetrate the enemy's front, and in time—there beyond Percote, along the edge of the Troad—I made a name, going not unhonored amongst my peers.

—The Panther, for that was my regiment, was then commanded by Hicetaon, offshoot of the War-god, elder of Troy, gray-bearded veteran of both the Thracian and Mysian wars. As such, he knew well both the elder Ucalegon and the wise Antenor, and when—some eight or nine moons before the Greek War commenced—they visited Percote on a tour of close inspection, I went down from our upland camp with Hicetaon in order to meet them, in the way of the warrior, and act as commander of their escort along our sector of the frontier. In short, both men took my measure, and before even their inspection tour ended, I was on my way, moving south under orders, toward the isolated rendezvous of the Spider.

—I was surprised, Warrior, when I finally reached my destination—a narrow valley deep within the mountain fastness east of Troy—to find not many others then in camp. And my surprise continued, for at the end of a week no more than three hundred warriors had assembled beneath a newly issued regimental standard which had been planted dead center on the valley's floor. Clearly we had not even the fighting strength of a Trojan battalion of the line, and in that hour, during those first few days, I could not understand how such an assemblage might be of the slightest use in any war that Priam chose to conduct. To confuse the matter further, no one seemed to be in charge, save a single old bald-headed warrior of some three score or more years whose back was bent but whose hawk-like eyes penetrated everywhere. "I am Pharos," he said to me when I first reached the camp, "Wait and study patience." And study patience I did, and so in fact did the remainder of the command . . . for twelve long days until finally, beneath the wane of the moon, flint-eyed Polydamas appeared suddenly and with him my Lord Polybus. Then, Warrior, things began to happen.

—Within a matter of moments, I remember, we were called to assembly, and there for the first time we heard the name of the Spider. Immediately we were sworn to secrecy about the unit's identity, our place in it, and all further operations that it might conduct, and then, with short ceremony but clear, Polydamas invested my Lord Polybus with command and departed into the night. We had not time, I think, even to contemplate his going, for almost in the same moment that he received his standard, Polybus raised it, and hawk-eyed Pharos emerged from the ranks to stand by his side. "Listen well," Polybus commanded, "for in the months to come, the wisest amongst us will teach us the way of the Spider." We thought to cheer, but even before the sound could burst from our throats, my Lord Polybus withdrew himself into our ranks, leaving naught before us save the gaunt countenance of that hawk-eyed apparition. "Cheer not!" Pharos suddenly commanded, striking the earth once with the butt of his spear, "for the way of the Spider is silence, combining patience with stealth, and the Spider cheers not in the wake of its victory." —In that moment, Warrior, we first heard the Spider's authority, first began to learn its ways, and in the days and moons that followed, we quickly learned to respect those ways, and in the end we trusted them implicitly.

—Who, you ask? —He was the oldest and certainly the wisest warrior at Troy. Indeed, as I was to learn, ancient Pharos of the hawk's eye had once been Priam's most important general. The elder Ucalegon, Antenor, Lampus, and Thymoetes had all served at one time under his command during our long-gone wars with Thrace. Even noble Hicetaon had once been Pharos's runner. Long before my birth, it seemed, Pharos had held high place at Troy, counseling the king, but then, owing to the pitfalls of a palace intrigue, he had fallen forever from favor, and his life had become obscure. What precisely had led to his downfall, none of us—certainly not I—had ever been able to learn, but the effects were clear enough, no matter what the political reasoning behind them: clearly the best military mind at Troy had been denied command, and in the end this affected not only himself but his protégé, flint-eyed Polydamas, to whom Pharos had imparted the most assiduous training during those long, dark years after he had fallen from favor. That, Warrior, is as much as I know and as much as I am ever likely to learn, but this much is certain: in denying merit, for whatever reason, the royal house of Priam hastened its own destruction. I have thought both long and hard on the matter since the last days of Troy, and even now I still believe that had Pharos, or Polydamas, commanded on the Plain, Ilium might have survived.

—As you say, Warrior, to rethink the past is idle speculation, and yet the exercise has value when one wishes not to repeat a mistake.

—I am coming to that, so wait, my impetuous friend, and study patience, for it is beyond my power to answer two of your questions at once. First, then, my knowledge of him who commanded on the Plain.

—Clearly, Warrior, he was blunt and hard, imposing a stern discipline that was good for the army and which bound our allies to us even under the greatest stress. I admired him for that, as did all Trojans, and in his political acumen I knew of few who ever found Hector wanting. But even so, he had not the foresight in battle that flint-eyed Polydamas showed, and his grand design proved ever more reaction than action. He was a good defensive fighter—that much is clear enough, for he managed to hold back the Greeks through nine long years—but before Troy the situation demanded more than defense, more than blunt, frontal assault, and in that Hector came up wanting. —Say you again? —In a phrase, lack of imagination. Know you, Warrior, that Hector was ever the practical administrator, ever the competent man of affairs, but on the field, face to face with the intuitive fluidity of the Greek, he lacked that quickness of imagination that would have allowed the army to exploit the enemy's weakness and drive the Greek to destruction. —Mind you, I found no fault with the man, only with the general, for to the bitter end the man demonstrated a matchless, admirable integrity, and in doing so he taught all Ilium how to die. How much better had he possessed the insight to find for us the key to life.

—Just so, for your second question concerned our training. Know you, Warrior, that each amongst us was already well skilled in the conventional use of arms and tactics before we were ever selected to join the Spider. In fact, by my measure prowess in battle was the prime requirement for entry, but once in, Pharos introduced a training regimen surpassing anything I had ever seen. We already knew how to kill;

in the ranks of the Spider we learned how to kill silently, with patience and stealth.

—Our training was endless. Night and day we studied in the field a new form of warfare that taught each man to rely on himself, and yet at the same time we became masters of what Pharos called small unit tactics. Working individually at first and later in groups of five or ten, we learned how to infiltrate into the enemy camp and kill him sleeping in his bed, how to sow the seeds of fear and disorder behind his lines, how to destroy his food supply, how . . .

—Pardon? —Indeed, Warrior. Would you know the matter now? —So be it.

—Know you, then, that in the war's fourth year, long after my mission to reclaim our captives had ended and long after I had rejoined the ranks of the Spider, the grain harvest was everywhere light in the land owing to a prolonged summer's drouth. Furthermore, this condition prevailed apparently across the length and breadth of the Aegaean. Owing to foresight among Priam's administrators, Trojan granaries were already filled to capacity as a result of careful rationing after a surplus during the summer before, but amongst the Greeks, who relied upon merchant hulls to bring in their stocks, shortened supply was almost immediately felt—useful information that we quickly gleaned from a variety of Argive captives taken on the Plain.

—My Lord Polybus, who had a fine and independent mind, considered the problem alone, I remember, for several hours, and then, calling me in, he gave me command of an independent operation to be directed against the Greek staging areas on Tenedos.

—Know you, Warrior, that Tenedos, once the home base of the Shark, the Whale, and the fighting elements of the Trojan fleet, had fallen in the opening days of the war to the warriors of Crete who had stormed ashore there in overpowering numbers and, after two days of hard fighting in the field, succeeded in annihilating a veteran battalion of Whales which was then acting as garrison.

—There, during the weeks and moons that followed, the Argive Greeks consolidated their gains by creating an immense base from which their entire army on the Plain was to be supplied. Lacking war hulls, we had not the capacity to make an effective, fighting counterassault against the island, but even so, had we attempted such an attack using Mysian or Carian hulls, the issue would have remained doubtful owing to the ninety-hull fleet from Crete, which controlled all of the island's sea approaches. —Such were the facts, but such too was the quality of Polybus's imagination that he found for us an effective way to damage the base by stealth.

—In short, Warrior, on a dark night in the autumn of that year I contrived—by means of two small boats—to put myself and nine legs of the Spider ashore on Tenedos's northeast cape. The boats were small enough, you see, so that to escape detection, we could tip them, fill them with stones and water, and sink them out of sight beneath the placid waters of a cove, and then, moving swiftly in silence, we worked inland under the cry of a nighthawk and there made ourselves secure in a copse. Almost immediately I became aware that we were doomed to failure, for in the cold light of day, as we reconnoitered the base, we found to our shock that it was more than thrice as large as we had supposed and very well guarded. Nevertheless, in the moment that Helios descended, plunging the world into the darkest of nights, I moved my warriors, dividing them first into two teams for the purpose of broadening our effect. During the preceding day, while making our distant, visual survey of the area from the cover of a ridge, we had identified what we believed to be as many as sixteen separate areas of grain storage across nearly half a league of beach. Knowing that we could never hope to deal with all, we moved, instead, directly against the center of the area, for it was my intention that we should begin with the largest stores and then, as time passed, work out toward the edges of the base, putting as much distance between teams as possible in case one or the other were detected.

—We moved then, down from the copse in utter silence, covering our track with the cloak of night, and within less than an hour we managed to infiltrate between sentry posts which the Greeks had arranged inland at irregular intervals. Indeed, at the time I remember thinking that I might have brought in safely as many as fifty legs of the Spider, for the Argive garrison, having never before experienced our kind of attack, seemed blind to the threat.

—On the beach some cover was afforded by the immense stacks of supplies that were everywhere in evidence: cord wood for winter fires, animals in pens, fodder, hides for making shields and armor, cordage, stores of long pine oars, and cut timber for ship repair. Had we gone in with enough strength, we might easily have fired the entire base and withdrawn safely to tell the tale, but such was its immensity, such its wide and varied spacing, that fires, even those compounded of pitch and wind, seemed to have little chance of spreading so as to engulf the whole, and this I thought to be the key element—and a shrewd one—in the Argive camp's design.

—We moved then against the largest areas of grain storage, many of them easily identified by row after row of immense clay jars standing as high as a man's chest. Those storage jars, narrow near the top, were sealed with beeswax to the thickness of a man's hand, and it was simple enough, using a sword blade, to cut straight through the wax and lift out the seal. This I did, moving swiftly from jar to jar down those long, endless rows while the men behind me—working two to a team—mixed copious amounts of goat's dung, gathered from the surrounding pens, with sea water brought up from the beach, and this spoiling mixture, in quantity, we added to each storage jar before replacing the seal.

—Effectively, we polluted more than two hundred storage jars in the first area alone; the time required to complete this work proved lengthy, so in the end, seeking to speed our pace, we contented ourselves with the addition of sea water alone until we had gone through the storage capacity of two separate areas, but then, as we were about to begin working our way through a third—not many hours, I think, before the dawn—in the distance an alarm went up, and I knew instantly that our second team had been discovered.

—By training, Warrior, and without the slightest hesitation we melted immediately into the night, dropping some five or six Greeks of an alerted inland guard with stones from our slings so as to make clear the pathway of our withdrawal. We went to ground then in a variety of well-concealed upland caves, and on the following night three men from my second team rejoined us, reporting our other two men killed by lance thrusts on the beach. Some nights later, after refloating our boats, we put to sea and beached before morning in the Troad, having come safely away from Tenedos under the very eyes of the Argive war fleet.

—In retrospect our raid on Tenedos proved a strategic failure but a tactical success. Had we gone in with greater numbers, we might have achieved a far greater success and forced a Greek withdrawal. As it was, lean winter rations crippled considerably the Argive's ability to make war during that year, and in that I must own a hand, for including the nine who went with me, my understrength raid on Tenedos succeeded in cutting the Greek bread ration by as much as one fifth. —Thus, Warrior, the stealth of the Spider.

—Indeed, refresh thy cup and draw closer to the fire. Tell me, Wielder of the Axe, does hunger yet gnaw at thy innards? —*Ah,* that is even as I suspected, for the mortality of man demands ever to be fed. Help thyself to a barley cake and wait no more on ceremony to fulfill thy needs.

—Defame not the sling, Warrior, for the Hatti would be wise to employ it. 'Tis no axe, that much is certain, but it kills with precision in silence, and such was the mark of the Spider. Twice, at least, in close combat, I have seen it make the difference between victory and defeat, and thus my sling is ever with me, even now. At a distance, Warrior, it is as sure as a spear.

—Just so, for the first time was in the war's sixth year when I saw the Locrians paralyze and then destroy a company of our own noble Mysians who were about to turn the Argive flank. Lord Hector, that morning, had extended our line, and from a ridge in the Dardanian hills, where I was acting as scout to warn against inland penetrations, I saw the Mysians go in rapidly around the exposed Greek wing, charging hard, throwing a tough battalion of Boeotian infantry back in disarray. It looked then like the beginning of the end, like the long-awaited collapse of the Greek battle line, but in the same moment that I rose to my feet in anticipation of victory, the Argive general commanding threw in his last reserve, a battalion of close-cropped Locrians who moved up swiftly in good order to support their fleeing infantry. At no less than one hundred paces they let fly, and their first volley brought our hard-charging Mysians to their knees, paralyzing all further movement. As quickly as he could, Hector threw in archers to support the Mysians, but by that time the damage had already been done; the best the archers could do was cover the Mysian retreat. —That, Warrior, was the first encounter in which I saw the massed power of the sling. In the second I employed it myself.

—As you wish. —Know you, then, that in the ninth year, after our great offensive on the Plain had crumbled, the Greeks assailed us from all sides. To the north Percote, holy Arisbe, Abydus-by-the-sea, and even Dardanos had fallen, while to the south the Greeks were pressing hard along the upper reaches of Scamander, preparing to cross over en masse in order to sever our supply routes from Mysia and all points beyond. Thymbra remained yet secure and Ilium and that single sector of the Troad, backing on Phrygia, which lies between the Simoeis and Ida's upland heights. But all else had fallen beneath the hard Argive heel.

—The role of the Spider in that last deadly year—aside from infiltration and reconnaissance—was to act in such a way as to draw off units of the Argive army from pursuing their main objective, and clearly that objective was to close a ring around Troy so as to starve the city into submission. Since we were better fed than ordinary Trojan units, for we were living off the land, my Lord Polybus thought the Spider still to be capable of long-range penetration behind the Greek lines, and thus, setting aside some forty warriors to continue meeting the main reconnaissance needs of the army, he reorganized the remainder of us into two fast-moving combat commands numbering about one hundred warriors each. As next senior in rank, it fell my lot to command one of these; Eteocles, my closest friend—the man you met in Cilicia— commanded the other. Our respective assignments took us far apart; indeed, I never saw him again, and until you, Warrior, brought me news of his breath, I had believed him to be dead.

—No, in keeping with my long familiarity with the area I was sent north. Having been born and brought up in the vicinity of Ida, Eteocles was, to my judgement, rightly assigned to the South, to the upland region west of Scamander but south of Besika Bay, and there, as I later learned, he made his command seem like a Trojan corps, slowing the Greek advance through a deft series of feints. For myself, I preferred to hit and run, moving in under cover of darkness to inflict as much death and damage as possible upon unsuspecting, isolated Greek commands and then withdrawing in haste only to reappear on the following night

at some distance from my previous point of attack. Thus, throughout
that last long summer and fall, while the weather held, the Spider
moved with great speed and stealth, disrupting supply and communication, striking again and again to sow as much death and destruction as
possible at the heart of the enemy's rear.

—Clearly we achieved some success, for from the moment of our
first attack—against an exposed Spartan bivouac south of Percote—the
Greeks came after us in close pursuit, first in company and battalion
strength but later, as we became steadily more daring, with a light
regiment and then a fully reinforced corps. This, I own, had been our
objective from the start, and once we achieved it, I might have been
well advised to withdraw. But by that time, you see, there was little left
to withdraw to and small hope to survive by any means other than our
continued hard resistance. As a result, we remained in the field and
fought on, enduring ever greater dangers from the pursuing Greeks,
who hunted us in a state of blind fury for having so slowed the progress
of their northern advance toward Troy.

—And then, Warrior, I awoke one morning early to feel the first
flakes of snow touch my face, and in that hour I knew that we could no
longer survive without warm shelter and an ensured supply of food.
And I knew something else too: I knew that when we moved we would
be forced to move with more speed than we had ever used before, for
there, in those cold Dardanian hills, our firm track on the snow would
be clear, and it would only be a short matter of time before the relentless Greeks ran us to ground to drive us fighting into the dark, deep
chambers of Hades. I called my warriors together then, ordered them
to discard spears and shields and body armor, and told them all that
henceforth they were to rely on their slings and the sharpest throwing
stones that they could find, and in the same hour, after we finished the
remains of our food, I began running the survivors of my command,
some seventy men, south in the direction of the Simoeis.

—Even now, Warrior, I remember the journey for its weightless
sounds of silence, for the soft footfalls of my men, running ankle deep
through newly settled powder, for the quiet drift of the wind as it
covered our heads with flakes, for the long, slow fall of the snow as it
drifted silently down from a gray sky. Throughout the whole of the war,
across a span of ten long years, that moment—there in the Dardanian

hills—brought me, I think, the only feeling of tranquility that I ever experienced. And then, like an unexpected thrust of thunder, it ended instantly with the screams of two of my fast-moving warriors, point men both, who had burst unexpectedly through an ice-clad willow thicket to find themselves utterly exposed on the snowbound floor of the Simoeis. In the same instant that they had broken from cover, Greek archers, waiting in ambush on the river's opposite bank, had struck them down from the mists, striking each man with a hard volley of sharp-barbed arrows.

—Alerted, I did what I could, halted the Spider's movement, reversed its advance, and withdrew in haste up the sloping, wooded ridge to our rear, slipping steadily west so as to put myself on the flank of what I supposed would be immediate Greek pursuit. In time we cut a shallow, snowbound meadow, not a large one by any measure, but as I recall, its width must have spanned the distance of a well-thrown javelin cast while its length was, perhaps, longer. Hurrying my command across that ground, I put them immediately into cover under the upland tree line, and there, hunkering behind the pines, we awaited the coming of the Greeks.

—When they came, they came in far greater strength than I had anticipated, moving quickly up through the trees and mists and slow-falling snow like a powerful, silent tide, and then I knew that my tactics were strong, for in that moment I perceived that I was facing not a single company but a battalion and that by slipping continually west during our retreat up the slope, I had indeed succeeded in moving the Spider athwart the Argives' left wing. We waited, then, breathing hard from the rigors of our withdrawal, and slowly, carefully, from the depths of the lower road, seeming to float above the mists like snow-shrouded ghosts, spear-wielding Corinthian infantry began to emerge onto the meadow's floor. They were hard to see, I remember, for each had wrapped himself in a sea cloak cut from the whitest of sail cloth, but the rounds of their helms, which seemed made of leather, remained fully in view, and it was by those that we marked their progress.

—No, Warrior, for as I have tried to imply, patience is the way of the Spider, and it must always be so. I waited then, allowing the infantry to move well into the midst of the meadow, drawing them forward, step by step, with an illusion of growing security. And then, at last, one by one, their supporting archers began to appear behind them, moving quietly up from the wood, their short, curved bows held at the ready. I waited for a length of ten long heartbeats, and *then,* Warrior, at my sharp command, the Spider rose as one and let fly, and in the dim, shrouded distance, just before the cover of the lower wood, the Corinthian archers went down under the sharpness of our stones like felled, frozen timbers, and the snow turned red with their blood. No man cried out, I remember, for the shock of our volley was too sudden, too swift, too deadly, and the exposed infantry reacted in those first fleeting seconds as though struck dumb by the hand of Zeus. Then, their danger fully apparent, they rallied to their ram's horn and charged, shouting their war cries together as they roared through the snow like a pride of enraged lions thirsting for our blood. Had they been armed with javelins or throwing darts, none of us would have survived, but instead, according to Corinthian custom, their infantry carried the long ash spear, and in the end it proved their undoing. As they charged forward, their heavy spears at the ready, we were able to get off two rapid volleys even before they could close to throwing range, and the effect was devastating. All along the Corinthian line, warrior after warrior went down, some with skulls and faces smashed, others with gaping wounds to their legs, and still others with chest wounds where the strength and sharpness of our missiles had penetrated their ox-hide shields. Thus, within the briefest span it was over, with more than a full Corinthian company laying dead or badly wounded in the snow while survivors fell back in panic toward the east, searching through the snow and mist for the safety of their battalion center. In their wake I gave immediate command, and the entire Spider rose again, sprinting south and west for the cover of the trees, the snowbound valley of the Simoeis, and the safety of the Trojan hinterland beyond. Five days later, gaunt and worn, we returned to the Spider's camp only to find it burned and deserted, and from there, moving individually or in pairs, we made our slow way down toward the citadel on the Plain.

—Know you, then, Warrior, never to denigrate the sling, for in the main it is an effective weapon whose bite proves lethal and precise. In the right hands, at the right time, it can even break the strength of the line as I twice saw it do in my youth, once in the hands of the Spider.

—If it please you, Warrior, add fuel to the fire, for the night has turned bitter cold as if often does here in the hours before dawn.

—Indeed, the words I used are true: *burned* and *deserted*—the result, I think, of a long-range Argive penetration into the heart of the Troad. —No, the dead lay where they had fallen, covered by kites—each leg of the Spider and some four or five lightly armed Athenians, or so the markings on their shields informed us. In ways unknown to me, the Spider had somehow been taken unawares; several of its warriors had been killed outright while others, including my Lord Polybus, had withdrawn up the nearest ridge. We knew as much, for we found their snow-covered bodies frozen stiff, there on the ridge, amidst a larger number of Athenians. My Lord Polybus was still, in death, gripping both his spear and his standard, and that—with some difficulty—I removed from his hand and bore away to Troy to hide beneath the stones of the citadel. We were two days, I remember, making mounds over the dead, and then we departed in silence, reentering the Trojan perimeter through the shortened lines of my Lord Aeneas, whose once-strong corps had been reduced to the size of a regiment but whose spirit remained ever firm.

—No, in that, Wielder of the Axe, Eteocles was mistaken, for in the wretched hour that Troy fell, I was far upcountry near the shores of wide Propontis, recruiting mercenaries from the same barbarian tribes that I had once fought to quell. Flint-eyed Polydamas had sent me, with a last bag of Priam's gold, and in that—the final spin of the Spider—I failed. —Even in the moment of my negotiations, word of Troy's fall was borne upcountry on the winds of rumor, and the barbarians turned immediately hostile. I escaped, without Priam's gold, and then, while making my return, true report finally reached me that the end had come, and since that hour the secret of the Spider has been ever within my keeping.

—Nay, Warrior, I am not weary. Seat thyself again and listen, for in the days to come, with patience and precision, I intend to teach you all the stealthy ways of the Spider. Study well my words, for unless I miss the mark, the safety and survival of the Hatti depend solely upon the lingering strength of the web, and it is your fate to carry home the silk. Now, Warrior, attend me.

Nastes at Miletus

—Seat yourself, my Lord, here, beside my gray right hand in the place of honor, and when—with the coming of spring—you return to Hattusas, let it be known to your king that his right royal ambassador was warmly greeted.

—Huzziyas, you are called? —It is a noble name that carries the strength of your forebearers, and in their honor I welcome you to Miletus, where lordly Helios blesses the soil with his strength. If it please you, lift with me your cup, and together we will pour libations to the all-knowing gods whose divine faces we may ask to shine on the countenance of our meeting.

—And now, my Lord, please you to partake of our food. Beside the table of your king, Carian fare will seem humble, I know. Nevertheless, our food is nourishing, sufficient to its purpose, and plentiful in its kind, and the masters of my cooking fires are not altogether without merit. Try—if it please you—the boiled gull's eggs; here in Miletus we like to strip away their shells and flavor them with tiny pinches of salt before each bite. Or, if you prefer, the oysters are fresh from the sea, and the hands of my table slaves are deft in opening their shells. Would it please you, then, to have one slave so charged . . . to stand beside you and open each shell at your will? —A wise choice, my Lord, for know you, too, that here in Caria, oyster flesh—when eaten raw with the plentiful juices of the lime—is thought to improve the strength of a warrior's seed.

—Indeed, Lord Huzziyas, even as we speak, the line regiments of Caria are gathering strength and training hard for war. Presently the

Borean winds will begin nipping at their shins, but with the first spring melt I intend three of my front line commands to march swiftly north in your wake. Know you, too, that among the Argive Greeks who have been driven by fate to seek shelter along our shores, my agents are recruiting mercenaries, and these, too—hard men all and armed at my expense—will march north to join the Hatti in a fourth regimental body. —That is so, for clearly the stability of Hattusas to the east supports us all; if your line of protection should falter, we of Caria would be thrown by the invader like a handful of dust onto the swirling currents of the wind.

—No, Lord, that must not be, although permit me, in my refusal, to say that your skill as a diplomatist is exceeded only by the courtesy of your request. But *no,* for observe, my Lord, not only do the veins on my spear hand stand high and blue with age, but now the wounds which I received in my youth cripple the strength of my stride, and I am a man who walks slowly on the strength of three legs. So *no,* my gracious Huzziyas, at the head of the Carian regiments Nastes no longer commands. Instead, the entire Carian corps—citizen warriors and Argive outlanders alike—will march to the orders of my son, and each Carian regiment of the line will follow the standard of one or more of my bronze-armed grandsons. Thus, when the spring melt ends, the Hatti may swell their ranks with the best warriors that Caria can send forth.

—If it please you, noble Huzziyas, permit my slave to cut for you from the flank of the boar where the meat is thick and full of juice. —Epeian, show the Hatti ambassador your skill with the blade and garnish his slices with a faint hint of cheese and a sprinkling of wine.

—In my youth, Huzziyas, in my youth. —Just so, for during those long years I fought hard across the Plain, leading my warriors in the service of royal Priam, and in the end the war went against us and Troy fell, burning white in the fires of its own ash.

—My battles before Troy? —I fought many, for we were ten long years on the Plain, and the war was relentless—hard, cold, and bitter to the mind, and I survived by pure chance.

—Victories, you ask? —There were some . . . some, one in particular that carried weight, although in the end the results proved meaningless, but I remember it—above others, perhaps, for it was the one engagement that Carians fought alone, relying only on the strength of their own right arms. We fought the battle in the autumn of that long last year, high up across the mountain valley of Scamander in the hour after dawn, and the outcome, I think, remains a lingering testament to Carian war-craft and the strength of our discipline.

—Just so, my Lord, at dawn. Aurora blushed only dimly that morning, touching the rain-soaked uplands behind us with no more than the faintest hint of pink. Before us, through the mist-bound distances beyond Scamander, thick Greek movement, muffled but still audible above the noises of the river, penetrated the dawn. Close in, amidst the barley fields, I remember—where my entire command lay prone beneath the shelter of their shields—rain-moistened grain drooped heavily toward the ground, its autumn ripeness rich with the scent of the earth.

—Indeed, we were cold, shivering beneath a close, clinging damp, and yet no man made a sound. We had gone early into concealment there, to defend Scamander's upland fords. We had moved, I remember, well in advance of the midnight hour, and when the rains struck us, not long after we had crept into position, they struck hard, rolling in from the sea and up across the Heights of Heracles in a dark line of squalls that obliterated the stars. There, gathering strength above the heights, a tempest had formed, and then, throughout the remainder of the night, it had smashed down hard onto the entire upland valley. Hunched beneath our shields, we endured hour after hour of cold, pelting rain until shortly before dawn the storm moved on, climbing before a westerly wind onto Ida's lower slopes and up toward the peaks beyond.

—We waited in silence—cold, hungry, wet—knowing that the relentless Greeks would advance in the storm's wake, knowing too that we men of Miletus and the snowy slopes of Latmus—dark-eyed warriors all of the Carian regiment of the Wind—were Priam's last hope in the South, where Scamander's broad, upland fords lay open to attack. On the far bank, you see, during the moon preceding, a Trojan regiment of the line . . . the Bull, I think, had been whittled down and mercilessly cut to pieces by the combined strength of a Greek corps sent into the area especially for the purpose. During the days that followed, as one party of survivors after another retreated back across the river, they reported to us that the Greeks were moving men and supplies across all interior trails along the Heights of Heracles. From that time forward we knew that their attempt on the fords merely awaited an opportune moment; we knew too that if their assault succeeded our lines of communication with Mysia, Lydia, Maeonia, and Caria beyond would be immediately endangered, for then the Greeks would be well positioned for a sudden strike against the high mountain passes over Ida. Thus, at my Lord Priam's command I withdrew from battle on the Plain, marched my command into the southern uplands, and positioned them squarely athwart the most probable route of the Greek advance. There, with strong words and clear, I ordered the Wind to stand or die in defense of holy Ilium.

—Something—and to this day, noble Huzziyas, I do not know with certainty *what,* although I often heard rumors of a mysterious Trojan company that operated deep behind Greek lines, so that or something like it . . . perhaps, even, the gods—thwarted the Greek design, bringing their first rolling advance to a standstill not long after it had crushed the Bull. During those hours and days, as I marched my Carians swiftly up from the Plain through the last season of a long, dry summer, wide Scamander's rushing course had shrunk to less than half its normal depth. During those anxious hours, had they moved with speed, the Greeks might have easily seized the fords, assaulting hard on the heels of the retreating Bull. But as I say, for reasons that remain obscure the Greek general commanding failed utterly to exploit his clear advantage. And then later, after he had regrouped and fully consolidated his gains along the Heights but before he could launch his attack, the first autumn rains poured from the sky. Overnight the Greek option for winning an unopposed, swift victory at the fords was destroyed forever. Unseen during that hour, beneath the cover of the rains, my noble Carians moved silently onto Scamander's eastern heights, went quietly into a series of concealed bivouacs, and waited, watching with satisfaction as the autumn downpour transformed the river into a white, raging torrent, for in that same hour, my Lord, the gods themselves slammed shut the gates to Ida and the whole of the lower Troad.

—Unabated, the rains continued for nine straight days, and then on the tenth morning they ended, Aurora rising a brilliant pink from

Tithonus's autumn bed. Immediately I fixed my attention on the river, watching carefully its every change. At first the torrent's drop was imperceptible, but then, as the days passed and the last Trojan harvest ripened into gold, the water level began to fall, foot by threatening foot, toward a broadly fordable depth. I offered my libations then to the War-god, waited, and when the moment came, moved the Wind silently down from the heights and into the barley fields below the deep cover of darkness, and there to my relief the dense rains began again, pouring down heavily from the direction of the sea, soaking my warriors to the skin beneath the cold shelter of their shields, and when the dawn broke beneath a hard gray sky, the Wind made itself ready for war.

—The Greeks, that morning, moved with the first light, putting out a long line of skirmishers well in advance of their collected regiments. Knowing that they had only a few hours in which to effect a crossing—before Scamander again reached flood level—they moved swiftly, lunging forward in rapid, silent order, their spears and shields held at the ready. Once they came out of the hills, the western bank afforded them little cover, for days before, in the wake of the Bull, we had set fire to the fields there, seeking to discourage any close approach by the Argive reconnaissance scouts, deft men who were known amongst us to be adroit at concealment and daring in their methods. By burning to ash all grain, undergrowth, vines, and trees, the fierce Carian Wind had created a desert before the fords to a depth of some four or five hundred paces, and it was across this blackened ground that the Greeks were forced to advance. Throughout, I held the whole of my command motionless amidst the barley fields, silent, prone beneath the wet exteriors of their shields where they gripped their hard, bronze arms against the soft, soundless face of the earth. From somewhere above, I remember, a single oak leaf floated into view, its seared edges twisting slowly on the wind as it drifted out over the river and down onto the waters below. And in that moment the Greek skirmishers reached Scamander's edge.

—Heavily swollen with the night's runoff, the fords had already risen to thigh depth, and when suddenly faced with this, the river's unexpected strength, the Greek skirmish line first hesitated and then froze, knowing well the dangers they would face if caught by surprise amidst Scamander's rising flood. In that crucial instant the commanding Greek should have halted his main body and come forward himself to reconnoiter, for the risk in crossing—then, there, with Scamander rising fast—was indeed great and growing greater by the moment. Instead—sensing perhaps yet another opportunity to be slipping through his fingers—he must have given the attack order, for without even so much as the sound of a ram's horn, the entire Greek line surged suddenly forward toward the fords.

—Within moments, then, two heavily armed regiments of the line, an entire Argive corps numbering more than four thousand spears, had moved en masse onto the river's edge, bumping up hard against their all but stationary skirmish line. So pressed—and in response to angry commands—the skirmishers, in twos and threes, waded tentatively into the flood. Some, having missed their footing, were immediately thrown down and swallowed by the white, rushing waters while others, after first discarding their armor and bracing themselves with the butts of their spears, felt their way forward to thigh depth where they were barely able to stand. In short, given the river's strength, the crossing was already impassable, the unseized opportunity lost.

—Just so. Had the Greeks crossed during the night under the storm's cover, as we had expected them to do, mere strength of numbers might have given them a quick, sure victory in securing the fords. Instead, moving at dawn, they had arrived too late, only to find the gates of the Troad once more closing against them.

—So one might think, noble Huzziyas, but to my shocked amazement, these Greeks—Myrmidons all—threw caution to the winds and persisted in their attempt. Stripping off their armor, whole companies of them plunged into the flood, forming arm-locked human chains that swayed before the force of the current but did not break, and these, working man by man across the fords, soon spanned the course. Then, finally, the Greek commanding sounded one long blast on his ram's horn, and like molten bronze flowing from the forge, company after Myrmidon company poured quickly down Scamander's banks and into the river.

—Motionless beneath a swaying sea of barley, silent beneath the gray cloak of the sky, I waited, watching, until as many as six hundred Argive warriors had rushed into the river to string themselves singly along the length of their several human chains. Then, my Lord, like the grim heights of Ida rising behind me, I rose in silence, lifting my standard of command, and the fierce Carian Wind rose at my back and came forward through the grain with a rustling of spears. So intent were the Greeks on effecting their crossing, so loud the torrent of the river above their shouted commands, so confidently certain of success were they that none of their number even seemed aware of our advance until I finally lowered my standard, calling up a thousand Carian javelins into blood-hungry flight. Then, as Greek after Greek went down, the Myrmidons finally sounded the alarm—moments too late, for hundreds of our sharp, bronzed darts had already found their marks, and wide, white Scamander ran red with Argive blood. Within seconds, I remember, each warrior chain collapsed; those who were not struck instantly dead by our first well-thrown cast were, instead, adrift in the flood, fighting the fast-swirling currents, struggling under the heavy weight of their armor, or lunging out with hand or arm to recover the grip of a comrade. Well beyond anything like an effective retaliatory range, horrified, white with rage, screaming to vent their fury, the remaining Greeks—the mass of their bronze-armed corps—stormed and seethed atop the opposite bank, powerless to attack us in revenge and utterly helpless to save their friends who went down fast beneath the blood-chilling waters of the flood. —For days afterward . . . along the entire length of lower Scamander, all the way down to the Plain . . . rooks and kites and lean, hungry dogs picked sharply at the bloated flesh of their bones.

—We withdrew then, as silently as we had advanced, and went again to ground beneath the ripe, swaying waves of the barley: in a matter of moments nothing moved save the wind where all trace of our existence had disappeared. Across the river, athwart the opposite bank, the Greeks seemed stunned. Slowly their piercing screams quieted and died to be replaced by the low moan of the Myrmidon death chant, and then, turning their backs on the river's wide expanse, the Greeks withdrew, disappearing like night thieves onto the wooded Heights of Heracles, leaving the voiceless Carian Wind in sole possession of the field.

—Thus we secured the upper fords and won a significant victory over the bronze-armed Greeks, and throughout the remainder of the moon, and a part of the moon that followed, the gates of Ida remained hard shut before the advancing Greeks. But then in late autumn—in fact, beneath the first Borean winds—the rains gave way to snow, and the river fell, and after amassing more than four bronze-armed regiments, the Argives poured from their heights and rolled across the river like a tide. Within a matter of hours, fighting hard against the swell, my entire command was turned, swept off its feet, and overrun, and there, on a moonless night before Scamander's upland fords, the voiceless Carian Wind went down forever beneath relentless waves of Greeks.

—If it please you, Lord, partake of the fowl: the meat is well roasted, stuffed with almonds and bread, and the skin has been basted with honey that is fresh from the hive. —Epeian, see to my guest's cup, for in the halls of Nastes no guest waits in need.

—No, my noble Lord, for in fact the threat against us before Scamander was well known at Troy. Daily, you see, I dispatched runners to the citadel with close reports concerning my well-formed apprehensions about the enemy, and those, received and acknowledged, formed a basis for our planned reinforcement. Flint-eyed Polydamas himself worked out the plan, but it fell to lordly Aeneas to appoint commanders, and there, I think, our survival foundered, for bowing to royal pressure, what should have been a unified command under the capable leadership of Keas became instead a divided standard, and much the larger part of it—fully two-thirds of a newly created regiment—was given over to royal Alexandros. According to the last message I received from Ilium, word borne to me by a runner mere hours before the Greeks finally brought us to battle, noble Keas was to have moved up across our rear onto the heights of Ida while Alexandros, following immediately in his wake, thrust the main body of his own new command into the gap between us. That Keas took up the proper position, I am reasonably certain because two of my scouts reported him in place, but royal Alexandros . . . he never appeared, and when the Greeks struck, his absence proved our undoing: it took them only a short time, you see, to find the gap and pour through a swift-footed regiment onto our rear while still holding us engaged to the front. Then they simply rolled us up and overwhelmed us with their numbers.

—My Lord, they were not well known to me, for I was always a warrior of the Wind and preferred, unlike some others, to remain in the field with my men.

—No, your words are just, and the clarity of your statement does not offend me. Clearly, to the Trojan ear the accents of the Carian tongue were thought unmusical, uncouth, and dull, and beyond our appointed officers of liaison, few men, if any, amongst them ever mastered enough Carian to communicate with us in the speech of our native land. Flint-eyed Polydamas was one who did; wise Antenor was another. Both men, I remember, spoke Carian with some difficulty and with no true accent, but even so, they honored us by learning our tongue with the result that the warriors of the Wind were much inspired to respect them. That lesson, noble Huzziyas, may prove an invaluable gift to your king, for in the spring, when the snows melt and the great army assembles before Hattusas, the royal king of the Hatti, like Priam before him, must face the immense problem of command through the medium of multiple languages. Before Troy, Priam summoned regiments speaking more than twelve distinct tongues, and the ensuing problems of command numbered in their thousands. How many, my friend, will be the tongues spoken before Hattusas when the spring winds blow? —Just so, just so, and to the minds of your staff, each tongue must be perfectly known, or the defense will prove a disaster.

—Pardon, Lord, for in speaking to the point, I have drifted from its source, and its source was the truth of your statement: among the Trojan princes, the warriors of the Wind went seldom on a social footing. Partly, that was due to our tongue and partly to theirs, but a part, too, must be ascribed to the character of the royal house, for it was ever aloof, treating allies and outlanders alike with a tolerant, distant courtesy that discouraged the firmer bonds of intercourse. Amongst their fighting commands, the case was different, and there we of the Wind formed reliable friendships and were warmly received. Even now, I remember some of their names and faces, but like my own brave warriors, all—in the end—were driven deep into the chambers of decay by a tide of relentless Greeks.

—I knew him not, my Lord, for he was ever in the company of Mysians and remained much within the confines of their high, dark fortress at Thymbra. Whether he attended them owing to his natural inclinations or, as some said, as a matter of royal policy, I never knew, for politics were not my sphere during my years as a warrior in the field. I heard rumors, of course, about the beauty of the Spartan whore but never saw her and cannot believe, to this hour, that the war had much to do with her. Clearly the Argive kings coveted the prosperity of the Troad, finding it grounds enough to urge their hot attack. Better for all, themselves included, had they remained at home, minding the security of their shores, for had they done so, rather than bleeding themselves white across the length of the dusty Plain, they might have been able to withstand the hard barbarian attacks from their north—the same attacks that *now,* in this very hour, continue to drive one Argive hull after another to seek refuge here at Miletus. But to return to your question—*no,* I knew not Alexandros of Troy, whose failure to appear on my left wing doomed the Carian Wind. —I could, my Lord, but let me condemn no man from the midst of ignorance: clearly Alexandros failed to appear; clearly the Wind fell. That much is certain, I think, but *why* remains obscure, and now, as my thread runs short and the hand of Smintheus presses hard against my chest, I know in my brittle bones that I will never know the truth of it, so I refuse to condemn. That, I believe, to be the way of the warrior and, certainly, the way of the judge. In the end—just as I did in my youth so many long years ago—I leave Alexandros and Hector and Deiphobus . . . the lot, the entire house of Priam—to the will and judgement of the iron-eyed gods.

—Epeian, place venison before my guest, and a round, bright bowl of honey cakes and figs. And replenish his wine cup as its level drops. —You were saying, my Lord Huzziyas?

—Indeed, *him* I did know and knew him well, for he was a master of war and came often amongst us in the midst of the field, fighting beside us in the face of the enemy. Iron-eyed Polydamas, my Lord, was a man among men, a commoner who—on the strength of his merit and on merit alone—had risen faster and higher than any other man at Troy, save one—right royal Hector, son of Priam—he who went down fighting before the walls in the war's ninth year.

—Nay, for that would be inaccurate. For strength in battle lordly Hector exceeded all the fine, brave warriors at Troy, but for penetration of mind, for the hard devising of stratagems, for mastery of war-craft, Polydamas knew no peer, and on the strength of his mind, and his mind alone, the long defense of Troy depended. And then, if what wise Antenor spoke to me was true, a vote in the council chamber went hard against him, and in that dark hour Hector opened his last great offensive across the Plain, planting deeply the seeds of Ilium's final defeat. Polydamas, I was told, advised delay, for even then, Memnon of Ethiopia to the south and the Amazon, Penthesilea, to the east were marching toward Troy, leading some twelve new regiments to join our allied command, and with those he hoped to match the Greek's strength. But in the end the offensive went forward—a desperate gamble for a sharp, quick victory on the beach—and in the end it failed. —Priam's Hector, noble Sir, was ever the hard, face-to-face fighter who believed implicitly in the supremacy of Troy, but dauntless Polydamas was a general— the best, I think, that Troy ever produced—and therein rested all the difference between them.

—Just as you say, for the work of the Trojan staff was both deep and broad, and as chief, there, in the staff rooms of the citadel, Polydamas was much occupied. Even so, as I have said, he came often amongst us, measuring the strength of my warriors, checking to see that we were fit and well supplied, marking our readiness for battle. I never ceased to wonder, I remember, at the strength of his eye, which penetrated deep even into the smallest matters . . . the condition of the men's sandals as they made ready to march, the number of sling stones each man was set to carry. Once, even before I had noticed the symptoms myself, his flint-sharp eyes caught signs of the running sickness, just as it began to break among some ten or twenty of my men. Immediately, he ordered Trojan healers to attend us, and narrowly, after first pulling back from the line to consume a newly prepared diet of goat's cheese and bread, the Wind avoided an epidemic that might otherwise have crushed our strength beneath Apollo's hard fist. Thrice, even in the heat of battle, Polydamas came up unexpectedly at the most critical moments, offering me sound tactical advice and close support, and in each of those three dangerous hours his sound grasp of the action served to stem a rising Greek tide that threatened to engulf us. Clearly, to Carian and Trojan alike, Polydamas was a rock, the anchor of Troy's defense and peerless in his war-craft.

—In the great offensive? —In the great offensive Polydamas commanded the entire Dardanian corps—outlanders like himself who had trained long in the arts of war and defended the Troad with their blood. He fought beside Hector there, for a length of three long days, casting his spear with the strength of ten men, and the Greeks went down hard before him. He advised withdrawal, I remember, near the end of the second day, for by then Hector had thrown all Trojan reserves into the line, and still the Greeks held. —Clearly Polydamas had been right in his assessment. Clearly the assembled strength of the Troad, including the entire allied command, was insufficient to the purpose. Nevertheless, following Hector's certain orders, we fought on, taking heavy losses, hammering hard against the unyielding anvil of the hard Greek line. And then, on the third day, like a raging fire crashing across the crown of a forest, a fresh Argive army, Myrmidons all, appeared suddenly on our flank and exploded through our line, scattering our weary, bleeding warriors headlong across the Plain. The result was catastrophic, but even so—even in the midst of such an irrevocable reverse— Polydamas managed to extricate the main body of his corps intact, and in the process of his withdrawal he extracted, too, the grateful warriors of the Wind: owing to the speed of the Greek advance, we had been pinned, without mercy, against Scamander's bank. There iron-eyed Polydamas saw us and instantly sent two battalions of the Kite crashing into the side of the Greek advance, and these—in the brightest moment of the day—opened a path for our escape. Polydamas, my friend, was a general; throughout the long span of my life, I have known none better.

—If it please you, noble Ambassador, permit the Epeian to set before you the tally sticks by which I mean to number in your presence the spears of my warriors as I intend them for service at Hattusas. The black stick pertains to the Thunder, men from our southern shores to the number of two thousand. The white stick, which is notched and grooved, counts the Carian Fire. Warriors of the Fire come from the slopes of Latmus; they are trained for shock, by night assault or day, and their strength exceeds twelve hundred spears. The blue stick marks the cold Carian Rain that freezes the enemy in his tracks, and its warriors are as numberless as the waters of the sky: three thousand bronze-armed infantry, my Lord, for service in the Hatti's main body. These, then, are the pick of Miletus, with Argive mercenaries to follow, and with the first melt, I will send them north toward Hattusas beneath the returning flights of geese; may they prove strong and invincible in the Hatti's defense.

—The Wind? —The Wind died forever on the slopes of Ida in the faraway Troad, hard by the banks of Scamander. Not even Carian singers
recall their deeds, and in the end that is a death beyond measure.
—There were no survivors . . . none at all, and their names live only
in my memory. Take that away, and the Wind's death is final.

—Indeed, gracious Huzziyas, by pure chance I survived. Know you
then that on the night that the Greeks crossed the fords, I stood and fell
beside my men, stunned by a sword stroke that must have been turned
by the ridges of my helm so that I received the blow's strength only
with the flat of the blade. I went down then, as darkness rolled over my
eyes, and there, pressed against the earth, I was buried beneath the
bleeding bodies of my warriors as they fell in their numbers to the
onrushing Greeks.

—By the time that I regained consciousness, it was almost dawn.
Before me, around me, the whole face of the earth was white with new-
fallen snow that covered even the bodies of the Wind. The weight of the
dead that had fallen on top of me was crushing, but I dared not move,
for in the shallows of the fords the last units of the Greek rear guard
were still crossing Scamander, still working up across the fields toward
the snow-covered slopes of Ida.

—I waited, then until broad mid-morning, until well after the last
Greek had passed, until I could stand the weight and stench of the dead
no longer, and then, inch by inch, I extricated myself from the fleshly
confines of that grave. By that time the snow was again falling in thick,
wet flakes that stuck to hair, arms, and legs before melting into a thin,
liquid ice, and in order to protect myself against the growing cold, I
stripped a white sea cloak from the dead body of a Greek, wrapped it
about my shoulders, and began making my way inland in the direction
of Thymbra.

—Almost immediately I found my way barred by the bivouacs of the
Greek rear guard that had passed me at dawn. With the way east closed
to me, I turned north toward Ilium, only to find another Argive battalion placed squarely athwart my path, and in that hour I knew finally
and without doubt that Troy had been surrounded by an impregnable
Argive ring. I took, then, the only route left open to me, doubled back
on my track, crossed west over the fords of Scamander, and began

working my way south down the Heights of Heracles in the direction of the Trojan citadel at Assus. Three days later, before a driving wind, I came down out of the hills to find Assus deserted, her walls and citadel burned to the ground. Not even the dogs were left alive, and the stench of death was everywhere.

—I waited five days before Assus, sheltering myself in a cave at the base of a hill, surviving as best I could on the flesh of a sea fowl that I had fortune enough to bring down with a sling. Throughout, I saw neither man nor beast, but in the sea beyond, amidst the winter waves, high-beaked Argive war hulls sailed menacingly before the wind. What they were doing there, I have never determined; I can only suppose that they sought to prevent any Mysian grain hulls from beaching before Assus to replenish the Troad. But they might just as easily have been sent to sea to prevent our escape, and in view of their presence I kept myself concealed.

—In the end, counting my chances for survival as slim, I marched east along the sharp, forested ridges of the coast, toward Ida's southern slopes and the brown Mysian breaks beyond. And then for the first time, I saw the face of starvation, for there, across the bitter slopes of Ida where the snow was knee deep and the earth lay frozen hard, no sign of life beyond my own so much as stirred. Across a span of ten long days I moved slowly east, surviving on roots and bark and a precious few acorns that I was able to dig from the earth after first clearing the snow away from the base of an oak. At night, beneath Ida's fierce winds, I wrapped myself in my cloak and burrowed deep into the snow like an animal gone to ground, surviving—I know not how—by the hands of the gods. On the eleventh day, gaunt and drawn and half-blinded by the glare of the snow, I staggered into an outpost of the Mysian frontier guard and lived to speak my name.

—Four moons later, while I was still recovering from my ordeal in the Mysian barracks at Chrysa, word reached me that Troy had fallen. Not long after, I heard that Lord Aeneas and some few hundred survivors had gotten out by escaping deep into Phrygia before doubling back to the coast in the wake of the Greek withdrawal. Such may have been the case; if it please the gods, I hope it may be so, for Aeneas was a noble warrior. But I doubt, Lord; I doubt . . . to the best of my knowledge, I am the only man living who fought at Troy and survived.

—If it please you, noble Huzziyas, let us rise and go into the field. There, beneath the moon's full beams, I will sound the ram's horn and unfold to you the full strength of the Carian corps. May the Hatti rejoice in their bronze-armed might.

Polydamas on the Plain

—No, Lords, *no* . . . you speak of a thing that cannot be, for know you, all, that I will fight no more. I have long since broken the shaft of my spear and flattened the curve from my bow, and my hard, bronze sword I have cast deep into Scamander's swirling stream. Like the season of my youth, the way of the warrior has faded behind me, and now I am done with war forever. Return, then, to the distant halls of Hattusas, to the warm hearths of your families, and take my words to your king: say "*Here* died Polydamas, warrior of Troy, in obedience to Priam's command. In the warrior's place, in the midst of the dark, cold Plain of ash, which spreads now where once stood holy Ilium, only one gray man remains alive—Polydamas, son of Panthous: a priest to Hermes the Guide, a burier of long-dead warriors' bones." —Say that, Lords . . . and say, too, "The Burier sends the salt and bread of respect to royal Suppiluliumas, Lord of the Hatti, He who recalled the once-great glory of Troy and honored me in your sending." Say that, Lords, and let the matter be done, for in these, my last days, as my life lingers to measure out my thread, I will go on, as I have, collecting the bones, raising their mounds, and burying the Trojan dead so that finally the wandering shades of all my once-bright warriors may pass to rest, working down through the sleeping earth, following the Guide into the immortal chambers of decay.

—Your words are gracious, but *no*: the facts, examined, are otherwise, so let us speak true in the way of men. My right eye, Lords, is blind, where a sharp Argive arrow pierced its light during the last hour of the war. My spear-arm has withered, owing to severed muscles and tendons, and on my hands the veins are both hard and blue with age. Even my legs are stiff, like twisted oaks, with the debilitating wounds of war. Observe—there—in the hut's corner: those staffs, Lords, are not Trojan spears; they are the pillars with which I support my frame when, with bitter will, I leave this hearth to move afield across the dusty Plain. Thus, Lords, the truth: I am not what I once was, not even what I might have been; rather, like a long body shield of lead, my life hangs heavy on my spine; my strength is forever gone. Know you, Lords, that I have seen ninety white winters pass coldly before my eye, and now, in the midst of this—daily—here on this last naked shingle of the world, I pour libations to the honor of Zeus the Thunderer and Hermes the Guide, praying with urgent fervor that the gods will not desert me, praying that *this,* my ninetieth year, *will be* the last lingering winter of my life. With my own hands, across sixty dark years, I have buried more than forty thousand men, and now I am ready to die. I will not command at Hattusas, Lords, no matter how severe the need, for the measure of my thread has run, and with the wisdom of my flint-eyed age I am done with war forever.

—Even so, Lords, for my answer is irrevocable. But wait; depart not. Remain and share the warmth of my hearth, for the hours of darkness fly swiftly upon us. Outside, across the whole length and breadth of the Troad, for upwards of forty leagues to the east, you will find naught but the desolate wasteland through which you came to seek me, and that, by morning, will be completely buried by snow. —Doubt me not, Lords. Listen to the evidence of your ears. Know you the strength of that wind? Thus blows Boreas, hard from the mountains of Thrace, hurling frozen snows onto the long-silent Troad. Wait, Lords; remain until morning when the storm will have spent its strength. I have barley loaves here, which we may break four ways; they are made from native grains which grow wild in the fields where spent Trojan blood has manured the ground. I have no wine, but in the krator there you will find water from Simoeis that is clear and pure. Seat yourselves, Lords. I will add faggots to the fire so that you may warm your Hatti bones with the last flickering hospitality of the Troad. Please, Lords, to remain and speak to me your names.

—Your words honor me, Zidantas. But even so, they remain inaccurate: the best military mind that Troy ever produced belonged to my tutor, to Pharos the Gray, who first commanded the Shark and then, for a time, the whole Trojan army. Like myself, he was a commoner, an outlander, the son of a soldier. He was born, I think, in the shadow of the citadel at Dardanos, in the time when Laomedon still ruled over Ilium, and he reached his majority in the same year that lordly Priam ascended to the Trojan throne. As a company commander, Pharos fought hard and well against all of the various barbarian tribes on the northeast frontier, playing a strong part in silencing forever the dangerous Phrygian threat to the Troad. In the years that followed, he was promoted swiftly to battalion command in the Boar, and then, on orders from Priam himself, he was handed his standard and ordered onto Tenedos to establish the Shark, a wholly new regiment designed for swift assault from the sea.

—The Shark, noble Zidantas, contained the pick of the army, men especially recruited from the best standing regiments in the Troad. It was smaller than other commands by nearly five hundred men, but its training was far more rigorous, and in its first campaign it exceeded all expectations for battle-hard performance, winning victory after victory under Pharos's capable hand. At that time, know you, the Thracian lords of Thynia made sudden rebellion against Troy, and in consequence the Shark was sent in against the rebel stronghold at Sestus. There, after landing at night and showing, by day, only one of his bright-eyed companies, Pharos lured the rebellious lords to battle amidst an open plain, crushing them irrevocably with an ambush of regimental proportions. So sudden, so swift, so unexpected was his stroke that he prevailed over a force that exceeded his own by a strength of five. In the weeks that followed, showing an unparalleled brilliance of mind, he moved swiftly to subdue all Thynia, bringing the entire peninsula—including its huge copper and tin deposits—under well-governed Trojan control. So mild was the application of his policy, so just the force of his hand, that in all the moons that followed Thynia remained peacefully quiet under a benign Trojan administration that afforded all of the line regiments of the army a plentiful supply of bronze. Thus, having tested no more than the hard war-strength of the Shark, Pharos returned, Victor of Thynia, after capturing seven enemy standards.

—Indeed, Telipinus, at the end of the campaign both Pharos and the Shark removed to Tenedos, but in less than a moon Pharos was summoned to Ilium, and there, with full rites and ceremonies, he was taken onto the council and made army commander in preparation for Priam's wars in Thrace. Over the ten-years' course that followed, Pharos organized victory after Trojan victory across the length and breadth of the North, subduing tribe after barbarian tribe of topknotted Thracians until in the end Priam's influence stretched even to the shores of the dark, black sea, and all of wide Propontis became little more than a placid Dardanian lake. In those years Pharos's name was known far and wide throughout the Troad, for not only did he win victories, his victories conserved men, and Troy gained much at little cost in warrior's lives or bright Trojan blood. And then—as the Thracian Wars concluded—for the first time Mysia looked down hungrily on the treasures of the Troad, and in the spring, when the high mountain flowers bloomed white and blue, a sharp Mysian army attacked us in strength across the entire southern frontier, and the forested slopes of Ida ran wet with warrior's blood.

—Just so, Arnuwandis, for the twenty long years of the Mysian Wars sapped away our strength and bled us white; in truth, neither Troy nor Mysia ever fully recovered. But in one point, Lord, you are mistaken: on the Mysian front Pharos did not command, for at the war's beginning he fell from influence, struck down by a palace intrigue, and his fall annihilated both his power and his name.

—The intrigue? It is simple in description, Lords: he interfered with a royal birth. Know you, then, that on the night before Hecuba gave birth to a son—the one that we later believed to be Alexandros—the queen dreamed that she was possessed of a firebrand. On the following morning, even as she labored to deliver, Priam and the high council listened with pain as dream interpreters rendered their accounts, warning beyond hope that if the boy lived he would surely, someday, be responsible for the utter and complete destruction of Troy. In the hours that followed, when it became apparent that the shocked king would decline to act, Pharos forced the vote, carrying the broad majority with the implicit consent of Antenor, Laocoön, Ucalegon, and several others, who rendered their decision in secret after electing Pharos to bear their word to the king. That he did is a matter beyond dispute, for not long after, bearing the child on his back, he moved swiftly upcountry onto Ida to leave it exposed. For this attention he earned the queen's undying enmity and no strong love from Priam, and with the first opportunity they acted decisively to bring him down and take their hard revenge. What they did, simply, was charge Pharos with attempted rape—with the attempted rape of Cassandra, royal princess of Troy. Cassandra, then in the first bloom of her beauty, harbored a genuine affection for Pharos, even though he was many years her senior—or so it always seemed to me when I later came to know her—and this emotion, I believe, her mother had noticed and determined to manipulate to her own dark advantage. Thus Hecuba brought each, mutually unaware of the other's presence, by separate summons into a darkened room of the palace, and there, by means of lamps brought quickly forward by a party of sycophantic courtiers, royal Cassandra and my Lord Pharos were surprised within the confines of a palace bedchamber. Pharos was, of course, denounced and threatened with immediate death, for even in cases of attempted rape death was ever the Trojan law. Cassandra, running hot salt tears of shame for the malignance of her mother's trap, protested loudly and long but to this effect: the more she proclaimed the truth, the more she was disbelieved, and in the end, in an act of singular injustice, her parents confined her to the temple of Apollo to repent of her "crime" and cleanse away her shame. When she finally reemerged after a confinement of some years, her bearing, I remember, had become truly regal, but by all but a few she was thought to be demonstrably strange.

—In that, Lord Zidantas, Pharos proved fortunate because, before the sentence of death could be passed, wise Antenor, the noble Laocoön, Ucalegon, and some others of independent mind took a hand in the proceedings, protesting scant evidence and clearly disputable testimony on all sides, and in the end the affair stopped just short of Pharos's death. Even so, he was banished from the city, stripped of his rights and titles, and set afoot on the Plain; not even the singers were permitted to remember his name, and in time the full measure of his identity—except to a few—passed wholly from sight. It was then, Lords, for my father's coin, that he became my tutor, and it was from him, and from him alone, that I learned the art of command.

—If it please you, Lords, draw closer to the fire, for the night turns bitter cold, and Boreas hurls hard out of Thrace without mercy.

—What you say, bold Telipinus, is true: for reasons of politics and personal enmity royal Priam deprived Troy of her greatest military mind, and in the end the results proved disastrous. Brute, unimaginative generalship characterized most of our Mysian campaigns, for with Pharos gone the old, defensive generals returned to power, and under their rough hands whole regiments were decimated and then halved in bitter fighting before Thymbra and up across Ida's northern slopes. I fought there myself during the First Mysian War, from the moment I came of age, and the bloodletting suffered by both sides exceeded anything yet seen in living Trojan memory.

—Pharos did not remain completely out of it. He could not: he was Trojan to the core, you see, and knew his duty, so by means of secretly concealed contacts he gave consistent, sound advise to wise Antenor, Ucalegon, and gray Laocoön, and in time, even against the prevailing, defensive mind-set at Troy, some of what he advised became policy. As a result, not long before the Mysians initiated their second war against us, I was unexpectedly given my standard and elevated to command the Shark, whose potential for offensive assault had never been fully comprehended by the old commanders of the line. Immediately, then, I made my way to Tenedos, and there, using Pharos's precise advice, I initiated a vigorous prosecution of the war at sea. For five years running, owing to light rains and long, hot summers, Trojan and Mysian harvests alike had been light, and this Pharos advised me to exploit, and I did so, consistently, by stopping all Mysian imports from Egypt, Greece, and Crete. In time the efforts of the Shark were so successful, our hard raids and close blockades so effective, that we twice—in the Second and Third Wars—simply starved Mysia into submission and might have done so in the Fourth War had not the Mysians themselves enacted the means of their defeat.

—Late in the last lingering autumn of the Fourth Mysian War the enemy gambled all on a swiftly sudden, cold weather attack that began well after the close of the summer's campaign. In short they quickly overran the upper reaches of Scamander and very nearly succeeded in achieving their aim, which was to take and hold Thymbra before the first deep snows made Ida impassable. Faced with the sudden and unexpected severity of this threat, which would have left an entire Mysian army comfortably quartered not more than four leagues above Ilium, the old line generals finally stirred and gave way, and in the week following I put three Trojan regiments ashore at Chrysa, seized the granaries and the citadel, and cut off at their base the enemy's long lines of supply over Ida. Then some two weeks later, when the first heavy snows fell hard on the north face of Ida, my Lord Hector brought a weak and starving Mysian army to battle before Thymbra and annihilated it in the field, and at last those long desperate wars came swiftly to an end.

—Indeed, we had won, but the cost of victory surpassed all reasonable limits. Across twenty long years of war, with a sound reckoning taken, fully one third of the bronze-armed Trojans who had fought before Thymbra had fallen; adding the wounded and maimed, our regiments of the line were hard pressed to muster half their pre-war strength. In Mysia, which swiftly recanted its greed to become a close Trojan ally, the case was even worse, for there—apart from those commands which had been totally destroyed and apart from the starving— all regular regiments of the line had been reduced by attrition to battalion strength. Such, then, was the condition of the Troad, of Mysia, and of all our fighting commands at the bitter end of the last Mysian war, and in the spring of that year, not long after the geese had flown north, nine of our broad-beamed hulls made sail in the Hellespont, departing for Greece to carry young Alexandros on his royal embassy to Sparta.

—Fear not, Lords, for on the morrow I will show you the way to icebound Simoeis, and *that* will be your guide east toward the open passes into Phrygia and the land of the Hatti beyond. The route has this advantage over the way that you came: the high ridges of the valley will shelter you from the Borean force of the wind. Better that, Lords, than the shores of wide Propontis, for there, beside an iron-gray sea, the sleet blows sharp, hard, and unyielding.

—In truth, Zidantis, only a slim case may be made for such conclusions. If it please you, consider: Achaian Greece held wealth beyond bounds in men, in cattle, in the bounty of the land. Her trade was far-reaching across the whole of the wide Aegaean, and nowhere, to my knowledge, were her merchants rejected. Even here in the Troad Priam accorded the Argive kings a specialty of treatment in the land shipment of their goods to all northern climes and points beyond, and as a result, across the length and breadth of the East a warrior would be hard pressed to enter a home, villa, or citadel that was not well stocked with bright Greek goods. No, Lords, to my mind the relentless Greeks came neither to plunder nor in envy of the wealth of the Troad. Rather, they came to do justice, to fulfill the hard terms of the law. They came, Lords, to make the doer suffer, and with cold finality they did so without mercy as an example to the world.

—What you say, Arnuwandis, is true: such was the explanation that was given currency among us and particularly among our many allies, but consider the source and consider the reason. We of Troy observed the same laws as the Greeks: amongst us, ever, the penalty for wife-rape was swift and painful death. Had the law been upheld, royal Alexandros should have been stoned within the same hour that he returned from Sparta bringing his beautiful captive with him, but instead the law was not upheld, and within moments the lie had broken forth. —The lie? —The lie, Lords . . . the first lie . . . was that Helen was a Spartan whore, a sensual suppliant who had followed Alexandros of her own free will, seeking sanctuary from a bestial husband. Who— whether Hecuba, Priam, or Alexandros—first spoke its words, hatching it from its shell, I have never known, but in the days and weeks that followed, under the care of royal propagandists, that lie grew feathers and wings, taking swift flight over the Troad to all points beyond, and in the end, as intended, it was widely believed.

—It is a cold man, Lords, who can pass a death judgement on his son, and Priam could not do it—not then, when Alexandros first returned to Troy after seizing and raping Helen, and not in the beginning, when the assembled wisdom of the council first declared the boy a firebrand and called for him to be exposed. In either case, had the sentence been carried out, Ilium might have survived, but in the second—as in the first—Priam acted the lie. —Pardon me, Lords, for I wish not to be unclear: indeed, Pharos *had* exposed the boy on Ida, but agents—of Hecuba or Priam or both—followed onto the mountain, rescued the child, and gave him over in keeping to an old Mysian shepherd, who raised the boy to a man before sending him back at last to the high citadel at Ilium. As a father, then, and as a man Priam twice acted to preserve Alexandros's life, and in that I find small fault with a loving, paternal nature. *But* . . . consider, Lords, Priam was also king, head of the royal house, Lord of the Troad, a beacon to his people, the rock of the law: when he circumvented the law, he shattered the rock upon which Troy was founded, and the high, white walls of Ilium came crashing down in ash.

—Just so, and thus the second great lie: the lasting charge that the relentless Argive Greeks made war for plunder . . . that they came not for justice but to dominate the land and the golden wealth of the Troad. Look carefully, my Lords; can the eye's evidence support such a lie? Where are the prosperous Argive farms that were supposed to have supplanted us? Where are their bright villas, their teeming harbors, their broad upland estates, the high stone citadels of their power? —Tomorrow, as you move east toward Hattusas, Lords, you will see naught but the long, hard winter of our desolation and the high mounds of our bones, for know you that the Greeks came for justice, not to rape or dominate the land, and in the hour of their darkly bitter victory, they made an end, recovered Helen, and sailed swiftly for home, leaving the empty Troad behind. So no, Lords, the Greeks came not to plunder and not to destroy the allied security of the East, but only to make Troy suffer under the great weight of Alexandros's crime. Thus, after the first lie—the lie that debased the law—the second became a desperate necessity, an urgent matter of both domestic and foreign policy, as Priam sought to rally all of Troy and all of his many allies in a hard, sustained defense of what, in reality, was forever indefensible. And in the end, like the debased pillar of the law, Troy shattered and fell.

—Indeed, at almost any point in the war before the deadly end of Hector's last great offensive, the final disaster might have been averted, and the Greeks, even after long labor, might have been placated by Helen's return. So argued the many elders of Troy, and so argued the Greeks, who warned us again and again through the secret voices of their heralds to let the woman go or face complete and utter destruction. But to all and each—even to my Lord Antenor, who proclaimed in council that we had made everlasting perjurers of ourselves—Priam turned a stone-deaf ear. Thus the war dragged on, year after bloody year, our bronze-eyed warriors fighting hard for the politic lie while we who led them fought equally hard for time, hoping beyond hope that each new dawn would bring a reversal of Priam's decision and a quick finish to the killing. But in the end Priam never rectified his mistake, and at the finish Troy's high, bright flames ate us alive.

—Past the midnight hour, Lords, Boreas invariably slacks his fury: from now until dawn the only sound you will hear will be the long, silent fall of the snow.

—How say you? —No, my noble Telipinus, in that you have been much misinformed. Know, then—from my own lips—that Hector was my much admired friend. That we had differences, I will not deny: Hector trained for command with the Boar under a host of old line generals, and many of his methods were theirs, but not all, and on the whole he retained a fresh, flexible mind. That we should differ on points of command was right and proper to our professional relationship. Clearly Priam chose Hector to command before Troy because—as a most experienced warrior and the immediate heir to the throne—he had both the strength and the bright, personal magnetism to unite our many allies into a loyal and effective army. For reasons that were made equally clear to me by aging Laocoön, Priam chose me to be Hector's chief of staff, knowing full well that as a result of my training I would bring to our deliberations an entirely different habit of command and act consistently as Hector's foil. Thus, by our forceful yoking together, Priam hoped to strike a balance between us, believing that from just such a union would develop the best military decisions. —Clearly. As you say, Priam was far from being a fool. Blind he might have been to the transgressions of Alexandros and the many dangers that they created for us, but in the political manipulation of men Priam was often wise. In command, then, Hector and I functioned with determined effort over the course of nine long years, each of us counterbalancing the opinions and propensities of the other, and in time we came to respect one another, and in time we became friends, and the hard hour of his death still sits heavy on my soul.

—You are correct, Zidantas; for lack of manpower I opposed the great offensive and argued hard against it for some twelve long days.

By the ninth year, you see, our ranks were pitifully thinned, and to this day I believe that we had not the strength to go forward. Royal Memnon of Ethiopia then marched to reinforce us from the south, but the host of his army was marching through Mysia and had not yet entered the Troad. Distant, too, were the Amazons. Commanded by dark-eyed Penthesilea, regiments of those fierce female warriors were hurrying to join us from the east, and it was my strong advice that Hector wait, that he delay his planned offensive until both fresh armies entered the Troad to bolster our strength with their spears. We argued long, I remember, over the merits of such a decision, and in the end I think I might have prevailed. But then, on the very eve of battle, just as Hector was about to send out the order for the army to stand its ground, we received an intelligence direct from the Greek camp: a frog-eyed, hump-backed animal named Thersites. Winters before, in the war's fifth year, Hector had captured the creature during an advance along the Simoeis. Quickly reading Thersites' character, Hector corrupted him with a promise of gold, recruited him for our spy, and released him on the field to make his own crooked way back into the depths of the Argive camp. Later Hector laughed about the man, reporting him to be, surely, the least erected spirit on the Plain, and for four long years he never crossed our paths again, and then suddenly, he made his way into our lines and was brought before us, reporting a major political rift in the Greek camp—a quarrel, I remember, that had broken out between Agamamnon, Lord of the Argive Alliance, and one of his subordinates, Achilles, King of the Myrmidons and the fiercest fighter on the field. According to the creature, who reported the matter in precise detail, Achilles had withdrawn from the battle and from the war, finally and irrevocably, taking his hard Myrmidon regiments with him; even in that hour, Thersites told us, Achilles was sailing for Greece on a strong night tide.

—Throughout the remaining hours of darkness Hector questioned the creature at length. For myself, I remained skeptical, but even so, Hector did not, for by morning he was convinced, and as Aurora rose blushing in the east, with great strength of will, Hector seized what seemed to be a golden opportunity to prevail and sent us hurtling across the Plain in broad frontal assault.

—We fought well, I remember, throughout the first dusty day of the

offensive and then through a part of the next, and in sum we pressed
the Greeks hard, but we could not break their line, and as the day
waned, it became increasingly clear to me that we could not win, for
we had not the necessary strength in numbers and were bleeding ourselves slowly to death in nothing more imaginative than a brutal contest
of force. Clearly we had lost our momentum, and the battle had passed
out of control. I hastened then to Hector's side and warned him, and
warned him again, and yet again, urging him to withdraw in order to
conserve the strength of our men and preserve the army intact. By that
time, too, it had become clear to me that the Myrmidons, while with-
held from the field, had in fact not sailed but remained fresh in their
camp, a threat in being that seemed fully capable, at any moment, of
unleashing against us. —Hector heard me out but rejected my argument, and then, after first tightening his control over the army, he
renewed our attack, leading—himself—at the forefront, and I followed
in his wake. Less than an hour later, like a flowing tide of fire the
merciless Myrmidons struck us hard on the front, and with great loss
of life we were thrown back to Troy. Somehow, after first killing the
Myrmidon general who led the Greek counterattack, Hector rallied the
army to the hardest fighting of the day and regained the lost ground,
and then, during the twilight hour, he made a fatal and irrevocable
error in judgement, and it cost us the war.

—The Greeks, my Lords, had gone to ground behind the low,
wooden walls of their stockade while the warriors of Troy, around a
thousand flickering campfires, waited through the night for Aurora's
first blush across the Plain. Then at the midnight hour I went to Hector,
urging him to retire on Troy. "The Myrmidons fought today," I told
him. "Achilles will fight tomorrow. Let me persuade you to retire, for
the army cannot prevail, so weakened are they by the offensive's hard
strain. Let us husband our strength, go back over to the defensive, and
survive to fight, for we, Hector, are the true towers of Troy and great is
her strength while we live." For several moments, I remember, he said
nothing, and then he looked to the stars. "Are you not tired," he asked
me, "of being caged behind Ilium's walls?" He looked on for a moment at the broad night sky, and then slowly he lowered his head,
looking squarely in the direction of the Argive ships. "We are within
sight of victory," he said simply. "Tomorrow, at first light, we will arm

and attack them fiercely. If the War-god is willing, we will burn their ships and drive them howling into the sea."

—On the following morning, beneath Helios's most radiant beams, the enraged Argive Greeks burst like thunder from their camps and succeeded, finally, in breaking our weary line. Then, across the length of a long and terrible hour, they trapped fully half of the Trojan army against the high, rushing waters of Scamander and butchered them to the last man. By mere chance, Lords, I managed to withdraw the Dardanian corps intact and survived, but my Lord Hector did not. Unlike Priam, who had let slip his integrity to preserve the all-but-worthless life of a son, Hector sacrificed himself to restore the integrity of Troy, willing his own death at the brutal hands of Achilles.

—Hector was my friend, Lords, and when the hour came in which to make recompense for his mistake, he stood his ground and died the death of a warrior. I miss him greatly, even now, so many long years after. Let us raise our cups to honor his memory.

—Of the deaths of the royal family, Lords, I cannot speak, for even in the hour that they died, I was fighting beside Pharos in a narrow street east of the citadel. But of Alexandros, yes, for I saw him fall from the walls of the palace with a bronze-bright Argive arrow through his neck. That he stood his ground and died like a Trojan warrior, I believe to be true.

—Pharos? —Yes, Zidantas, at the bitter end Pharos broke his proscription and came home to Ilium. Throughout the war I had relied often upon his sound, war-wise advice, but he had never come within the walls, and thus I traveled often to a secret reconnaissance camp in the hills east of Troy, where he made his bivouac or exchanged words with him by means of well-disciplined runners from that same clandestine unit. He was gone, then, when the great horse was drawn into the city and gone too when the Greeks broke out, but when the flames rose high over Ilium, he came home at last and found me, I know not how, beneath the wall of the citadel. Together, we gathered a party of some forty warriors and attempted to relieve the palace so as to rescue royal Priam, but in that pointless effort we were immediately unsuccessful because even before we could come within sight of the gates, we were bumped and then overrun by swarms of Athenian infantry coming up from the streets below. Pharos saved my life there, by leaping through a doorway and dragging me quickly through behind him, and then quickly we scaled a wall and escaped over the rooftops into an adjacent street. Collecting more men as they dashed from their homes, we next attempted to storm a passage toward the temple of Apollo, where ox-eyed Cassandra was thought to have taken refuge, but again, in the moment that we moved, we were struck, both front and back, by relentless Pylian spearmen whose sharp war cries pierced the chaos of the night. Again Pharos saved me by darting through a door to scale the wall beyond, but then we found ourselves in a narrow, doorless street, no more than one strong spear-cast from a boiling company of Spartans who attacked us with the swiftness of the wind.

—We had no place left to retreat, Lords, so there, in that narrow street, fighting side by side, we gave battle to the Greeks, killing many and wounding more as we were pressed back hard into the smoking confines of a courtyard. On that ground, with our backs to the wall, we took a last, desperate stand, littering the earth with Greeks and the dark, smoking flow of their blood. And then, Lords, the Spartans brought up archers, and that was the end. We did not hesitate, I remember—we did not wait to die—we charged, shouting the war cry of the Shark. The last thing I recall clearly is the sight of Pharos, his ancient body already pierced by a hard flight of arrows, lunging forward, driving his long ash spear into the collapsing form of a Greek. In that second, with blinding pain, I took an arrow to the eye, and night came down swiftly over my screams.

—Observe, my Lords, the dawn: through the crack above my door comes the thin, gray light. Listen . . . above the silence you may hear the long, withdrawing roar of the tide falling back across the Hellespont. I think the hour of your departure is near.

—*How*? —*How* did I survive? —Surely by the hand of Hermes, Conveyor of Shades, for in the hour of my deepest wound, he found me waiting before the death-gates to Hades from whence, against my will, he returned me here, to *this,* to this ash-white desert of my desolation, to make me fulfill the terms of my fate and become the final burier of my people. —No, the specifics are beyond my ken. My assumption has always been that the Greeks, moved by the hand of the Guide, overlooked me or, worse, left me to my long, lingering pain after first stripping away my armor and casting me deep into the dry hollow of a well, for there, on the following day, atop a lifeless mound of corpses, I recovered my senses and knew that I had survived. Then, when I knew that it was true, that—indeed—I lived, with great effort and pain I emerged again into the world and made my way here to the Plain, knowing for the first time that I was destined to live out my days alone, forever obeying Priam's last command by burying the remains of my failure.

—Ride, Lords of the Hatti, toward the windswept plains of the East, toward the distant halls of Hattusas, and take these words to your king: say "Polydamas the Warrior is dead in obedience to Priam's command." Say "Polydamas the Burier will fight no more, for he is done with war forever."

Glossary

ABAS. Keas's faithful squire.

ACAMAS. An elder of Troy.

The ACHAIANS (ACHAEANS, ARGIVES, DANAANS). Homer's terms for describing the people who fight against Troy (Ilium). The word *Greek* is not used by Homer.

ACHILLES. The son of Peleus and Thetis, a sea nymph. In battle he commands the Myrmidons of Phthia. In the war's ninth year, following a quarrel with Agamemnon, he withdraws from the fighting to sulk beside his hut. Later, sending Patroclus to command in his place, Achilles is responsible for his friend's death in battle. These events are the subject of *The Iliad*.

AENEAS. The son of Anchises and the goddess Aphrodite, he is also Hector's cousin and an important field commander at Troy. Following Hector's death, he commands the army. Later, having survived the sack of Ilium, Aeneas escapes to the West where he eventually founds Rome. He is the hero of *The Aeneid*.

AEOLUS. The Keeper of the Winds.

AGAMEMNON. The king of Mycenae and supreme commander of the expedition against Troy. He is often called ATREIDES. Elder son of the ill-fated House of Atreus, Agamemnon is overlord of the Argives.

AGATHON. The braggart son of Priam.

AGELAUS. Priam's chief herdsman, who may also have acted as Hecuba's agent.

AGENOR. An elder of Troy.

ALEXANDROS (PARIS). Repeller of men. The abductor and seducer of Helen, the pretty son of Priam and Hecuba, and younger brother of Hector, he is the source of Troy's troubles. Opting for the bow, he eventually kills Achilles by shooting him from a distance. On the last night of the war, as he stands atop Troy's wall, the Argive bowman, Philoctetes, kills him with a bronze-tipped arrow.

ANCHISES. Father of Aeneas. He escapes from Troy's flames on the shoulders of his son.

ANDROMACHE. Hector's wife.

ANTENOR. An elder of Troy who wants to return Helen to Menelaus.

ANTIPHORUS. A son of Priam and Laothoë. He commands a battalion of the Guards.

ANTIPHUS. Son of Talaemenes. He commands the Maeonian Uplands before Troy.

APHRODITE. The daughter of Zeus and Dione, she is the goddess of love and beauty. She is married to Hephestus, the god of craft and fire.

APOLLO. Variously the god of music, poetry, the arts, medicine, and prophesy. Falling in love with Cassandra, he grants her the gift of divine sight, only to find himself rejected by her. Thereafter, he is responsible for the fact that no one believes her when she speaks the truth. When death by disease is attributed to the penetration of his arrows, Apollo is called SMINTHEUS (See *Iliad*, I). He is the son of Zeus and Leto.

ARNUWANDIS. An ambassador from Hattusas.

ARTEMIS. Goddess of the moon, the hunt, and chastity.

ASIUS. Son of Hyrtaeus, he commands the Lion of Percote.

ASSARACUS. Son of Tros, he is brother to Ilus and Ganymede.

ASTYNAX. The infant son of Hector and Andromache, he is sometimes called SCAMANDROS.

ATHENE. Having sprung fully formed from the forehead of her father, Zeus, she is the goddess of forethought and wisdom.

AURORA. The goddess of the dawn, she is wife to Tithonus and mother of Memnon, leader of the Ethiopians.

BELLEROPHON. A descendant of Sisyphus, he is a heroic ancestor both to Sarpedon and to Glaucus.

BOREAS. The north wind.

CASSANDRA. The daughter of Priam and Hecuba, she has the divine gift of foresight and the divine curse that no one believes her prophecies.

CHARON. The boatman who ferries dead souls across the river Lethe in Hades.

The CICONES. The Trojan allies who live in western Thrace beneath the shadow of Mount Ismarus.

CLYTIUS. Son of Laomedon and brother to Priam.

CREUSA. The wife of Aeneas, she dies in the sack of Troy.

DARDANIANS. The Trojan outlanders who inhabit the northwestern Troad.

DARDANOS. Son of Zeus and ancestor of the House of Priam.

DEIPHOBUS. Son of Priam and Hecuba, he commands elements of the Leopard.

DIATOR. The Younger Diator commands the Hawk's Talons before Troy. The Elder Diator commands the Grays.

The DORIANS. Barbarian Greeks who overrun and conquer Achaia not long after the end of the Trojan War.

EPEIAN. Nastes' slave at Miletus.

EPISTROPHUS. Father of Odios, he is king of the Alizones at Alybe until near the end of the war.

ERICHTHONIUS. Son of Dardonos and father of Tros.

ERIS (ATE). The goddess of strife.

ETEOCLES. An officer in the Spider and a close friend of Heptaphoros.

EUPHEMUS. Commander of the Cicones before Troy. He is the son of King Troezenus, who rules at Zone.

The FATES (The MOIRAI). Three old women who determine man's fate by spinning, measuring, and cutting his thread. Clotho spins, Lachesis measures, and Atropos severs the string.

GANYMEDE. Son of Tros. Prized by Zeus, he is made cupbearer to the god.

GLAUCUS. Son of Hippolochus, he is Sarpedon's cousin and second-in-command of the Lycian allies.

HECTOR. Son of Priam and Hecuba, he is supreme commander of the Trojan army and all allied commands.

HECUBA. Daughter of Dymas and Eunoë, she is the wife of Priam and mother to Hector, Alexandros, Polites, Cassandra, and others.

HELEN. Daughter of Zeus and Leda, Helen is the most beautiful woman in the world. Electing from among many suiters to marry Menelaus, son of Atreus and younger brother to Agamemnon, she becomes queen of Sparta. And from Sparta Paris abducts her, an act of wife-rape that infuriates all of the Argive kings, who had sworn to protect her.

HELENUS. Son of Priam and Hecuba, he is thought to have divine vision.

HELIOS. God of the sun.

HEPHESTUS. God of fire, craft, and forge, he is the lame husband of Aphrodite.

HEPTAPOROS. The last commander of the Spider.

HERMES (The GUIDE). Messenger of the gods. Hermes also conducts dead souls to Hades.

HERA. Queen of the gods, she is wife and sister to Zeus.

HICETAON. (1). Son of Laomedon and brother to Priam. (2). Son of Eurytion, commander of the Trojan regiment of the Panther, and Priam's general of the northeast frontier beyond Percote.

HIPPOLOCHUS. The father of Glaucus, he rules Lycia in Sarpedon's absence.

HIPPOTHOUS. A son of Priam known for his cruelty.

The HITTITES (The HATTI). Lords of Hattusas, they rule a vast empire in the East, in the area known today as central Anatolia.

HUZZIYAS. The Hatti ambassador to the Carian court at Miletus.

IDAEUS. Priam's faithful charioteer.

IDOMENEUS. The aging king of Crete whose hard sea warriors open the war by assaulting and capturing Tenedos.

ILUS. (1). Son of Tros and father of Laomedon. (2). A son of Priam.

The ITHACAN. Probably Odysseus, king of Ithaca.

KEAS. A Trojan general much favored by Aeneas.

LAMPUS. A son of Laomedon, he is also Priam's brother and an elder of Troy.

LAOCOÖN. A Trojan elder and a priest of Poseidon. When he tries to warn the people of Troy about the wooden horse, sea serpents appear suddenly, attacking and suffocating Laocoön and his two sons within their coils.

LAOMEDON. Son of Ilus, he enlarges the boundaries of Dardania and builds the towers of Ilium. He is the father of Tithonus, Priam, Lampus, Clytius, and Hicetaon.

LAOTHOË. Another of Priam's wives.

LYCAON. Hector's younger brother. He commands a battalion of the Guards.

MEDESICASTE. The wife of Keas.

MEDON. One of the Trojan generals charged with the wall's defense.

MEMNON. Son of Tithonus and Aurora, the Dawn. He is king of the Ethiopians, who live at the world's end. In the tenth year of the war, he strikes the Achaians hard in open battle on the plain; there he is killed by Achilles.

MENELAUS. The Atreides, the injured husband of Helen, and king of Sparta. On his account, his older brother, Agamemnon, leads the Argive expedition against Troy.

MEROPS. A runner from Percote who rises, eventually, to command the Lion.

MESTHLES. Brother to Antiphus, he commands the Maeonian Lowlands.

MORYS. An old-line Trojan general who commands the Boar during the First Mysian War.

The MYRMIDONS. Warriors of Phthia commanded by Achilles. During the attempted river crossing against Scamander's upland fords, when so many of their number are annihilated by Nastes and the fierce Carian Wind, they are probably commanded by Neoptolemus, Achilles' impulsive son who came late to the war in the wake of his father's death.

NASTES. King of Caria who commands the Wind before Troy.

ODIOS. Ruler of Alybe. He is the son of Epistrophus and commands the Alizones on the Plain.

OENONE. A water nymph seduced and deserted by Paris during his sojourn on Ida.

PAMMON. A son of Priam whose arrogance is public knowledge.

PARIS. (See ALEXANDROS).

PATROCLUS. Achilles' best friend and squire who is killed by Hector on the second day of the great Trojan counteroffensive.

PELEUS. Mortal husband to the sea nymph Thetis and father of Achilles.

PENTHESILEA. The queen of the Amazons who allies herself with the Trojans in the final year of the war. Her beauty is reputed to be great.

PHAROS. Polydamas's tutor.

PHILOCTETES. The Argive bowman who kills Paris after making a long and trying journey to Troy.

POLYBUS. The son of Antenor, he commands the Spider. He is killed in the closing days of the war by an Argive penetration behind Trojan lines. The evidence suggests that Menestheus of Athens led the attack.

POLYDAMAS. Son of Panthous, he is a commoner and Hector's chief of staff.

POSEIDON. Brother to Zeus and Hades, he is Lord of the Sea, the Earthshaker.

PRIAM. King of Troy, husband of Hecuba, he is father to Hector, Alexandros, Deiphobus, Helenus, and many others.

PROTESILAUS. The first Argive warrior to leap ashore on the Plain. He is killed by Hector.

PYRACCHMES. Commander of the bright-eyed Paeonian archers along the Wall of Heracles.

RHEA. The Earth-Mother.

RHESUS. The king of Thrace. He is killed in his sleep by Odysseus and Diomedes (*Iliad*, X) during a night raid behind Trojan lines.

SARPEDON. The king of Lycia, he is the son of Zeus and Laodameia, the beautiful daughter of Bellerophon.

SMINTHEUS (see APOLLO).

SUPPILULIUMAS. The last king of the Hatti, the last Lord of Hattusas.

TALAEMENES. The king of Maeonia. He is the father of Antiphus.

TELIPINUS. An ambassador from the lords of Hattusas.

THERSITES. A hump-backed, frog-like man who is the least erected warrior at Troy (*Iliad,* II).

THETIS. A sea nymph, she is the wife of Peleus and mother to Achilles.

THOAS. The Argive sea commander from Aetolia who gains control of the Hellespont for Agamemnon.

THYMOETES. An elder of Troy.

TITHONUS. Son of Laomedon. A mortal who married Aurora, goddess of the Dawn, he is also father of Prince Memnon of Ethiopia. For aspiring to union with a divinity, he is usually cast as a type for pride because at the time he also asked for immortality. Forgetting to ask as well for immortal youth, Tithonus steadily withered with age but could not die. Finally Zeus took pity on the man and transformed him into a cicada, and thus Tithonus was permitted to expire. *Sôphrosynê,* a kind of temperance, suggests that man must recognize and accept his own mortality. This is an important element in the heroic code by which the Trojans and Greeks live.

TROEZENUS. King of the Cicones, he rules at Zone.

TROS. (1). Lord of the Trojans and father of Ilus, Assaracus, and Ganymede. (2). Son of Keas.

ZEPHYR. The west wind.

ZEUS. Father of gods and men. Lord of Thunder, the Cloud Gatherer, he is also Hera's husband and brother.

ZIDANTAS. The chief Hatti ambassador sent by Suppiluliumas to recruit Polydamas to command at Hattusas.

Gazetteer

For ease of notation, the following symbols will be used for map references in the Gazetteer:

Map I—Achaia (Greece)	I
Map II—Troia	II
Map III—Ilium	III
Map IV—Asia Minor	IV

Map references will be included in parentheses following place names.

ABYDUS (Abydus-by-the-sea) (II, III). Blue city by the water's edge, Abydus is located in the eye of the "fishhook," on the coast of the Hellespont due south of the Thynian citadel of Sestus.

ACHELOUS (I). Principal river of western Greece. The river's west fork originates at the head of the Pindus Mountains; the eastern fork springs from the foot of the Pindus.

AETOLIA (I). A region in western Greece bounded, roughly, by the Ionian Sea to the west, the gulfs of Patrai and Corinth to the south, the river Achelous to the north, and Locris to the east.

ALYBE (II). Located in the Phrygian hinterland east of Troy, Alybe is the chief citadel of the Alizones.

AMYDON (I). A Paeonian citadel located along the banks of the Axius River.

ANATOLIA (IV). The East—the domain of the Hittites in Asia Minor.

ANTISSA (II). Port city on the north coast of Lesbos.

ARCADIA (I). A region in the central Peloponnese west of Mycenae.

ASSUS (II). The Trojan citadel located on the southwestern cape of the Troad to guard the sea approaches from Lesbos and all points south.

ATHENS (I). Directly north of the Saronic Gulf, Athens is the chief city of the region known as Attica.

AXIUS (I). Principal river in Paeonia, the Axius courses south to empty into the Gulf of Thermais.

BESIKA BAY (III). Southwest of Troy, Besika Bay fronts on the Aegean Sea, looking toward Tenedos.

BOEOTIA (I). This region in central Greece is located north of Attica and west of Euboea.

CARIA (II, IV). Caria is allied with Troy. It is located in the southwest corner of Asia Minor immediately north of Rhodes.

CAYSTER (II). Draining the slopes of Mount Tmolus, the Cayster River runs west out of Maeonia through Lydia toward the sea.

CHIOS (II). A large island west of Lydia.

CHRYSA (II). An important Mysian port, citadel, and supply center located south of Mount Ida on the Mysian coast.

CILICIA (IV). That part of Asia Minor fronting the Mediterranean Sea directly north of the island of Cyprus. Cilicia backs on the Taurus Mountains.

COLONAE (II). A Trojan citadel located near wide Propontis on Ilium's northeast frontier.

COS (II). A small Greek island northwest of Rhodes in the Sporades.

CRANAË (I). The offshore island, possibly Cythera, where Paris first seduced Helen.

CYPRUS (IV). South of Cilicia and west of the Phoenician coast, Cyprus is the largest island in the eastern Mediterranean.

DARDANIA (II). Troy is the chief city of Dardania, the coastal region north of Mount Ida and the River Scamander, bordered by the Aegean Sea to the west and the Hellespont to the north. The region also encompasses the Plain, the River Simoeis, and the citadels of Dardanos, Abydus, Arisbe, Percote, and Colonae.

DARDANOS (III). The Trojan citadel at the tip of the "fishhook" on the Hellespont.

DOLOPIA (I). This triangular region of Greece is bounded on the west and south by the two forks of the Archelous River.

EUBOEA (I, IV). Running northwest and southeast, Euboea is the long island which separates Locris, Boeotia, and Attica—the Greek mainland—from the Aegean Sea.

GARGARON (II). One of Ida's many peaks which overlook the passes into Mysia.

HADES. The Underworld.

HATTUSAS (IV). The administrative and military center of the Hittite empire in Asia Minor. The site may be approximately located on a modern map by the intersection of two lines, one running east from Ankara, the other running north from Beirut.

HELLESPONT (II, III). The body of water separating the Troad from Thynia.

ICARIA (II). A Greek island located west of Samos at the head of the Sporades.

Mount IDA (II, IV). Home of the Trojan gods, Mount Ida separates the Troad from Mysia.

Mount ISMARUS (II, IV). Located in western Thrace, Mount Ismarus faces the Aegean. The Cicones live along the mountain's southern slopes, which overlook their citadel at Zone.

LACONIAN GULF (I). The closest sea approach to Sparta in the lower Peloponnese.

LARISA (I). An Argive citadel located in northern Thessalia along the banks of the Peneus River.

Mount LATMUS (II). Mount Latmus is located in Caria northeast of Miletus.

HEIGHTS of HERACLES (III). The southern extension of the Wall of Heracles.

Mount LAURION (I, IV). Located in Maronea in southeastern Attica, Mount Laurion is the source of Athenian silver.

LEMNOS (II). This island is located west of Troy. It is a thriving trade center and slave market where the Greeks exchange their spoils for war material.

LESBOS (II). West of Mysia and south of Assus, the huge island of Lesbos is allied with Priam. Its chief cities of Antissa and Mytilene are trade centers.

LOCRIS (I). East of Aetolia, Locris is home to the Locrians, who are adept with the sling.

LYCIA (IV). Located northeast of Rhodes and east of Caria, Lycia borders Cilicia to the east and Maeonia to the north. Its chief citadel is Xanthus.

LYDIA (II, IV). Located south of Mysia and north of Caria, Lydia is allied with Troy.

MAEONIA (II, IV). Athwart the banks of the Cayster River, Maeonia lies in the shadow of Mount Tmolus, east of Lydia.

MARONEA (I). The eastern tip of Attica. The area is dominated by Mount Laurion.

MILETUS (II). Situated in the shadow of Mount Latmus, Miletus is the chief port city and citadel of Caria.

MYRINA. (II). A trade center and slave market on Lemnos's western coast.

MYSIA (II, IV). The warrior nation south of the Troad.

NISYRUS (II). An island northwest of Rhodes, one of the Sporades.

Mount OLYMPUS (I). Home of the Argive gods, Mount Olympus is located in northern Achaia, immediately west of the Gulf of Thermais and south of the Haliacmon River.

PAEONIA (I, IV). West of Thrace, Paeonia is allied with Troy. Its three southern fingers extend into the northern Aegean east of the Gulf of Thermais.

PATMOS (II). One of the Sporades located south of Icaria and west of Caria.

PERCOTE (II, III). A Dardanian citadel located on the Hellespont north-east of Abydus.

PHOENICIA (IV). An ancient region of city states located at the eastern end of the Mediterranean Sea. Modern coastal Syria and Lebanon roughly mark the region's borders.

PHRYGIA (II, III, IV). The vast hinterland extending from Troy's eastern borders into the heart of Asia Minor. The peoples of this region are allied with Troy, although some barbarian tribes remain hostile.

The PINDUS (I). Running roughly northwest and southeast, the Pindus Mountains form the backbone of central Greece.

PITANE (II). Citadel of the Mysian kings and a major port city north of Cyme.

PROPONTIS (Sea of Marmara) (II). The broad island sea which connects the Hellespont with the Bosporus and the Black Sea. Prior to the Trojan War, the area was a Trojan lake, owing to the fact that access was controlled by Priam.

RHODES (II, IV). The large Greek island south of Caria.

SAMOTHRACE (II). A large island west of Thynia and south of Zone.

SCAMANDER (II, III). The largest river on the Trojan Plain. Running west from the Mysian and Phrygian highlands, Scamander passes Thymbra, joins the south fork running down from Ida, and runs north across the Plain until it empties into the Hellespont.

SCYROS (I, II). Birthplace of Neoptolemus, Achilles' son, the island of

Scyros rises from the Aegean between Euboea and Lesbos.

SESTUS (II, III). Thracian stronghold on the Thynian peninsula.

SIDON (IV). A port city in Phoenicia.

SIMOEIS (II, III). The second largest river on the Plain. The course of Simoeis roughly parallels the Hellespont until, like Scamander, it turns north and empties across the Plain into the sea.

SMYRNA (II). South of the Hermus River, Smyrna is located at the tip of a finger-shaped gulf that recesses into Lydia.

SPARTA (I). The domain of Menelaus located north of the Gulf of Laconia in the lower Peleponnese.

TELOS (II). One of the Sporades, the island is located west of Rhodes and south of Nisyrus.

TENEDOS (II, III). This offshore island, which covers the mouth of Besika Bay, also guards the western approaches to the Troad.

THESSALIA (I). Thessalia is bounded to the north by the Peneus River, to the west by the Pindus, and to the south by Phthia.

THRACE (II, III, IV). The vast lands which lie north of the Hellespont and wide Propontis.

THYMBRA (III). A mountain citadel guarding the southern and eastern approaches to Troy along the banks of Scamander.

THYNIA (II, III). The peninsula which forms the northern shore of the Hellespont.

Mount TMOLUS (II, IV). The high mountain which separates Maeonia from Lydia.

TYRE (IV). A port city in Phoenicia.

WALL of HERACLES (III). The low coastal mountain range which separates the Plain of Ilium from the sea. The southern tip of the Wall slopes down to Besika Bay.

XANTHUS (IV). The primary port city and citadel of Lycia. Xanthus is built along the banks of a Lycian river having the same name.

ZIPPASLA (IV). A plain located in Asia Minor midway between Mount Tmolus and Hattusas

ZONE (II, IV). Built in the shadow of Mount Ismarus, Zone is the citadel of the Cicones.

ILLINOIS SHORT FICTION

Pastorale by Susan Engberg
Home Fires by David Long
The Canyons of Grace by Levi Peterson
Babaru by B. Wongar

Bodies of the Rich by John J. Clayton
Music Lesson by Martha Lacy Hall
Fetching the Dead by Scott R. Sanders
Some of the Things I Did Not Do by Janet Beeler Shaw

Honeymoon by Merrill Joan Gerber
Tentacles of Unreason by Joan Givner
The Christmas Wife by Helen Norris
Getting to Know the Weather by Pamela Painter

Birds Landing by Ernest Finney
Serious Trouble by Paul Friedman
Tigers in the Wood by Rebecca Kavaler
The Greek Generals Talk by Phillip Parotti

Singing on the Titanic by Perry Glasser
Legacies by Nancy Potter
Beyond This Bitter Air by Sarah Rossiter
Scenes from the Homefront by Sara Vogan

Tumbling by Kermit Moyer
Water into Wine by Helen Norris
The Trojan Generals Talk by Phillip Parotti
Playing with Shadows by Gloria Whelan